TALES OF STRELIT
THE BATTLE OF LIFE

STERLING DAVIES

To my Mum, who will always be my inspiration and my biggest supporter. I love you more.

TABLE OF CONTENTS

CHAPTER ONE..7

CHAPTER TWO.. 19

CHAPTER THREE...25

CHAPTER FOUR 33

CHAPTER FIVE..45

CHAPTER SIX 53

CHAPTER SEVEN 61

CHAPTER EIGHT 71

CHAPTER NINE 83

CHAPTER TEN 91

CHAPTER ELEVEN 101

CHAPTER TWELVE..111

CHAPTER THIRTEEN 123

CHAPTER FOURTEEN 137

CHAPTER FIFTEEN... 149

CHAPTER SIXTEEN 159

CHAPTER SEVENTEEN...................................167

CHAPTER EIGHTEEN 177

CHAPTER NINETEEN... 193

CHAPTER TWENTY...203

CHAPTER TWENTY-ONE 211

CHAPTER TWENTY-TWO 223

CHAPTER TWENTY-THREE.....................................233

CHAPTER TWENTY-FOUR 247

CHAPTER TWENTY-FIVE...257

CHAPTER TWENTY-SIX 275

CHAPTER TWENTY-SEVEN.......................................285

CHAPTER TWENTY-EIGHT.......................................297

CHAPTER TWENTY-NINE...317

CHAPTER THIRTY 331

CHAPTER THIRTY-ONE...347

CHAPTER THIRTY-TWO 359

CHAPTER THIRTY-THREE 373

CHAPTER ONE

*D*ing! The elevator door opened. People poured out, leaving me there alone. I shuffled out too, and instantly was overwhelmed by the smell of coffee and donuts.

Dozens of police officers, detectives, and other staff passed by, but I made eye contact with no one. Instinctively, I took a right turn at the end of the hallway, then knocked on the second door to the left, the one with a sign that read DETECTIVE BOOKER.

"Booker, listen to me! They're out there!" a voice shouted through the door. "They're flying over our sky like comets! Do something about it!"

The door swung open, and the man who had been yelling stormed out.

I poked my head inside. Booker sat at his desk, looking at some case files. He sighed heavily as he leaned back in his chair. "Come in, Leon," he said in his deep voice. I trudged into his office littered with coffee cups and wrappers.

Sunbeams lit up the space. That was strange: only twenty minutes ago it was raining.

"How are you doing?"

"Good," I mumbled, hands jammed in my pockets, looking at the ground.

"Well, what brings you here? I bet I can guess, though."

"Can I look at the files for my sister's disappearance?"

He rubbed his temple. "Sure, Leon. But you've looked at it three times in the last month. There's nothin' else you're gonna find." He got out of his chair and walked out.

A few minutes later, he came back and handed me a wrinkled yellow folder crammed with a stack of white pages. "Our best connections in Boston discovered everything there is about what happened. We had our police, detectives, forensic scientists, investigators, private investigators, and anybody else on the police squad trying to find out what happened to Rebecca. And we talked to everybody she knew also. They all said they hadn't heard from her after the crash. Remember, part of the reason you moved here to Hawaii was to get away from it. It's been eight years. Try to get some closure."

"Thanks, Booker," I said, to be polite. I put the folder in my backpack.

"I'll just look again, though."

I pushed the door open, headed back to the elevator, and headed outside.

How was I supposed to get closure on what happened that day? Rebecca's disappearance ruined my life.

The sky was turning gray again. Dark clouds rolled in, blocking out the sun. I hopped on my rusted bike and pedaled home.

The wind picked up. It howled as I whistled along the dirt road. The trees shook violently like they were going to rip out from the ground. The rain started again and pattered against my rain jacket. My tires sloshed in the mud. I needed to get home before the storm became too much to handle.

I made my way to the main road, but the storm was too strong now. I could hardly see through the pounding rain and flashes of lighting. I swerved on the slick concrete, but as I turned a corner, my bike flew out from beneath me.

I crashed down to the sidewalk. My right elbow hit hard, making me cry out in pain. I clambered to my feet, holding my elbow. To the left of me, my bike lay smashed against the side of a building. The chain had come off, and the spokes were sticking out at every angle. There was no way I could keep biking. I needed to wait out the storm and hopefully find some help. But where?

Across the street, a huge LED sign reading OPEN glowed in the window of a sandwich shop. I hobbled with my dismantled bike and sought shelter inside.

The door chimed as I entered. The place smelled of stale bread and cheese. Fluorescent lights flickered above and gave off a hum that buzzed beneath the patter of the rain. The tables and booths were packed with chattering people also waiting for the storm to pass.

Everyone stopped and looked at me; even the rain seemed to stop. Some snickered as I passed their tables or pointed at my mangled bike.

I made my way to an empty table in the corner. I leaned my bike against the booth, but it crashed to the floor, sending pieces scattering. Everyone just laughed as I crawled around to collect them all. A kid I knew from school kicked a spring that had fallen next to his foot.

I looked like a fool. I was making a mockery of myself.

Once I had gathered all of the pieces, I hurried to sit down. The clock read seven forty p.m. when I took out the police files and started to read.

The truck swerved into the lane of the victims. The victims' car rolled down a ditch and crashed into a tree.

All of a sudden, a girl came to my table. She propped her bike against the booth, but it slid down and clanged to the floor too. Some people laughed, but she didn't even look their way or bother to pick it back up. She took the seat across from me and propped her feet up on the table. Mud dripped from her shoes, nearly messing up my file. I organized the papers and set them away from her.

"What are you working on? Huh?" Her voice was loud and penetrating. She reached over the table and grabbed the file from me. She smacked her chewing gum as she scanned the grim details of the report. "Aren't you too young to look at stuff like this? What are you, like, ten years old?"

"Um … those are mine." I grabbed for the papers, and she rolled her eyes as she handed them over. I glanced at the clock again: seven forty-three. "And I'm fourteen."

"Huh, you're the same age as me." She gestured to the file. "What even is that?"

"It's nothing." Now the clock said seven forty-five. I had to be back at my aunt's in eight minutes. Or else it wasn't going to go well for me.

I packed up the file and slung my backpack over my shoulder.

"Where are you going?" the girl scoffed. "You can't go outside, it's pouring. You're going to wind up dead on the side of the road."

"I-I'll be fine," I said as I maneuvered my broken bike to the exit.

The left pedal came loose and clanged to the floor. Snickers rang through the room, and people started making comments again. I rushed to pick up the part, and I could feel my face redden. I went outside.

Thunder rolled in the gray sky as the rain poured down. I tried walking my bike home, but it was no use. Pieces kept falling off, and the wheels bent every which way. Not to mention, my clothes were already soaked.

The girl that was at my table in the shop pulled up next to me on her bike. "Go into the alley!" she yelled over the whips of wind.

I stared at her, confused. Why would I trust a stranger and go into an alley? But I didn't really have a choice: it was either get help or be late. And I didn't want to be late.

I ran into the alley and took shelter from the rain.

She followed me. "What happened to your bike?" She looked at my bike in horror. "I saw it in the sandwich shop, but it didn't look *this* bad. It looks like you ran it into a wall."

"I slipped, and the bike hit a building."

The kid who had kicked the spring away sped by the alley and shouted, "LOSER!" He skidded his bicycle into a puddle and sprayed water all over me. He laughed like a maniac as he rushed away.

"Hey, you!" the girl yelled. She picked up a rock and chucked it with deadly accuracy. It shot through the rain like a bullet and got caught right between the spokes of the front wheel. The kid went swerving and ended up flipping over his bike and face-planting into the sidewalk.

I was speechless.

She dusted off her hands like her deadly aim was no big deal, and picked up the broken parts of my bike. "Give me a second," she said. "I'll fix this."

"How are you going to fix it?" I asked, about to hyperventilate. "My aunt is going to go nuts. She's going to kill me. I'm never going to be able to leave the house again."

"Oh my gosh!" the girl said, rolling her eyes again. "Just give me a second, alright?!"

I quieted down as she fixed my bike. But what she did shocked me. It was like clockwork for her. She hardly even had to look at what she was doing. Her hands wrapped around the bike and maneuvered through the metal with ease. Pretty soon, she was done.

"How did you do that?"

"Don't you have someplace to be?" she snapped back. "And you're welcome. Now come on, go!"

"Thank you. Um … what's your name?"

"Maria. Now go, before you're late."

"Thank you, Maria," I said. "I'm Leon and—"

"Go!" she yelled. "Before we're both late!" She mounted her bike and pedaled away from the little shelter we had.

I left as well. The rain pelted my jacket, creating a thunderous patter. I took a left and saw Maria ahead. She then took a right. I needed to take a right too. And then I needed to go left. But she went left as well!

"Why are you following me?!" Maria yelled over her shoulder.

"I'm not!" I yelled back. She must live nearby; there were only two neighborhoods this way.

I couldn't keep up with Maria, and I lost her and was left alone in the storm. After continuing down a slippery hill and turning the corner to my street, I reached my aunt's house.

I laid my bike in the bushes, then fumbled with the keys in my pocket before I managed to grab the right one and unlock the door.

I crept in slowly, trying not to make a sound. I was five minutes late. If my aunt caught me, it wouldn't be good.

I nudged the door closed, took off my shoes, and placed them on the rug. The TV blared from the living room, so she had to be there. I held my breath and tiptoed to the stairs that led to my room. I slowly made my way up.

But the fourth step creaked like it was groaning underneath me.

I froze in fear. Did she hear me? The talking on the TV paused.

I was going to get caught. My aunt was going to kill me.

She groaned as she got off the couch. Her feet stomped toward me, and the floorboards groaned under the enormous weight.

Then she walked into view. She waddled from side to side, like an oversized penguin. Her pajamas were stained from who-knew-how-many meals. Her blond hair went every which way; some strands matted against her droopy eyes and cheeks, others stood up as though she had rubbed them with a staticky balloon.

"Look who decided to show up," she said in her deep voice. "Don't you know how late it is?! I have places to be!"

"I'm sorry, Aunt Pat," I mumbled. "I'll just be in my room." I rushed up the stairs before she could say another word.

"Nuh-uh-uh. I'm not finished with you yet," she sneered. I trudged back down the stairs. "Where were you? Huh? Cuz clearly you were *somewhere* that made you come home so late."

"There was a really bad storm," I grumbled. "I had to wait for it to pass." I tried to turn back, but she pulled me by the hood of my jacket.

"The storm didn't start until seven forty. You should've been home before seven twenty-five. Where were you?!"

I didn't say anything. I kept my eyes glued on the floor, hoping something would take her attention off me. Maybe the phone would ring?

"Look at me when I'm talking to you!" she snapped. "You're lucky I even took you in after the car accident! If it wasn't for me, you would have nowhere to go!" Her face turned red under her arching eyebrows. "Now, I'm gonna ask you for the last time. Where were you?!"

Like a miracle, the doorbell rang. *DING-DONG.*

I exhaled as Pat glanced at the door with narrowing eyes. But she ignored the interruption and continued to direct her anger at me.

But the doorbell rang again. And again and again and again. *DING-DONG DING-DONG DING-DONG.* Whoever was behind that door just kept hammering that button. And then they added knocking too.

"Ugh!" Pat groaned. She marched toward the door and flung it open.

"It's not a toy. You're gonna break it!"

Maria was standing outside. What was she doing here? But she was acting differently. Her eyes were wide and didn't narrow like usual. She shifted from side to side with unease.

"I-I-I'm sorry to bother you at this ungodly hour, ma'am," Maria said, stumbling over her words. Her quivering voice was two octaves higher. "I just wanted to say my thanks to Leon. H-h-he helped me with my school project, and we spent all day on it."

"Oh," my aunt said with surprise. "Well, okay. Go then, you said your thanks now."

Maria gave a warm smile to my aunt, but when Pat turned away to close the door, she winked at me.

What was that all about? Well, whatever that act was, she got me out of a lot of trouble.

"Go up to your room," my aunt said. "Dinner will be ready in thirty minutes. And you better be down by then."

Her hands balled into fists as she trudged back to the couch. My aunt couldn't stand being corrected, especially if her error had anything to do with me.

I went upstairs to my room, set my backpack on my floor, and hung my jacket across my chair. My keys were still in my hand. I set them on the desk, right next to a picture of my family. My mom, dad, sister, and I stood on a boat. We had taken a trip to Alaska. That was the last trip we ever took as a family before the car accident.

The light turned green, and we drove through the intersection.

"Finally, the light turned green," my dad said. "We were waiting for that forev—"

A deafening crash exploded around me, and in a blurry instant our car was rolling down a ditch. The car thudded and jostled me until it slammed into a tree. My body flung against the seatbelt as I whipped back into my seat, and Rebecca's door smashed against the tree trunk.

My ears were ringing. Something warm and sticky ran down my head. I was disoriented and seeing double.

My mom and dad were unconscious in the front seats. I unbuckled my seatbelt and Rebecca did the same. We both tugged at our doors, but they wouldn't budge. My body felt twisted, like it had been thrown into a tornado.

The smell of burnt rubber and leaking oil filled the car. A fire ignited in the engine. It grew quickly.

We were trapped.

I banged on the shatterproof glass while the flames licked the entire car.

My sister hurled a metal water bottle at the window and broke it. Shards of glass flew everywhere and cut my arms. I squirmed through the opening, the glass slicing my body.

After what seemed like forever, I pushed myself through and crashed onto the dirt, panting.

But I was the only one that made it out.

Flames engulfed the car. My eyes went wide with horror. The firemen came and doused the car, but all that remained were the bodies of my mom and dad.

And Rebecca was nowhere to be found.

CHAPTER TWO

After dinner, I decided to go on the roof after the storm. I could get some air up here and take a chance to think. I thought about Maria and why she had showed up at my house. Did she hear me getting in trouble? How did she even know I lived here?

It was, like, four in the morning now. I couldn't fall asleep for some reason. But all of a sudden, I saw a streak in the sky, ablaze like a meteor, barreling toward the ocean. What was that?

I wanted to go find out, but I didn't want to sneak out in the middle of the night. If I got caught, I would be in so much trouble.

But then I saw Maria. She was walking out the front door of the house next door. That's weird: she lived right next to me. I thought that house was empty. And why would she go out now? Maybe the timing had something to do with the streak in the sky.

I quickly got off the roof and went back to my room. I had to find a way out and go talk to Maria. She might tell me what happened last night, or something about the meteor-thing.

But I couldn't go out the front door, or else my aunt would know. I tried to find something in my room that would spark an idea. My window, which was right above my desk, was broken, so it was always ajar and constantly let the wind come into my room. I could use that to get out.

I moved my desk out of the way and opened the window. The hinges let out a loud creak like a rusty door untouched for years.

I winced and froze. Did my aunt hear? I waited to see if there was any movement, but there was none.

I continued opening the window as my heart raced. I had to push hard with both hands as it was pretty sturdy for a broken window.

I didn't know why I was doing this. I never did anything against the rules, let alone sneak out in the middle of the night. I never got in trouble. Why was I suddenly following this random girl that I met yesterday?

It was weird: there was something about her that was different. I needed to go talk to her, but I had no idea why.

Once the window opened wide enough for me to fit through, I peered out at the twenty-foot gap to where hedges lined the edge of the house. I needed something to rope myself down.

I grabbed my bedsheets and tied one end around the bedpost. I then flung the rest out the window.

I stood on the windowsill. I tugged the bedsheets to check the safety. It didn't budge.

I put my right foot out first and leaned back. I put my left foot back, and then steadied myself. So far, so good.

I continued to lower myself, slowly and steadily. Maria was crouching at the front of her house. What was she doing?

But then a bird flew around me. It looked like a pigeon. It circled my face and made it hard for me to see.

"Go away," I said, shooing the bird with one hand.

That was my mistake.

I lost my grip with my other hand and crashed into the hedges. Branches and twigs poked me in every direction. I groaned as I managed my way out. I had scraped myself all over.

"Who's there?" Maria said. "I will call the cops on you." She turned the corner of a hedge and saw me. "Leon, what are you doing?"

"I was going to see the streak that was in the sky." I picked out the leaves that were sticking in my hair. "What are you doing?"

"I was going to see it too," Maria said. "Come on, let's go."

She started running toward the beach, and I followed her. But I was out of breath. Why did she run so fast?

"Wait," I panted. "Why did you come to my house yesterday?"

She looked back as she ran. "Well, I heard the yelling. And I thought I could get you out of trouble. So, you're welcome."

"But you turned into a completely different person," I said. "Do you take acting classes or something?"

"My mom's an actress. You pick up on things. And my dad's a cyclist. That's why I knew how to fix your bike. Now come on, hurry up."

"Wait," I said. "But *why* did you do it?" It didn't make any sense for her to help me, especially because she came off as a selfish person.

She rolled her eyes. "Because I could get you out of trouble. So I did it. Now come on!"

We ran down to the beach and stepped on the cool sand. It crunched under my feet as we searched for the meteor. I still had no idea why I was outside on the beach at four a.m. with Maria. But I needed to do it, even though I still had no idea why.

I waded into the water a bit. The choppy waves were slapping against me, making it difficult to push through the current. My wet clothes clung to my skin, but the water wasn't cold to me. I tried to find where the meteor had landed, but couldn't find it anywhere. Maybe I should just go back? What I was doing was crazy.

But then, I stepped on a rock. It pierced my foot and sent a shock up my body. I picked the rock off my foot and held it up.

That's when I realized it wasn't a rock.

"Maria?" I called out. "Come look at this."

In less than a second, she was standing right in front of me. "What is it?" She touched the object, but yelped, "It's so cold! How are you touching it?!"

I looked at her, confused. It didn't feel cold to me at all. Maybe she was just being dramatic. What I was holding looked like a cone, except the end was pointy enough to make someone bleed. The color was icy blue, and it had a scale-like pattern. It also shimmered a bit. What was it?

We looked around for a while, but we couldn't find the meteor, or anything else. We plopped down on the shore as the sun began to peek out.

My feet were wet from the water, but my forehead glistened with sweat. Sand crunched between my toes.

So many questions ran through my head at once. Why was there some weird cone thing on the ground? Did that have something to do with the meteor? The shimmer of the sunset sparkled on the ocean's surface as I pondered everything at once.

My thoughts were interrupted when the ground started moving. We both got up and shared a worried look.

Everything around us was shaking. The umbrellas fell down, and the water started shaking. We got off the beach and ran to the sidewalks, but the concrete was cracking all over the place.

The ground shook so hard that I fell down on my side. It was an earthquake!

CHAPTER THREE

I didn't know what to do. I couldn't concentrate. What was I supposed to do in an earthquake? I held on to a tree and prayed that nothing fell on me. I could hear pieces of the sidewalk breaking off. Each crack and thunderous boom was followed by a plume of powder.

"Get away from the tree!" Maria yelled. But there wasn't any other safe place. Why would I leave?

But before I had time to think, Maria grabbed my arm as she ran back onto the beach. She dragged me along as she sprinted toward a lifeguard tower. My heart was racing and leaping out of my chest.

She ran underneath the tower, and I ran behind her.

"W-what are we doing underneath here?" I asked. I was panting, and my hands were on my knees. But the ground shook even more, and I fell down again.

"You're supposed to seek shelter under something," Maria said. "Just lay low! Don't stand up!"

The tower shook, and debris fell on top of us. The ground started shaking harder. I could hear stuff falling around us with deafening crashes. It was chaos. Car alarms were going off, and people screamed all around me.

One of the legs of the lifeguard tower cracked and started leaning. My heart was racing, and my blood was rushing. The thing was going to collapse, and we were going to be stuck inside of it.

I ran out from underneath the tower and tried to move away from it, but as I was going out, the tower collapsed. It was falling in my direction. It was going to land on top of me! I ran as fast as I could, but I wasn't going to make it. I was going to die!

I fell to the sand and shielded my face. Tears streamed down as I braced myself. But nothing happened. There was no crash. And the earthquake had stopped.

I peered up from the sand, and my jaw dropped.

The broken tower was being held in the air by a dragon.

I rubbed my eyes. Was I seeing this right? The dragon was flying in midair, holding up the lifeguard tower on his back. It pulled the lifeguard tower out of the ground and laid it down onto the sand.

My hands trembled. What was happening? Maria walked to me. Her face was frozen and her eyes were wide.

"W-w-what is this?" Maria was shaking. "Oh great, now it's walking toward us."

The dragon was an almost-golden color. Its scales shimmered against the sun. It stood on all four legs and had four giant claws coming out of each one. Two huge wings sprouted from its back and, behind it, a tail curled to a pointed tip. The tail looked a lot like the piece we'd found on the shore. Its two narrow red eyes stared at us.

"Hello," the dragon said. "I am Bruno."

"And now he's talking!" Maria said, throwing her hands in the air and walking in circles. "This is too much. It's too much!"

I was still frozen in shock.

The dragon gave a small chuckle. "There is nothing to be afraid of." He had a deep voice, and it boomed a little. His voice commanded attention, but in a peaceful way. "As I mentioned, my name is Bruno. I assume this might come as a shock, but I can assure you two, there is nothing wrong, you are safe. But you need to come with me."

"O-o-okay?" I managed to get out.

"No!" Maria shouted. "No, not okay! So not okay! Why would you say that's okay?"

I shrugged.

"Look, Bruce, or whatever your name is. We aren't following you to some magical place or something. I don't even know why you're here!"

"I'm sorry," Bruno said. "Allow me to explain my appearance. You two are in grave danger. I am from a land named Strelit, and I am the leader of it. However, you two are part of Strelit as well. A long time ago, shards of powers scattered across the US, especially in Boston, where both of you are from. But two of the shards landed in your ancestors. You, Leon, you have powers that are related to me, the leader of Strelit, and so you are becoming the leader of that land now. And you, Maria, have powers as well. And so, we need you two to come to Strelit, because there is a species of creatures named *demons* who are trying to take over Strelit and will do so by attacking you both."

I blinked twice. I was still frozen, and what he said didn't make the situation any better. I was a leader because of my family, and there were dragons and demons, and they were trying to kidnap me?

This sounded ridiculous.

"M-my powers came from my ancestors." I could hardly get a sentence out. "S-so, w-why would they come from you? W-wouldn't you have been d-dead?"

"Well, I have been the leader for over two hundred years and I have been alive for much more than that. And so my blood has been passed down to you, which is why you have the power to become the next leader. Trust me, it will all make sense later on."

"You expect us to believe you?" Maria scoffed. "Please. We weren't born yesterday. You're probably just some kid underneath a costume."

She walked up to Bruno and tugged at his face. It didn't move. She went to the tail and tried to pull it off.

"Why isn't it coming off? Wait, Leon, gimme the piece you found at the beach."

"H-h-here," I said, giving it to her. As it touched her hand, she yelped and dropped it. "Why is it cold?! Why is it freezing cold?!" She decided to kick it through the sand.

She went back to the dragon's tail and put it against the tip. "What? The piece looks like your tail. What is this?"

"That is a dragon tail from an ice dragon," Bruno said. "That thing that you might have seen falling from the sky not too long ago was the ice dragon to which that belonged to. There are dragons all over right now looking for you two."

That must have been the meteor-thing we were looking for. Could it possibly be?

"No," Maria said, "you're not fooling me, Bryan. This is just some joke or something. Who set you up to do this? Huh?"

"My name is Bruno. And I am not here to fool you. I am telling you the truth. You both have powers, and—"

"Whoa whoa whoa," Maria cut him off. "We do not have any powers, okay? That is ridiculous!"

"Why is it that Leon can hold the tail of the ice dragon and you cannot?"

"Wait." Maria looked at me, then back at Bruno, then at her hands. "No. No, there has to be another explanation. Th-there's no way."

"I cannot stay for much longer," he continued. "You two are in danger. Strelit is in danger as well. I cannot lead Strelit anymore. Leon, you must come to be the leader. Strelit needs your help."

What was he talking about? Me, a leader? There was no way. And yet, there was a dragon in front of me, and another dragon's tail in the sand. What if he was telling the truth?

"I understand that this is quite abrupt, but would you both be willing to come with me back to Strelit?" Bruno said, looking at me first, and then Maria.

"Ummm," I said. "I can't go with you. I'm sorry."

"Yeah," Maria said. "We can't just pick up and leave with you. We have lives here." Maria walked back to me and crossed her arms.

Bruno bowed his head and said, "I understand your priorities and desires. Just remember your powers are awakened and that earthquake wasn't a normal earthquake. That was just a sign that more is coming. Stay close and protect each other, for they are coming for you two."

He pulled out two golden necklaces, each with a pendant of a dragon with wings spread in midair. The colors kept changing like a shimmering rainbow.

"You should each put this on," Bruno said. "It will keep you safe."

Maria rolled her eyes. She snatched both necklaces and tossed one to me. I fumbled before I finally caught it. A warm tingling sensation started in my hands and spread throughout my body. The collar was intricately woven like a chain.

"I will leave now, but please be careful at all times. Good-bye for now." Bruno flew up into the sky and suddenly disappeared.

"That guy was weird," Maria said. "Come on, we should get back home. Your aunt's going to find out you're not in bed soon." Maria started walking back to the road and I followed her. "He just came here thinking he can prank us."

"W-what if he was telling the truth?"

"And that there is some magical place named Strelit or whatever? No way."

We walked in silence for the rest of the time, but we were both thinking. My mind was racing. Was he just messing with us? Or was what he said true?

We got back home, and Maria and I parted ways. I climbed back through the window and into my room. I put everything back where it was, and as soon as I was done, my aunt called my name.

"Hey, rat!" she shouted. "Get down here to eat breakfast!"

I put the necklace underneath my pillow and went down.

* * *

The day passed like usual, but I kept thinking about Bruno. Something about him made me believe him. And I contemplated going to Strelit the whole day. I had a horrible life here anyway. Nothing was keeping me here. I hated my aunt, I had nobody else—what was stopping me? And I could start a whole new life and be a new person.

But was Strelit even real? Would I just make myself look like a fool trying to find this random place?

That night, I had a weird dream. It was about my sister. I dreamed that I was in Strelit, but she was there also. And she was telling me to save her. Rebecca was telling me to come to Strelit to save her. The dream felt too real, like she was really trapped in Strelit and needed my help.

I woke up sweating and decided. I was going to Strelit.

CHAPTER FOUR

I went back to sleep, despite wanting to go to Strelit more than ever. I woke up a couple hours later at around seven thirty. The first thing I did was check if my necklace was underneath my pillow. Lifting the pillow, I didn't see a necklace. Panic rose and my heart thumped, leaping out of my chest. I had checked everywhere when I saw the intricate collar of the necklace placed on me. I followed it down my neck, and when I saw the pendant had somehow managed to get *inside* my body, I let out a scream loud enough for New York to hear. I suddenly closed my mouth, hoping my aunt wouldn't come up.

What was this necklace?

But I didn't have time to think about that. I heard my aunt's footsteps coming up the stairs. I had to think of an excuse to tell her. But she would see right through the lie.

She opened the door. "What's wrong with you, Leon? It's seven thirty in the morning, and you're screaming." Her eyes drooped, and she was barely awake.

"Um, sorry about that," I said. "I-I saw a-a-a spider." I smiled. She groaned and shut the door.

I got dressed and headed down. The whole house smelled of burnt toast. I grabbed a banana and headed out the door. I went to the house next door to see Maria, hoping she was home. I had to tell her about the necklace.

I knocked on the door, but there wasn't an answer. I knocked again, but nothing. Maybe she wasn't home?

"What are you doing?" Maria said behind me. I yelped and turned around.

"Why aren't you inside?" I asked.

"Well, why are *you* outside?"

"I-I thought you lived here."

"It's complicated," she said in a rush. "Let's just get away from here."

"Um, I wanted to tell you something. The necklace went inside of me."

"It happened to me too! It was, like, inside my body. That was so weird! It must be some kind of sick joke or something."

How could she still think Strelit was a joke? I mean, that stuff doesn't happen every day.

"I-I don't think it's a joke anymore," I said. "I don't think necklaces can do that."

"Well, it makes a whole lot more sense than a whole world full of dragons. I mean, come on. There's no way Bruno could be telling the truth."

We ended up on the beach again. Maria picked up a pebble and skipped it across the ocean. She picked up another one and skipped it again. *SLIP-SLIP-SLIP-PLOP.*

She kept skipping the rocks over and over again. Something was bothering her though, because she started chucking the pebbles instead.

She then picked up a huge rock, but before she could chuck that one too, I stepped in.

"Okay, okay," I said, putting my hands on the rock and lowering it. "What's wrong? Just put the rock down."

She dropped the rock back down on the beach. "It's nothing." She sat down and rested her head on her hands.

"Okay," I said, sitting down next to her.

"I mean, it's just crazy!" she ranted, out of nowhere. "My parents are always fighting, and it's just so hard. They completely ignore me all the time. You know how hard it is to hear it every day? Just the constant arguing. It's awful. That's why I stay in that house all the time. Just to get away from all the fighting."

"So, that's why you stay in the house next to me? So, you don't actually live there, but you just use it to get away."

Maria nodded. "I loved my parents. And we used to always do amazing things together. But as I grew older, they started fighting more and more. They never pay any attention to me, and half of the time, they take their anger out on me. I just wish I didn't have to be with them. It's so hard to be around it nonstop."

"Well, I wish I could say I knew what it's like. My parents died in a car crash when I was six. And my sister, Rebecca, was nowhere to be found. It happened when I lived in Boston."

"I'm sorry," Maria said. "That must've been awful."

"Yeah," I said. "But I had a dream about her last night. She was in Strelit, and she was asking me for my help. It seemed so real, like she might actually be there. And the more I think about it, the more I think it's a good idea to go to Strelit."

"I've thought about it too," Maria said. "There's nothing keeping me here. I can start fresh in Strelit and live a better life. I used to live in Boston too, when my mom was still acting. But you already knew that from Bruno. But still, there's no way that Strelit is real. It's just some fairy tale."

Maria picked up another pebble and skipped it. *SLIP-SLIP-SLIP-TONK*. That was strange. The rock had hit something in the ocean. Maria threw another pebble and the same thing happened. Something was in the water that wasn't there before.

The current of the water moved. Ripples formed at the surface. What was in the water?

A figure came out of the water.

Four figures, actually. They were all black and had two wings sprouting from their backs, plus two horns atop their heads. They stood on their hind legs. Even hunched down, they were a little over six feet tall, clearing my height by half a foot. Red veins ran across their entire body, and they had devilish red eyes.

Could they be the demons?

"I think we should go," Maria said.

We got up and ran, but the creatures caught up and surrounded us. We were trapped. What could we do?

"Greetings," one of them said. Its voice was crackly and garbled, like a scratchy record. "You need to come with us."

They stepped closer to us, and one tried to grab me. I stepped to the side and dodged the attacks.

Adrenaline surged through my veins, and my eyes were wide. I didn't know how long I could keep this up though. Another one came up behind me and grabbed me.

His scaly claws wrapped around me. I tried to struggle out, but it was no use. I tried to push out from behind the creature, but all of a sudden, the demons screamed.

I looked back in shock. All of them had clattered to the ground, and the sand around us was wet.

What had happened?

The demons looked at me in horror. Their veins glowed brighter and their wings tucked behind them a bit. They picked themselves up and flew in a hurry back to the ocean.

"What was that?" Maria asked. "You blasted water out of your hands."

"I did?" How had that happened? "But I didn't feel that." There was no way it could've been me.

"Let's just get out of here before something else comes back."

But before we could go, my necklace started shaking. It moved me across the beach. The force was so strong, it dragged me to the ground and kept pulling.

I couldn't stop. It was too strong, and I couldn't fight it. What was happening with this necklace?

Maria's necklace was doing the same. We were both being dragged down the beach toward a shack.

The ride was so bumpy, but I managed to say, "The necklace is dragging me to the shack over there!" The sand whipped my face and was sticking to my body.

Maria shouted, "We need to stop this thing before we crash into it!"

The old wooden shack was coming dangerously close. I tried to take the necklace off, but it was still inside of me.

What was I going to do?

I shielded my head with my arms as the shack approached. I hoped I could just break through the wood and then figure out how to get rid of the necklace later.

I closed my eyes and braced for impact.

But then, the necklace gradually came to a stop. We slowly floated back down to the ground. I opened my eyes to see the shack inches away from my face. I stood up and dusted my body off. I was alive.

Maria came up next to me. "I thought this necklace was supposed to keep us safe. Not try to ram us into shacks."

I shrugged. This shack was creepy. Spider webs covered the entire outside. It made a creaking sound as it swayed, as if it were speaking a warning.

"Let's just go back," I said, starting to walk back to the road, but the necklace dragged me back to the shack. I tried leaving again, but it wouldn't let me, and the necklace still wouldn't come off.

"Oh, come on," Maria said. "It's never going to let you go. Let's just go inside and see why it took us here."

I trembled with fear. I didn't want to go inside there. This shack was the stuff of nightmares.

Maria strode nonchalantly to the front of the shack as I closely followed.

An old wooden door sat there in the middle of two slabs of wood. Maria turned the doorknob, and it fell right off. She sighed and used her shoulder instead.

The door stood there like a boulder. She kept shoving at it but it didn't move. For such a flimsy building, the door should've come right off.

I tried shoving the door too. After a while, it finally budged. A centimeter. I groaned. This was going to take forever.

I was shoving and pushing the door when glass shattered nearby. I jumped. Maria had broken a cobwebbed window.

"What are you doing? That's illegal."

"So?" She rolled her eyes. "It's not like anyone's gonna know." I shook my head.

She checked to see if anyone was looking and slipped inside without making a sound. I followed her through the window. I slipped on a puddle on the floor and crashed to the ground with an immense thud.

"You just can't stay quiet, can you, Leon?" She helped me up.

A twenty-five-by-twenty-five-foot space stood in front of us. The ceiling seemed unusually tall. A central counter extended from one side of the room and almost touched the other side. A few windows and ledges lined the side we'd entered from, but other than that, there was nothing here.

I had taken a few steps around the shack when the necklace started buzzing.

"The necklace is vibrating," I told Maria. "I think it's some sort of

GPS. The closer we get to the thing, the more it vibrates."

What were we trying to find, though? I moved around the shack again. The necklace vibrated more or less, depending on where I was. I followed the vibration. It vibrated faster with every step I took. Meanwhile, Maria was giving herself a tour of the place.

As I reached the other side of the shack, the necklace started humming. I guessed I'd found the "treasure."

"I think this is it," I said, "but there's nothing here."

Maria started shoving the wall. I helped her out, but nothing moved, as expected. But then the wall gurgled, and part of it transformed into a door with a solid gold knob.

My mouth fell open. How did that door just appear? It wasn't there a second ago. I couldn't fathom how that had happened.

However, the knob wouldn't move, and there was no hint that the door was moving either, because it had no hinges. Maria just started kicking the door.

Behind the counter, something made a loud thud. Cans and metallic things started clanging to the floor. I screamed.

"Oh please," Maria said, rolling her eyes, "Don't be such a baby."

How could Maria not be scared? Someone could be trying to kill us right now. I grabbed a nail from the ground for a little bit of protection.

I handed Maria a nail too, but she scoffed and knocked it out of my hand. "That's not going to do anything."

It sounded like somebody was crawling out from underneath the counter. A gruff voice came from where the noise was.

"Kids these days just can't stay quiet, can they? When I was younger, if we made any noise, we would have to clean the dungeon."

I screamed. I grabbed Maria's arm so hard my knuckles turned white.

"Ow!" Maria pushed me away and rubbed her arm.

The thing knocked its head as it came out and muttered something foul. This person could be a murderer, waiting for someone to come inside the shack.

The person climbed out, but it wasn't a human being. We both screamed this time.

"What is that thing?" Maria said, her face twisting in disgust.

The creature had eight little stubs at the bottom of its body. And it had two arms as well. It wore a suit, but its skin was blue. Two round, sullen eyes made him look like he hadn't gotten a good night's sleep in three years.

"I'm not a thing," the creature grumbled. "My name is Simon, and I am a blubba gubba."

"A—a what?" I asked. All these creatures were really messing with my mind.

He scowled. "A blubba gubba. I am a threshold warrior. I protect one of the portals from this world to Strelit."

"Why are we here?" Maria asked him.

He sighed as if disappointed. "What do you think? Your necklaces, of course. Why else? Your necklace sensed that you were in danger, so it pulled you toward a safe location. Were you in trouble?"

"No," Maria answered, crossing her arms. "We were perfectly fine."

Simon scoffed. "Okay. Well, since you two are here, I think Bruno would want to see you and hear about your encounter. Would you two like to go to Strelit?"

"H-how would we get there?" I asked, which caused him to sigh again.

"Through the door behind you," Simon answered as he opened it with a key. The door swung open, revealing a set of stairs winding down to another floor.

Did I want to go down the stairs to Strelit? What was going to be down there? I mean, taking a look around couldn't do any harm.

I was starting down the stairs when Simon pulled me back.

"Don't you know anything?" Simon said. "Elders first." I stepped back and let Simon go first.

Maria and I shared a look. This creature was stubborn. It was as if he were just this grouchy old man. He had no patience.

He turned around and looked at me. "Oh, I will take the necklace now. You do not need them anymore."

I gave him my necklace, which thankfully came off without a problem.

Maria gave hers as well, and we went down after him.

The stairs were surprisingly sturdy, considering the rest of the shack looked like it was about fall over. The walls were smooth and had torches built into them. The air got colder the deeper we went. In front of us, light was coming closer and closer, until we reached the last step.

Torches lit up a vast room with absolutely nothing in it except a hobbit-hole-looking door. The edges glowed like something was beyond it. I wondered if Strelit was waiting outside the door. I had the jitters, my heart pulsing in worry but also excitement.

"Behind this door is Strelit," Simon said. "Are you positive you both want to cross this portal?"

Maria seemed confident, as if she had no regrets about going. I didn't really have anything to lose either. And I could always come back, right?

We both nodded yes.

He walked to the door with his eight legs squirming on the floor. I heard the key turn and the locks unlatch.

"Leon Rodriguez and Maria Salazar," Simon said. "I am proud to be the first person to say this to you two. Welcome to Strelit."

CHAPTER FIVE

The door swung open to reveal a flash of blinding light. I shielded my eyes for a moment and then opened them again to a world that seemed like paradise.

Flowers bloomed everywhere. The sky was filled by a rainbow of dragons of all different colors. Houses lined the street, and some bigger buildings were scattered near the road as well. Like a forest of pine trees, the air smelled fresh and clean. I could hear everything from the whoosh of dragons flying to the leaves swaying on the trees. In the distance, a white building towered above the rest of Strelit.

I stepped away from the door, and walked on the cobbled road, my shoes clacking. Little lanterns hung on the side of the street.

Child dragons played on the street with small blubba glubbas. Some dragons were red, others had icy scales, and others were camouflaged like the rough, brown dirt. The blubba gubbas were yellow, green, blue, and some were even purple.

A radiant dragon the color of sunlight approached us. The sun reflected off its scales.

"You two must be Leon and Maria!" the dragon shouted. "I am Angie, Bruno's daughter. Welcome." Maria and I both waved to her.

"I'm leaving now," Simon said. "Someone's gotta watch the portal." He squirmed away, but then he turned into a blue human. His body contorted and stretched until he looked like any other average person, except blue. Even his clothes stretched to fit him. My mouth gaped open.

"How did he do that?!" Maria exclaimed.

"Blubba gubbas can turn into any shape or creature," Angie said. "They just have to keep their color."

This new world was still shocking me, and the shock just kept growing and growing. My mind wasn't fast enough to process all of it.

"Come on, let's take a little tour," Angie said. "I'll guide you guys."

We followed her down the road, and she pointed out different things as we went by.

"Over on this side are the different kingdoms of Strelit. Each kingdom is for a different element of a dragon. There are four different elements for dragons. Fire, ice, earth, and light. There are also other creatures that live in Strelit. There's blubba gubbas, which you have met, and also unicorns."

Maria laughed.

What's funny?" Angie asked.

"Unicorns? Are you serious? Those are fake. Come on, what is this, Candy Land?"

"You don't want to mess with a unicorn," Angie said. "They can do a lot of harm. But anyhow, let's go see the Palace."

We had reached a forest, but a bright light shone through the woods.

"What's that over there?" I asked, pointing to the light.

"That's the tree that powers all of Wohna, but we'll save that for a later adventure," Angie said. "And for now, we have it in our possession."

What did that mean? Only *for now*? And I thought we were in Strelit— what's Wohna?

"What is that supposed to mean?" Maria asked. "Is it, like, *temporarily* here?"

Angie looked at us, confused. "You don't know about the Wohna Games?" We both shook our heads. She gasped. "You must know by now. The Wohna Games happen every fifty years. And the winner gets more land and takes away land from neighboring worlds. You're going to have to compete as well, Leon. It's happening this time next year."

I gulped. Why did I have to compete? Couldn't I just stay on the sidelines? I was already starting to panic, and the Wohna Games were a year away!

"W-what's Wohna?" I asked Angie. "I thought we were in Strelit."

"Well, Strelit is a part of Wohna," she answered as we walked away from the light. "Think of Wohna like the entire world, and each part, like Strelit, and where you're from, Midgard, are all little worlds, I think you would call them *countries*, and they make up the entire world, Wohna."

That made more sense, but what was *Midgard*? I didn't have time to ask because we were approaching the large building I saw before. It was a pearly white tower with a circular dome at the top, similar to the US Capitol. The building had dark wood accents and windows all around. It was breathtaking.

The two wooden doors at the front were at least twelve feet tall. Two dragons with spears blocked the entryway.

"Welcome, Angie," they said. "Who are the other two?"

"Leon Rodriguez and Maria Salazar," Angie replied.

They nodded. They slid the bar blocking the doors over to one side. Next, the two of them unlocked six different locks and latches.

"That's a lot of security," Maria said. "Like, a lot."

"We've had … some issues with security in the past," Angie said. "But those are all cleared up now. Let me show you inside."

The doors opened. The inside of the tower was stunning. It was huge, with one grand staircase on each side. A central hallway stretched as far as I could see, with larger rooms to the left and the right as well.

"This is the Grand Room," Angie said as she led us down the hallway. Our footsteps echoed along the walls. There were even more rooms here, but these seemed different. The doors had carvings in them. One had etched leaves. Another had flowers, and some were more abstract.

The hallway finally stopped. The biggest door of all stood at the end of the hall. The dark wooden double door had a design that wasn't like any others I'd seen. It looked like the yin-yang symbol but with four colors. The colors surrounded a gold circle in the middle, almost like the petals of a flower. The top section of the circle was red, the right was brown, the bottom was an icy blue, and the left was a blinding yellow.

Angie opened the door, and Bruno stood there on the other side. He was peering over a leather-bound book that looked unopened since the 1800s.

"Good afternoon. What can I help you with?" Bruno's voice was calm and peaceful, like a still lake. "Ah. Leon and Maria." He announced the words with a smile. "So nice to see you again. What brings you two here?"

"They've made their decisions," Angie said.

When did we make our decisions? We were dragged here by that crazy necklace.

"Oh," Bruno said. "And what is that decision? I'm hoping you are willing to stay?" He awaited our response and stood still. The whole room seemed to be waiting.

"Well," I started. "When we were still in Hawaii, four of these black creatures attacked us."

"Oh my," Bruno said. "Those must have been the demons. They came so soon. But I think the first shock is that you survived. How did you?"

"Um … there was water, and it pushed them back," I said. "But I don't know how it happened."

"Wait," Maria said. "I thought you knew that you did that. You shot it out of your hands."

I shot the water? No, that was impossible. There was no way I could've done it. But Bruno did say we had powers now. Could shooting water be mine?

"Is that possible?" I asked Bruno.

"Yes, of course. As I said before, you both have powers related to a type of element. Yours could be ice. But as the leader, you'll have access to all of the elements. If, that is, you want to become the leader. What is your decision?"

"I want to stay," Maria said. "How long do we need to stay for?"

"Well," Bruno started. "Forever."

Maria fell silent. She was never silent. And her face was completely blank. "You don't mean like *forever* forever, right? It's just, like, a long time?"

"Unfortunately, no," Bruno answered. "You would have to live here forever. And it would be too risky to travel back and forth."

Maria was still quiet, but her head fell down and her hair covered her face. Was everything okay?

"I-I mean, I'll be okay. It's not like I had a relationship with my family when I was there. I-I think I'll be fine. Yeah, I'll be fine, right?" Her words trailed off, and she looked at the ground.

"Are you sure you're okay?" I asked Maria.

"I said, I'll be fine!" she snapped. She faced Bruno. "I'm ready to stay."

Bruno nodded. "Only if you want to. But I am happy you chose to stay. Now, Leon?"

I thought for a second. If I went back to Earth, I would be able to live a normal life and go back to my daily routine. If I stayed in Strelit, I would never have to see my aunt again. But if I stayed, I'd never get to go back to school, and I wouldn't even get to see another human again or experience a regular life. It would be like I had been wiped off the face of the Earth. And I would have to be the leader of a whole kingdom! How was I going to rule a whole kingdom of unknown creatures?! Everything would change.

But I'd get the chance to start a new life and be respected for once. Strelit would be the greatest thing to ever happen to me. And maybe I could have a whole new family with everybody here.

"Well, make a decision!" Maria shouted. They all stared at me, waiting for an answer.

"I want to stay."

Bruno and Angie cheered and made whooping sounds. I guessed that was their way of clapping?

"Now," Bruno said. "Let's finish this tour."

CHAPTER SIX

We walked back to the front of the Palace and headed out the doors. The sun was setting, coloring the sky in a palette of pinks and oranges.

Rebecca and I would always watch the sunsets together. I wondered whether Angie knew my sister. Maybe she could tell me where she was.

"Is the sky always this beautiful?" Maria said, amazed.

"Breathtaking, right?" Angie answered. "The sunsets in Strelit are the best. Well, besides the ones in Asgard. Those are heavenly."

Wasn't Asgard some made-up place, where Thor's from? That guy from Norse mythology with the big hammer that can control storms?

"Um, Angie. Do you know of anyone named Rebecca here in Strelit?" I waited, hoping that she knew her.

"No. That's a very odd name for someone here to have. What type of creature is she?"

"Um, a human?"

"No. You two are the only humans in existence to come to Strelit. Do you know this Rebecca?"

"Yeah," I muttered, my head drooping. Well, just because Angie didn't know Rebecca didn't mean that she wasn't here. Maybe she was just lying low.

We turned to the right and headed to what looked like a volcano. The mountain loomed ahead, and smoke billowed out from the top.

I flew on Bruno's back as Maria flew on Angie's. Riding a dragon was so weird. Bruno lowered to the ground like a dog lying down, and then I had to clamber up to his back and saddle myself on his scales. Some scales jutted out far enough that I could hold on to them. The ride was incredibly bumpy, and I almost fell at every dip.

Once we were close to the volcano, the smoke seared my eyes and made them water. The ground bubbled, and pots of boiling lava were everywhere.

"Wait a minute," Maria said. "Why were we the ones chosen to come to Strelit? What's so special about us? Well, I know I'm special, but like, why us?"

Bruno chuckled a bit. "You certainly are special. But you two were brought here because your ancestors have ties to Strelit. It's a bit complicated, but to put it simply, a family member before you had a piece of DNA of someone from Strelit. And for Leon's case, that DNA was mine, which is why you are the leader."

So, Bruno was kind of like my great-great-great-great-grandfather?

We slowed down when someone greeted us. A small, chubby dragon flew towards us like a broken train moving uphill. His tiny wings looked like they shouldn't have been able to hold his weight. His skin was bright red, and his stomach was glowing.

"Welcome to Volcano Ignis." The dragon had a high-pitched, childlike voice. "My name's Chip, the leader of Fierys, the fire kingdom. You must be Leon?" I nodded my head.

He was a leader? He didn't even look old enough to be outside by himself!

Chip introduced himself to Maria, and then talked to Bruno and Angie for a while before coming back to us. "Please, follow me. I'll give you guys a tour inside."

He flew back to the volcano, which was shaking and teetering. Bruno caught up with Chip, and they whispered back and forth, as if they were arguing. I couldn't hear the conversation, but I caught phrases like "He's too young" and "He's not ready."

Were they talking about me? I mean, I was picked for a reason, right?

As we got closer to the volcano, I could hardly breathe. The air was so smoky you couldn't even see through it. All I could make out was the monstrous volcano, the bubbling lava, and Chip's fat, glowing belly.

The lava made me a bit uneasy. Ever since the car accident, fire had traumatized and scared me. But I needed to push through right now.

We came to a stop in front of Volcano Ignis. The only thing not covered in boiling lava was a small step made of obsidian. Chip took a deep breath and screamed. It sounded harsh and guttural, like someone was dying. I nearly fell back into the boiling lava.

Immediately, part of the volcano magically melted away, leading us inside.

Maria whispered to me, "Wouldn't knocking be easier?"

Chip led us in and announced, "Welcome to the inside of Volcano Ignis!"

The volcano was even bigger from the inside. So many dragons crowded the space, like a busy mall. Each dragon looked different, but they were all red.

"So," Chip said, "This first floor is the market. This is where you can buy all kinds of stuff."

"Why are all the dragons red?" Maria interrupted. "Is this where fire dragons live?"

"Yes. The fire dragons and all the other fire element creatures live here. Including me!"

The market was filled with different foods and snacks, but I didn't know any of them. One looked like a glass diamond, but with lava swirling inside of it.

"Those are lava rockets," Bruno said. "They are like—how do you call them in your world—oh, like chips."

"Have one!" Chip exclaimed and tossed one each to Maria and me. Maria popped it into her mouth without question.

My mind went back to the car accident with my parents and how the fire killed them. But I had to eat the lava rocket to make Bruno think of me as capable of being the leader. And I wasn't in any danger.

I put the snack in my mouth.

My mouth burned like it was on fire. The pain didn't go away. Heat flushed my entire face, and my forehead collected beads of sweat. What was this thing?

"It's kind of sweet," Maria said. "Like honey. Can I have another one?" Her eyes were wide, and she had a smile on her face.

This lava rocket did not taste like honey to me. This was the worst thing I could eat. My mouth felt singed.

"Oh," Bruno said. "You, Maria, must be a fire type. I'm glad we could find both of your elements so soon."

"Yes!" Chip shouted. "Now let's continue the tour! There's still so much to see!"

All of a sudden, the ground started shaking. Maria and I fell to the trembling ground.

"WHAT'S HAPPENING?!" Maria shouted.

The dragons didn't know what was happening either. The shaking made the floor heavily uneven as the cracks in the ground grew into massive holes.

"ISN'T THIS SUPPOSED TO BE A DORMANT VOLCANO?!" Maria was in a panic, and so was I.

Was I going to die?

A tail swooped me up and plopped me on a dragon's back. Bruno had picked me up, and Angie picked up Maria.

"Why is the volcano erupting?" I asked Bruno. The ground was rising and falling like an ocean.

"It's not erupting. Something awakened Yggdrasil," Chip said.

Wasn't that the Tree of Life from Norse mythology? There was no way Yggdrasil was here.

Something shot out of the ground like an arrow and struck the volcano's wall. It broke through the wall like it was made of butter.

I couldn't believe what I was seeing. A tree root the size of a skyscraper had punctured a volcano like it was a balloon. Was I in Hogwarts or something?

Everybody eyed me warily, as though I had somehow managed to pull a tree root out of the ground. But I couldn't even pick up my bike.

"Leon." Chip's voice was shaking. "Did you do that?" He spoke to me like I was dangerous and was threatening him.

"Chip, why is there a tree root sticking out of the ground?" I asked. There was no way something like that could even happen anywhere on the planet. But then again, I didn't think we were on planet Earth. Where was Strelit, anyway?

"Well, something awakened Yggdrasil, the Tree of Life that powers Strelit and other lands as well. So, it went all crazy and popped out. You might have something to do with this, Leon." Chip explained it like I should know everything by now.

"Something awakened Yggdra *what*?" My mind was already struggling to understand why a root that big had appeared, and now Chip's telling me that some tree powered the whole world *and* I could cause it to stir up like that?

"Yggdrasil. You know, the Tree of Life?" Chip was now rolling his eyes like Maria. Everybody was either still watching me, as though I might put the root back, or eyeing the root like it was supposed to put itself back.

"That's the tree that I was telling you about before," Angie said. "The one shining through the woods."

"But isn't Yggdrasil part of a myth though? Like in Norse or something?" I asked, still boggled by everything that was happening.

"Um, I mean, it's not a myth, it is right here. And this isn't Norse," Chip answered back, indicating the root. Maria stood next to Chip, nodding and acting like she knew, but in reality, she didn't know what was going on either.

Chip had been shocked by what I'd said about Norse myth. He even asked Bruno if he was sure that I was the new leader of Strelit.

"Leon, what are you saying?" Bruno explained. "We are in Wohna."

There was that word again. *Wohna.* What happened to planet Earth?

Maria dropped her act and said, "Where's Earth, then? You know, the fifth planet from the Sun."

"It's the third planet," I said.

"Whatever," she said, flapping her hand as if telling me to go away. "Is this a joke or something?" Maria looked at Bruno and Angie, and they both shook their heads to confirm that they were dead serious.

This conversation was so weird. Chip said he had never heard of Earth, which was like never hearing about the United States. And he also said that I was standing in a location from Norse mythology, which meant a made-up place.

"Leon, Wohna is the world," Bruno said. "That is where Strelit is. You just have to believe that. And your power is only growing. But not only does great power come with great responsibility, but also with great danger."

His words tied a knot in my stomach. I wasn't angry, but a fire was burning inside my stomach. It was growing stronger and gnawing at me, making me weak and tired. So weak and tired that I collapsed on the ground.

CHAPTER SEVEN

My eyes opened to Maria staring at me. "Oh! Leon, you're awake. Bruno said you weren't going to wake up for another half hour, so he wanted me to watch you in case something happened."

"Why would I be unconscious for another half hour, what happened?" I asked. My voice was so weak I thought she wouldn't hear me.

"You know that lava rocket thing you ate when Chip was taking us on the tour?" I nodded. "Well, it made you weak, and you fainted."

That explained the fire I felt in my stomach.

I noticed the room for the first time. I was lying in a bed so soft it felt like a cloud. The smell of freshly baked pastries wafted outside my room. The royal blue walls looked freshly painted. The view outside one of the many windows instantly made me realize I was in the Palace.

"How come *you* didn't pass out?" I asked.

"It's because I'm a fire type," she said. "They said that I have powers that I haven't discovered yet. Oh, also. There's a party tonight to appoint you the new leader. You should go get ready."

"But w-where am I supposed to get ready?"

"Oh, you have a room here. And I think they have clothes for you. I'll show you where it is."

I groaned as I got out of bed. I followed Maria down the corridor, and she opened a door for me.

The nice bedroom was furnished and everything. A wooden desk was on one wall, a bed on the other, plus a small room for a closet. But in the corner, there was a little thing curled up. It looked like a yorkie dog with a bow in its brown fur, but it had tiny wings on its back. What was it?

I went closer, and then it perked its head.

"Can't you see I'm trying to sleep?!" the thing shouted at me. "Don't wake me up!" It got up and shook itself off. "You're Leon. I'm Bubbles. I'm your companion. Now, get ready for your party!"

"H-h-how are you talking?" I asked. This world was so weird. Now there were talking dogs?

"I'm a Schnawegian," Bubbles said. "Us Schnawegians can talk. Get used to it!" She hopped onto the desk and looked at me with wide eyes.

"What is going on?!" Maria shouted. "You can talk? And you're Norwegian? This is crazy."

"I'm a Schnawegian," Bubbles said. "Not some Nor-whatever you're saying. But there's a party coming up, Leon. Let's get ready! Cuz this look, whatever it is, ain't gonna cut it." She walked on her four legs out of the room and yelled at somebody outside.

"What's with her?" Maria whispered. "She's nuts."

I shrugged as Bubbles came back in, followed by a dragon dragging a clothes rack with a bunch of suits.

"That's more like it," Bubbles said. "Now try them on!"

* * *

I walked down the hall, wearing a black suit with a bowtie and a white undershirt. I felt uncomfortable and awkward. I almost never put on a suit. The last time I did was at my parents' funeral.

The only thing that I had brought with me was a purple hat, which was now sitting on my desk. This hat was given to me by my parents and was the only thing I had left to remember them by. Every time I looked at it, it brought me closer to them and I felt more at ease.

Bubbles and I went downstairs to the main entrance. Maria was already there. Her brown hair flowed down in loose curls. Her blue dress went to just below her knees.

"Hi," I said. "Are you ready?"

"Yeah," Maria said. "I think the party is just outside. Bruno said to just take a right and then it should be there."

Creatures chattered outside. My stomach was twisting and turning. I didn't want to go meet all those people. But that's what a leader had to do.

I pushed through the doors to the green lawn. The grass was crammed with dragons, blubba gubbas, and all sorts of other creatures. The party smelled of delicious food and snacks.

Bruno came up to us. "Welcome! Come, I would like you two to meet some people."

He led us through the crowd. We bumped into dozens of creatures along the way, some who recognized us and some who didn't.

We got to the end of the crowd, where a group of three creatures were talking. One of them was Chip, another was a unicorn, and the other one was a black blubba gubba.

"Hello!" Bruno said to the crowd. "This is Leon and Maria. And you two have already met Chip, but Violet is the unicorn, and Professor Henchberry is the blubba gubba."

"So nice to meet you both," Violet said. Her voice was smooth and silky, like she worked at a spa. "Bruno has told me so much about you two."

"Hi," I said, my voice smoother and more relaxed. I didn't know why, but her voice and presence put me at ease.

"So *this* is the kid who's supposed to lead all of Strelit?" Professor Henchberry grunted. He had a mean look on his face, with his narrow eyes and curled lip, and he stared at me with pure hatred.

What did he have against me? I hadn't done anything to him. I just got here! Was he always like this?

"Henchberry, give him a break," Chip said. "You're so critical. You need to chill down a bit, ya know?"

"He's probably going to blow the whole Palace up," Henchberry said back.

"Mother Carla picked him," Bruno said.

"Hmph, *that* makes sense. She's a nutty lunatic." Henchberry still looked at me with disgust.

Who was Mother Carla?

"Anyhow," Violet interrupted. "Bruno, Chip, Henchberry, and I are the Council. We help make decisions in Strelit. We all represent the different creatures in Strelit and make sure everyone is taken into consideration. We will help you in your journey of being the leader. And both of you are joining the Council as well!"

Part of me didn't want to join, because a quarter of the members already hated my guts. But I didn't think I had a choice.

"We shall split up now," Bruno said. "But I'm glad both of you were able to meet the rest of the Council. Off to the party!"

Violet went over to some other unicorns, where she started laughing and chatting; Chip flew to the food bar; and Professor Henchberry suddenly disappeared.

"This is where we part; I must complete a few papers before I abdicate the throne and pass it down to you," Bruno said. "Good-bye." He flew high into the sky.

I enjoyed the party and met some new creatures. I ate some exotic food like nothing I had ever seen before. Then a horn sounded from the Palace.

Slowly, everyone started chattering excitedly like something special was about to happen. The creatures walked toward the huge stage-auditorium-thing attached to the side of the building. Maria and I followed the sea of everybody, which moved like a wave until it stopped.

Bruno came onstage. A spotlight shone on him and followed him to the center of the stage. He cleared his throat.

"Citizens of Strelit, I would like to thank you for being here today." His voice boomed as though he were speaking into a microphone. "I, unfortunately, do not have the power and strength to continue to rule Strelit like I have for the last two hundred sixty-seven years. But I know that the new ruler of Strelit will lead all citizens to a bright future." The creatures shouted, whooped, and hollered while Bruno bowed his head. "Leon, will you please step up onstage?"

I trembled like an earthquake. One pair of eyes turned to me, and then another, and another, and another, like a domino effect. Pretty soon, all eyes were staring at me. Beads of sweat dripped down my forehead as I walked to the stage. Everybody's eyes were locked onto me. When I finally got up onstage, my palms and head were drenched in sweat.

Bruno nodded his head at me. "The stage is all yours."

I got to center stage and gulped. I hadn't realized how many creatures actually lived in Strelit.

Thousands of creatures packed the grounds outside of the Palace. Most were dragons, but there were many unicorns and blubba gubbas, along with a few Schnawegians.

The way the creatures had arranged themselves was weird. There were no assigned seats or places, but each kingdom stayed in their own circle, with just them and nobody else. A group of ice dragons would be over here, and fire dragons over there, and some unicorns in the middle. From what I've heard, the unicorns don't belong to a certain element, so they wander wherever they want in Strelit.

Everyone looked eagerly at me, like they wanted me to say something inspirational or motivational. Their faces only made me even more nervous. I couldn't keep their hopes up forever. I was going to mess up eventually. I spotted Maria and Bubbles, who seemed to be arguing. I tensed up and spoke into the mic.

"Hello, I am Leon. Um, you know who I am, Bruno just said that. I'm from Midgard. I came here with my friend Maria because I was chosen to become the leader of Strelit. I was born in Boston. I'm not sure if the citizens of Strelit know where that is but it is on the east side of the United States of America, or USA. Then, when my parents died in a car accident, I moved to an island, Hawaii. Hawaii is actually many islands combined into one state, which was first settled by the Polynesians …"

I kept on talking about my life until Maria made a *talking-too-much* gesture with her hands, and then a gesture like she was going to fall asleep. What was I doing? Everyone was going to lose all interest!

"Anyway," I said. "Um … I'll do my best to lead Strelit in the best way possible."

Everyone erupted in cheers and shouts. I was shocked. I hadn't expected anyone to like me, let alone support me. I backed away from the mic as Bruno took my place.

"Now, to honor the tradition of Strelit," Bruno said, "would someone please bring the Goblet of Green Fire to the stage?

Was there going to be a fire? Fire, fire.

My mom decided to unbuckle her seatbelt right before the car rolled down the ditch. The car slammed into a tree, sending my mom crashing into the windshield. The gas started dripping, and it was only a matter of time before we would burn in flames.

I snapped out of my flashback when two dragons flew above us. They hovered down, holding a rustic goblet in their claws.

The goblet was as big as either of them, and it looked heavy. The two dragons let out a loud grunt as they set it down on the stage. Anxious and scared, I looked inside the goblet.

The inside was the same rusted color as the outside. Instead of the green flame, a white powder lined the inside of the goblet. Bruno walked opposite me and spat fire out of his mouth into the goblet, and then green flames appeared.

The flames started at the bottom and licked the sides until they curled to the top like a snake. The whole inside of the goblet was dancing in the green fire. My body froze and twitched like I was under the fire's will.

The car was doused with water, only to uncover my

mom and dad, burned.

"Now, Leon must repeat after me, and then he will be the official leader!"

No, no, no. The flame was like a constrictor, wrapping me in its coil until I couldn't take the pressure.

I screamed and lost control.

Water surged out of my hands and doused the fire, but it didn't stop there. Water swirled round and round me like a hurricane, growing bigger and bigger. The water hurricane stopped all of a sudden. I looked down at my feet, and they had turned into blue claws. My clothes had disappeared and I could feel two wings flapping behind me. I was a water dragon.

And then I roared and took to the sky.

I towered over everyone and stood ten times taller than a normal dragon—and they were already ten feet tall!

But I had no control of my body. The water dragon was like another being taking over my body. It showered everybody in water and destroyed everything in its way.

I crashed into the crowd and sent ten creatures soaring into the sky. All I could feel was the dragon's panic and terror. I was slipping away from my own conscience. There was no way I could control it.

Most of the dragons who had been sent flying were able to hover and stay safe, but two Schnawegians were trying to flap their tiny wings to keep from falling. Maria ran away and hid underneath a tree.

My body was getting weaker and weaker by the second. The water dragon acted more recklessly, and it flew full speed into the stage.

I tried to do something, but my body was so weak, I felt like a rag doll being tossed around. All I could see was the water dragon getting closer and closer to the stage. My eyesight went blurry, and black spots danced in my vision.

My eyelids began to droop—and then everything went black.

CHAPTER EIGHT

I was awakened by murmurs. To my right, Bruno was talking to Professor Henchberry.

"I can't believe you chose him to be the leader!" Henchberry said. "I mean, you could've chosen anybody else, and they would've been better than him."

"I didn't choose him," Bruno said. "Mother Carla chose him after I told her I would be resigning, and I trust Mother Carla."

I groggily looked around. I was lying on a hospital bed next to a small side table with yellow flowers. A needle in my arm hooked up to a bag that was infusing a yellow nectar into me. Two windows looked out onto the lawn and the Palace.

A unicorn was in the room as well. She must have been the doctor because she was fixing the bag hooked up to my arm.

The doctor noticed I was awake. "Leon, you're awake! How do you feel?"

Bruno came over to my side as well, but Professor Henchberry had slipped out the door as soon as he saw me awake.

"Um, I feel fine," I said. "What happened?" All I could remember was blacking out.

"You performed an emotional discharge," Bruno said. "An *emotional discharge* is when one uses their powers and subconsciously or consciously inputs emotion, which is what happened to you. You panicked and lost control of your powers and summoned a dragon, which is called your emotional creature. Your dragon was a water dragon, though, Leon. That is very unique since there isn't a water element, only ice."

So what I had was special? I guessed that's interesting, but summoning a creature was still just as scary whether it was a water dragon or an ice dragon.

"However, an emotional creature uses the creator's energy to thrive, which can cause the creator to die. You are lucky to survive such a dangerous act, Leon."

"How could I die because of that?" My voice was so weak it came out as a whisper.

"Emotional discharges happen based on emotions, and different emotions create different outcomes. Your outcome was most likely because of panic, based on how you reacted with the fire. And as the emotions grow stronger, the discharge becomes greater as well. However, when the emotions get too strong and the emotions discharge, there can be complications that can cause creatures to die."

"So, I have to not have any emotions?" I asked.

How was I supposed to have no emotions? Would I have to stop thinking about my aunt, and school, and family, and so many other things? But I was already thinking about them!

"Not necessarily," Bruno answered. "You have to learn how to keep your emotions calm and collected, and if they do get stronger, learn how to decrease them and express them without acting irrationally."

Professor Henchberry walked back through the door and huffed. "He's still here?" Henchberry said to Bruno. "So much for being strong enough to lead Strelit. He can't even survive his first day."

"I'm fine." Adamant to prove him wrong, I swung out of bed and tried to stand up, but I immediately collapsed back onto the bed and groaned.

Henchberry snickered. "Exactly my point."

I lowered my head, trying to hide my embarrassment.

"You should go visit Mother Carla," Bruno said to me. "It's good that you meet her and get to know her. She can provide a lot of help for you and Maria."

Henchberry scoffed. "Carla is a crazy, loopy, one-eyed bat who doesn't know her right from her left."

"Professor Henchberry," Bruno said, "please don't use that language to describe someone. She's not even a bat."

"She acts like one," Henchberry gruffed.

What was wrong with him? And who was Mother Carla?

"Um … who's Mother Carla?" I asked. They all looked confused, like they were surprised I didn't know.

"Are you— I mean, do you see this, Bruno?" Henchberry yelled. "He doesn't even know who that crazy lady is!"

"I-I-I'm sorry for asking." I lowered my head.

"Henchberry, please." Bruno was getting angry, but was still calmer than anyone I knew. "You did nothing wrong, Leon. Mother Carla is a Vanir God. She is a fortune-teller who has predicted many events in the past. She chooses the new leader when one resigns."

"There's no thought to what she does, anyone could do it. No wonder she picked you," Henchberry said.

Someone knocked. The doctor opened the door, and Maria and Bubbles burst in.

"We're here!" Maria exclaimed as she plopped Bubbles onto my bed.

"I said, let me down!" Bubbles barked at her. "Are you doing alright? Man, lemme tell you. You smacked down hard! *Bam*, right on the ground. And then Bruno carried you over to the hospital." Bubbles curled up next to me. "I'm glad you're okay though." She fell asleep.

"Well, I guess you're sleeping here tonight," Maria said. "How long does he have to be in the hospital for?"

"Probably just for the night," the doctor said. "He's healing very well. After an emotional discharge, it's usually three to four days. But I do think it's time for Leon to get some rest, so I think it would be best for him to be alone."

They all walked out except Bubbles, who stayed on the bed, snoring. Maria went to pick her up, but Bubbles nipped at her hand and went back to sleep.

"I think it's okay if Bubbles stays," Bruno said. "She shouldn't be a problem." He said thank-you to the doctor and walked out. The doctor stayed for a little while, checking a piece of paper, and then she started glowing. She created a blue aura around me and left. Maybe that was some sort of healing charm.

The room was silent except for some machines beeping and Bubbles snoring. As I lay there, all types of thoughts flooded my brain. Was I good enough to be a leader? I was in the hospital on my first day! Would everyone hate me now? Would I be able to handle the pressure? Would Bruno be proud of me?

Bubbles knew exactly what to say. "Hey, Leon. You'll be fine." She went back to snoring. Those words put me at ease, and I fell asleep.

*   *   *

I woke to rays of sun poking into my hospital room. Groggy, I stretched as much as I could in my hospital bed. Bubbles wasn't there.

The doctor came in and said, "Congrats, Leon! All your vitals seem perfect, and you're back to normal!" She helped me get out of bed. "Bruno and Maria are waiting in the lobby. I'll take you to them."

Bubbles was probably with them.

I followed the doctor down the hall, getting a glimpse of the hospital for the first time. The white walls were kind of plain, with a few paintings here and there.

Maria, Bruno, and Bubbles were all in the waiting room. Bubbles was pacing while Maria sat on a stool, looking lost. Bruno was chatting with another unicorn.

"Surprise!" the doctor said. Bubbles went to stand by my legs, but Maria didn't seem to have any emotion.

"You're alive," Maria said. She didn't seem to really care about me that much.

"When did you guys come back?" I asked.

"This morning. Bubbles stayed here through the night."

The doctor walked over to talk to Bruno. He said good-bye to her and the other unicorn, and then came over to us. "Leon," he said, "how are you feeling?"

"I feel fine." Nothing felt different except for some coldness, maybe from the blue aura.

"Excellent." Bruno smiled. "Now, we must be on our way. I would like you two to meet Mother Carla."

"Didn't Professor Henchberry say she's a crazy, loopy, one-eyed bat?" I asked. Was it safe to meet her?

Bruno sighed. "Sometimes Professor Henchberry doesn't always say things that are necessarily true. Mother Carla is a very nice lady. You have nothing to worry about."

We headed out the front door and onto the fresh green lawn. I hadn't noticed from my hospital window, but the hospital was right across the street from and a little to the right of the Palace. The streets looked surprisingly similar to the ones in the US. Each road had two lanes, one for each direction of traffic, but instead of cars, there were dragons, unicorns, and so many other creatures flying around. They flew better than people drive. On sidewalks on both sides of the street, blubba gubbas and other creatures that I didn't know walked, crawled, and even skipped by. Some flying creatures also pulled carriage-like taxis that took off into the sky.

Bruno walked to the sidewalk and hovered up. "Now, I will give you a ride to our next destination since you both don't know how to use your powers yet." We both hopped on his back, and I held Bubbles in my lap.

A couple minutes passed, and we were far past the busy part of Strelit, going into what seemed like a barren town. It was just us on the road now.

"Uh. Where exactly are we going?" Maria asked.

"We are almost there," Bruno said. "I would say two or three minutes."

But we kept flying and flying like we had no destination. The road became dirt, and the dirt became bark. Bruno slowed down as we got closer to the forest that surrounded Strelit. He stopped just in front of the first few trees, and we all hopped off.

"This is our destination," he said.

Maria and I were confused. There was nothing here. Bruno handed each of us a map of what looked like the forest ahead. Our location was marked at the bottom left of the page, and there was a red dot in the upper right-hand corner.

"What are we supposed to do with this?" Maria said, holding the paper out in front of her.

"It's a map of the forest," Bruno explained. "Your destination is marked in red. Part of this is to test your abilities to navigate through the forest on your own."

"And our destination is Mother Carla?" I asked. The forest was so thick; how were we supposed to find her?

"I'll leave the details of the destination a secret," Bruno said. "Are you ready?" We both nodded, a bit worried. "You may begin!"

We slowly made our way into the forest. The trees grew so tall and dense, the light was swallowed quickly. Twigs, dead branches, and tiny rocks covered the dirt. I could hear the *swoosh* of wind and the crunch of the ground beneath my feet. The air was bitter and cold, with a faint scent of rain. My forehead dripped with sweat, and my heart pounded with fear.

What if we got lost? What if we got ambushed? What if we didn't come out alive? There were so many things that could go wrong.

"Onward!" Bubbles shouted as she marched farther into the forest.

I gulped. This was a bad idea.

As we journeyed, we could only see by the small slivers of sun that managed to peek through the trees. We kept checking the map. As we moved, inky footprints appeared wherever we had gone, which made it much easier to know where we were going. The map also marked distinct rocks and trees that we could use to get a better sense of where we were.

The forest was quiet. We crunched the twigs and leaves underneath us. Every now and then, a creature would skitter along the ground.

Once we got close to the red dot, a pony-like figure with a long, dragon-like snout was wandering around the forest. They made eye contact with us.

"Ah!" the creature said. "It's you two! Come, come, Mother is waiting." She kept walking through the forest, but Maria and I stood there, completely confused. Were we supposed to follow her? "Well, let's not keep her waiting!" the creature said again. Maria and I caught up to the creature, who moved much faster than other creatures in Strelit.

"Wait," Maria said. "Slow down!" The creature slowed down so we could walk with her. "Who are you?"

"I'm Susan. I live in the same village as Mother Carla, and she sent me to go looking for you. She didn't want you to get lost!"

We kept following Susan, who seemed to know where she was going. A constant question nagged me, and finally, I just had to ask. "Um, Susan. I don't mean to be rude. But what are you?"

"Oh, it's not a bother at all," Susan replied, "I am a Vanir God. Some of the Vanir Gods have the ability to see someone's future. I can't do that, but you'll soon meet Mother Carla, who can." She spoke with a faint accent that sounded European, which was impossible. We kept trudging along in the forest, making turns around trees and boulders, until we reached a dirt path.

"Welcome to Vanir Village!" Susan announced, but there was nothing in sight. "Well, we have technically reached the village, but it'll be a couple of minutes before we see the actual village."

We followed the path, passing welcome signs as well as other Vanir Gods, who all waved and said hi. The dirt turned to paved stone, and the faint sound of an instrument grew louder. The Vanir Gods showed up everywhere, all greeting each other and chatting. The creatures were buying groceries, trading in small stores, and even picking up their kids from daycare. This place was so lively, it reminded me of small towns back in Hawaii.

A huge fountain stood at the center of the village. There was a band,

and one of the musicians was playing the instrument I'd heard before. It sounded like a piano mixed with a harp. Susan greeted the band members and kept walking.

We headed into what looked like the residential part of the village. Small houses and cottages lined both sides of the road. Most of the houses were neatly organized and taken care of. Then we came to a little cottage painted pearl white and made out of wood. A sign at the front of its little fence read All are welcome. The cottage made me feel like someone was giving me a warm hug.

I had started toward the cottage when Susan said, "That's not Mother Carla's home. It's this one." She pointed her head across the street, and I shuddered.

The house was made out of dark wood. Moss and vines grew everywhere, like the place hadn't been touched in ages. Crows perched on the moldy, splintered roof. There was no door, only a ragged piece of cloth. The house looked haunted.

Susan went toward it, with Maria and I nervously trailing behind.

"This does *not* look safe," Maria said to me.

Even Bubbles looked a bit scared, though she tried to cover it up. Susan had already reached the piece of cloth and was waiting for us.

"I agree," I said back to Maria as we hurried up.

Not one flower was alive on the lawn, and all of the grass was dead.

Something smelled like it was rotting. I held my breath as I stepped into the house.

82

CHAPTER EIGHT

CHAPTER NINE

Surprisingly, the house was really nice inside. The floor was shiny and clean, and the blue-and-white striped walls had been painted without a single mistake. There were three rooms: a kitchen, a sitting area, and a room with an oval rug and a bunch of candles.

As soon as I stepped in, my body relaxed and felt at ease. I took long, deep breaths, and even my eyes seemed to droop.

"Mother Carla!" Susan shouted. "The guests are here!" Shuffling footsteps came from the kitchen before another Vanir God popped out. This Vanir was white, though, with a few black spots here and there, like a cow.

"Welcome!" Mother Carla said. "I'm glad you could join me." She spoke in a soft, melodic voice that was soothing to hear. "Would anyone like a spot of tea?"

"I'll take one," Susan said. "And Maria and Leon should try your tea as well. It is amazing!" Mother Carla went back into the kitchen to prepare it while we made our way to the sitting room.

We sat on a floral printed sofa. Some sort of pet was lying asleep in the corner. It was a little smaller than Bubbles and had orange fur with two black lines going down its body.

The coffee table in front of us was spotless as well. The whole house seemed to be like that—well, except the outside. In the sitting room, a few black-and-white pictures hung on the wall. One was of young Mother Carla with a little Vanir God, and they were both laughing. Actually, most pictures showed Mother Carla and the kid. Only two pictures were not of the two of them. A really old Vanir God with a furry mustache that hung down to his legs was smiling in one picture. The other had Mother Carla with two other Vanir Gods. They all were enjoying themselves and having a good time.

Mother Carla came back with four cups of tea balanced on a plate that she was holding in her mouth. "Ah, you have found the pictures," she said after she set the plate down on the table. "These photos were when I was still young." She laughed.

We each picked up a cup of tea and drank a sip. It was the best tea I'd ever had. It was fresh like peppermint, but blended with green tea, and it also smelled really nice. Before I knew it, I had finished the whole thing. Maria had finished hers as well.

"My goodness!" Mother Carla exclaimed. "Would you two like another one?"

"Oh, no thank you," Maria said. I shook my head no as well. Mother Carla took our cups back to the kitchen and returned.

"I'm glad you could join me today," Mother Carla said. "Bruno wanted me to meet and get to know you two, and also read Leon's future. I would also like you to be able to know me a little bit more as well. Would you like to talk more in the garden?"

Maria and I said our good-byes to Susan, who left out the front door, and followed Mother Carla past the kitchen and out another door.

The garden wasn't really a garden because it followed the same trend as the rest of the outside. A dirt patch outside the door was enclosed by a rickety wooden fence, and a couple of growing crops were scattered here and there. There was also a small wooden table with four chairs, speckled with dirt and grime.

We all sat down at the table, but the way Mother Carla sat down was very odd. She first positioned herself so her fore legs were aligned with her hind legs, and then she just leaned back, lifting her fore legs off the ground and putting them on the table.

"So, tell me about your journey. How is it so far?" Mother Carla asked.

Without hesitation, Maria told her about everything so far, without even taking a break to breathe. She told her how I passed out too, which surprised Mother Carla.

"Seems like you have had an eventful time here so far," Mother Carla said. "Leon, what else happened? I would love to hear your side of the story."

"Um, Maria pretty much said everything." I hesitated quite a lot and avoided eye contact. "I summoned a water dragon, though, when I passed out the second time."

Mother Carla choked on her tea. "Oh, wow!" she exclaimed with more enthusiasm than seemed necessary. "I did not know that you summoned a water dragon. I'm sure Bruno already mentioned this to you, but the water element is pretty rare here in Strelit." She muttered something else under her breath, too faint for me to understand.

"There are four different dragon types," she continued. "You are probably already familiar with them, but there is the fire type, ice type, earth type, and light type. Each type comes with its own strengths and weaknesses. Ice types are more reserved and passive than the other types. You have the ability to breathe underwater and swim faster. Also, you can control water in any form and are extra powerful against fire types. However, you are extra vulnerable to light types."

That's strange, why light types? Maybe because the sun evaporates water?

"Yeah," Maria answered. "I'm a fire type. Bruno told me. What are my strengths and weaknesses?"

"Very interesting," Mother Carla said. "You two have contrasting elements. Fire types tend to be very energetic, outgoing, and daring. They have the ability to control fire and be immune to it. You are stronger against earth types, but weak against ice types."

"Do you have a certain type, Mother Carla?" I asked. Did Vanir Gods even have types? It couldn't hurt to ask.

"No, I, unfortunately, do not. Vanir Gods don't pertain to a specific element. The only creatures in Strelit who do are the dragons." She got up to put her teacup in the kitchen.

Maria and I sat there in silence as we waited for Mother Carla to come back. Across the street, some Vanir Gods entered their houses and others walked out. Everyone was so cheerful, like they lived without any worries or doubt. They all greeted each other and chitchatted a bit before parting ways. Their friendly manner was amazing to see! I imagined how life would be if everyone acted that way.

Mother Carla came back. "Now, Bruno does want me to read your future, Leon. Do you want to do it now?"

I stammered. "Uh, I guess we can do it now." I kind of didn't want to see my future, though. What if there were something bad?

"Alright, come along, then. Maria, you can stay here if you like, or come with us."

"I'll stay here," Maria said. Mother Carla nodded.

I followed her back into the house. We went into the room with the oval rug and candles.

"Please, have a seat on the rug." She brought some more candles and set them down on the floor. "Now, close your eyes and hold my hands." She extended her hooves, and I held on to them, which felt really odd. She didn't have any fingers, and her hooves were coarse and rough.

She hummed something in a foreign language. I noticed a pulling sensation in my arms. When I opened my eyes, Mother Carla was levitating off the ground! With her eyes still closed, she told me, "You must close your eyes in order for me to see your future." I quickly shut them and sat there in silence.

Was I supposed to see or feel something? Was she reading my future right that second? What did my future hold?

All of a sudden, a strange sensation came over my body, like I was spinning and stretching in a million pieces. I felt woozy, and I wanted to throw up. This feeling went on for what felt like three hours. I just kept spinning and spinning.

What was taking so long?

Finally, the spinning stopped. Mother Carla said, "You may open your eyes now."

My eyes had to adjust to the brightness again. "What did you see?"

I asked.

"Now, my powers work in mysterious ways. I can only see fragments of your future, like a puzzle. And then to tell you, I am only allowed to tell you in a riddle form. Here is the riddle. *Your life will not be a line, but an ocean. The feats will be big, but the crashes will be hard. But in the end, you will return home.* That is all I can tell you."

What was this supposed to mean? My life was going to be like an ocean? This riddle was too confusing. Did *home* mean I would go back to Hawaii?

"Thank you, Mother Carla," I told her as we both got up from the rug and moved back to the sofa. Everything was basked in a shimmery gold as the sun lowered and shone through the windows. Maria was sitting down, staring off into space.

"No worries, dear," Mother Carla said back to me. "If you ever need anything at all, you can always come to me."

Maria snapped back to reality and walked toward us. "How was it?" she whispered as Mother Carla went to the sitting room.

"I'll tell you more about it later."

Mother Carla came back with a scroll in her mouth and gave it to us. "This is a map. I want to test your abilities at an early stage. You will not be in any danger, you two just need to find something for me. Good luck to you both! It was very nice meeting the two of you."

"Nice meeting you too!" we both said as we left.

It was now late in the afternoon, and the sun was going to set in about an hour. Bubbles was outside playing with some of the Vanir Gods, but she came trotting back toward us. The handful of Vanir Gods still outside were returning to their homes.

"Should we open up the scroll?" Maria asked.

I opened it up and was almost blinded.

CHAPTER TEN

A bright light shone out of the scroll, almost directly into my eye. But Bubbles jumped up and knocked it out of my hand. The scroll flopped to the ground and stopped gleaming, and I was able to look at it. As Mother Carla said, it was another map, like the one Bruno had given us. Around a red *X* were outlines of other stuff like different roads and paths, and homes—and the Earth kingdom was on the way! Knowing more about the world might be helpful now that I was the leader. We should definitely go there.

"Should we start?" I asked. Maria nodded. We said many good-byes to multiple Vanir Gods, and to the band that was playing when we first arrived in the village. We also ran into Susan again.

"Hello! How was it?" She was accompanied by a little Vanir God who looked exactly like her. It must have been her child.

"Hello," Maria said. "It was great. She's a really good person."

"Yeah, she is really nice," I said. "Her tea was really good." Bubbles and the child Vanir God started to chat as well.

"I know, isn't it delish!" Susan exclaimed. "I could drink that every day all day. But how was the mind reading? What did she tell you?"

"Um, it was good. She just told a riddle of what my life will be like." I also didn't want to tell her everything that happened. It's called *personal* for a reason.

"Wow, isn't she just the best? I'm on my way back home, and I don't want to keep you two busy. Good-bye for now! James, say good-bye." The little Vanir God said good-bye to both of us and Bubbles, and we parted ways.

We headed back out into the deep and dark forest. This time, though, the journey went a lot quicker, and we were soon back on the road.

"You know what we should do?" Maria said. "We should find out exactly what our powers are. All we know is that I'm a fire type, and you are a water type and can turn into a water dragon. Let's find out!" She stuck her hands out in front of her and waved them in circles.

"N-no," I said. "I don't think that's a good idea. We should wait until we learn from a teacher or somebody."

"You worry too much," Maria snapped. "I'm just trying to summon fire, I'll be fi—"

All of a sudden, she was gone.

Where was she? I rapidly searched everywhere but couldn't find her. What had happened to her? I *knew* trying out our powers was a bad idea.

And then, Maria emerged from the forest. Her eyes were wide and her mouth gaped open. "I just teleported. W-w-what is happening?" She held her hands out, but I rushed to lower them before she could teleport again.

"Let's wait and ask Bruno about this," I said. "We don't want anything to happen."

"Relax, I'll be fine," Maria said as she held out her hands—and was gone again.

I started panicking. My heart beat faster in my chest. But she emerged from the forest, with twigs sticking out from her hair. She kept examining her hands in awe. "Let's just keep going. This teleportation thing is crazy."

We kept walking in silence toward the *X* on the map. Soon we saw a sign that read Earthy Way.

"I think that's the way to the Earth kingdom." Maria said. I agreed, and we took a right.

The road beneath us became less paved and more like packed dirt. Ahead was this big dome-shaped monument. We soon reached a banner that read WELCOME TO PHARAOH.

Earth dragons walked and chatted with each other. Everybody was busy doing something physical like building, carrying, or planting. A dragon looked down at a piece of paper and said commands like, "Perfect, that one goes there, Joe" and "Nice, Pablo. They look beautiful" and "Oh, careful, Joanne, make sure those are even" and "Beautiful job, everyone! This looks wonderful!"

We walked up to the dragon giving directions, and she gasped. "You two must be Leon and Maria! It is so nice to meet you guys! My name is Emily. We are getting ready for the Grand Festival."

"What's the Grand Festival?" Maria asked. Everyone within earshot gasped and stopped what they were doing.

"Surely you must know the Grand Festival," Emily said. We both shook our heads, which generated another round of gasps. "The Grand Festival is an annual celebration of the day Strelit became the protector of Yggdrasil, the tree of life. Every year a different element hosts it, and this year, it's our turn."

"Oh, that's cool," Maria said as she watched four dragons carry a huge fountain next to a banner. "When is it?"

"It's in a week. You two must come to the celebration," Emily said. "But anyways, would you like a tour of Pharaoh?"

"Um, sure," I said. We didn't have too much time, but I felt weird saying no, and I did want to see around.

"Perfect!" Emily shouted. "Everybody, I'll be back soon. Keep putting up the decorations. It looks amazing so far!"

We followed her into Pharaoh. A lot of farmers were selling different plants and herbs. The scene reminded me of a hippy town. Some dragons said hi to us, but some gave us disgusted looks.

"Ignore those disgraceful looks," Emily said. "They are just upset that you are wearing something to protect your feet. Some creatures think it harms the soil, but I think that's just some rumor."

Something to protect my feet? Did she mean *shoes*?

Emily took us down an alleyway. Small skinny dragon-like creatures were eating trash. "Those are dragots. They are able to eat and digest anything completely. So, they eat the trash or stuff the dragons don't need in Pharaoh."

That was cool, like a trash can that never needed to be dumped out.

Emily guided us to a gigantic farm. Crops, trees, bushes, and vines grew everywhere in neat rows, and earth dragons tended the plants, which were all were foreign to me.

One plant looked like a carrot but was two feet long. A dragon gave me and Maria a piece, and we each took a bite. It was amazing! The fruit didn't taste like a carrot at all. It was incredibly sweet and soft, like a mango, but tasted more like a plum.

"This is the Great Garden," Emily announced. "This garden provides vegetables, fruits, berries, and so much more to eighty percent of Strelit!" Wow, that was a lot of produce that comes just from one kingdom.

She took us back through the alley and toward the Taj Mahal–looking monument.

"Is that where we're going?" Maria asked. The ground also turned from dirt back to a stone pathway.

"Yes, we're going to what is called the Tower of Magic," Emily said back.

As we came closer, the buildings became nicer. The air smelled less of dirt and mud, and also seemed fresher and sweeter. Fewer dragons were on the road. We were entering some sort of business place, as all the buildings were offices, and all the dragons carried briefcase-like items. The ground was covered in some sort of glossy material that was so clear that I could see my reflection in it.

The Tower of Magic loomed over us, surrounded by a huge garden. Tall trees lined the sides of the spotless, grand walkway. The Tower itself was completely white, and the building was lined with long, rectangular windows. Two armored guards brandishing spears stood right in front of the tall wooden doors that led inside. When they saw us coming, they stepped to the side and said, "Good evening, Miss Emily, Lady Maria, and Sir Leon."

The doors swung open to reveal a vast library. The walls were lined floor to ceiling with bookshelves taking up every inch. There didn't seem to be space to add even one more book. A spiral staircase in the corner led to the second and third floors.

"The first floor isn't that interesting," Emily said. 'It's just a library with ancient scrolls and books. But the second and third floors are very interesting."

As we went upstairs, I could see that all the books were covered by an inch of dust. Spiderwebs hung in every corner of the bookshelves. The scrolls looked as though they'd been untouched for centuries, so brittle they might crumble at the slightest touch.

Like the first floor, the second floor was lined with shelves, but there wasn't a single book or scroll in sight. Instead, the shelves were filled with all kinds of gadgets. Some were flying, others made loud noises, some were walking around the floor, others were swimming in huge tanks—it was crazy. "This is the Hall of Things," Emily said. "You can find any sort of object that you might ever need right here."

Maria and I explored the gadgets. A little sphere that changed colors was floating in midair. A sign below it read, RESPHERE- REMEMBERS ANYTHING YOU NEED IT TO REMEMBER.

I peered inside one of the fish tanks. A real mini shark kept swimming back and forth, ignoring the other fish. Something about its behavior struck me as odd.

Emily walked up to me. "Ah, the pathwayers. You found them. They're interesting little creatures. Once they have an owner, they will find, search, and even spy on anything you want them to. They're extremely rare to obtain."

What other types of pathwayers were there?

There were so many other things to see and explore, but Emily said,

"Let's move up to the third floor. Trust me, you'll want to see what's there."

Emily floated up on her wings, and Maria and I took the staircase. The third floor was just one big room, and what we saw made our jaws drop.

There was a floating book.

The huge book hung right in the middle of the room. Its pinkish aura lit up the bare walls. There was nothing else on the third floor.

"This book is the Enchanter," Emily said to us. "This can make anything happen. If you need armor to be fire-resistant, check. If you need to heal a wound, check. This can literally do anything."

In awe, I cautiously went up to the Enchanter. The book was about six feet tall and at least ten feet wide. The pages were written in a tiny little text that was foreign to me. A faint harmonic hum came from it as well.

Emily scratched Maria's leg with one of her talons, making her bleed a little. "What was that for?!" Maria shouted. Emily hushed her and brought her up to the book.

"The Enchanter. Use your powers and heal this wound," Emily said.

The Enchanter glowed yellow. A golden wisp came out of its pages and went to Maria's leg. The wisp curled around and went inside her leg, and then the cut was gone.

"Did it hurt?" I asked. Maria shook her head, mouth agape.

This was amazing! Was there anything the Enchanter couldn't do?

Emily floated back to the first floor, and Maria and I took the stairs all the way down. The Tower of Magic was a jaw-dropping place. We said bye to the librarian and headed out the doors.

"Have a nice evening, Miss Emily, Lady Maria, and Sir Leon," the guards said. We said good-bye to them as well and headed back to the center of Pharaoh.

"Um, Emily," I said. "I was wondering if you could help us find this spot. Mother Carla told us to go there." I pulled out the map and showed her the *X*.

"Ah, that's a cactus berry," Emily said. "It's in the desert of Pharaoh, which is a little ways away. What do you need it for?" I shrugged. Emily's face had a hint of worry. "The cactus berry is a special kind of fruit, used very rarely. But you're going to want to head straight and take a left at the riverbank. After that, just keep going straight, and you will reach a spot where there's a cluster of them."

"Okay, thank you for the directions and the tour," I said. Emily smiled and bowed her head.

"Yes, thank you so much, the Tower of Magic was truly a sight to see," Maria said. I noticed that she changed her voice when she was talking to adults. She acted more mature and less snappy.

"Of course, the pleasure is all mine," Emily said as she was walking back. "And be careful with that berry. The cactus berry holds many unknown dangers. And whatever you do, don't touch the spike."

CHAPTER ELEVEN

We got to the riverbank and then took a left down a dirt road that led to an empty desert. The sky was getting darker as the sun hid behind the mountains. There weren't any dragons, roads, buildings. It was completely barren. The sand was so soft my feet kept sinking into the ground.

We walked in silence until Maria said, "Look over there!" She was pointing toward the ground. In the fading light, I saw an orange body with two black lines.

"It looks like Mother Carla's pet," I said to Maria. The animal spotted us and burrowed into the ground.

"Do you think it's the same one that Mother Carla has?" Maria asked.

I shrugged in response. What would it be doing here? "It could be.

Maybe they're native to this area?" Maria rolled her eyes.

We kept going forward. Except for a tumbleweed lying here or there, nothing else was in sight. We kept walking for around thirty minutes. And then, we finally saw something.

A little cluster of vegetation appeared in the distance.

"That's probably it," I said as Maria and I both zoomed towards it.

We got there quickly and saw a cactus berry for the first time. It wasn't anything surprising: the plant looked like a barrel cactus, but in a more vibrant green and with fewer spikes.

"And we're supposed to bring the whole thing?" Maria said.

Lines separated the cactus berry into parts. I carefully maneuvered around the spikes and got a hold of the cactus. Then, I just pulled, and a piece came off in my hand. The piece was half the height of the cactus and about as wide as four of my fingers.

"Okay, now let's get out of here," Maria said. We headed back toward Pharaoh.

All of a sudden, a harsh breeze washed over us. But it wasn't just a cold wind; I could sense someone was there. Maria and I looked at each other, and then turned around. Standing a couple yards away from us was a demon.

"Run!" Maria said. We both ran toward Pharaoh, but the demon flew and caught up to us.

"You two aren't going anywhere," he cackled. "I'm not going to let you get away with what happened at the beach!"

He must be the same demon we encountered back in Hawaii. What did he want with us?

The demon didn't attack but instead stared at us. His red eyes seemed to reach inside my soul and twist it into the tightest knot you could imagine. I wanted to throw up, but I couldn't. A heavy burden weighed on my shoulders now, and I couldn't stop thinking about the car crash with my parents.

The flames engulfed the car as I barely escaped.

My body filled with rage.

The ashes were the only thing left of my parents.

I didn't deserve to survive. I didn't deserve to be still here, walking on this Earth. Rebecca, Mom, and Dad should be with me, or I should be with them.

Maria was screaming and yelling at the ground.

All I could think about was the crash and how I didn't deserve to be here. My insides were boiling like a pot of water, and I could feel myself about to black out, like when I summoned the water dragon.

I had to calm myself down, but I couldn't. All I could feel was the guilt that I was the only one to survive the crash.

The demon laughed the whole time. He must have been doing this to us. His strength seemed to grow every time we got angrier.

The wisp of my water dragon formed in front of me. I couldn't die. Maria looked even angrier than I did. If we didn't calm down, we were going to die. I closed my eyes and tried to relax, but it was no use. We had nothing to fight with.

Wait, the cactus berry. Emily said not to touch the spikes. If I threw the berry at the demon and hit him with the spikes, then maybe we'd have a chance at surviving.

Through the anger clouding my mind, I mustered up all the strength I could. I held the cactus in my hand and chucked it. It soared and seemed to hang in the air, but it fell short and rolled to the demon's foot.

There was nothing else we could do. We were going to die.

"You think that was going to stop me?" The demon laughed. "Well, think agai—"

All of a sudden, the demon swelled up. Its limbs and face were getting bigger and bigger. It must have been reacting to the cactus spike. My idea worked.

The demon stumbled back and tripped in the sand. He tried flying away but couldn't. "This is only the beginning," the demon said. He half flew, half hobbled off toward the forest. We were safe.

"Are you okay?" Maria asked me. "What was that shriek?" I frowned in confusion. I hadn't heard a shriek.

"D-did you experience anything when we were fighting the demon?"

I asked.

"Why would you ask that?" Maria said quickly.

Was she trying to hide something?

I took a deep breath. I had to help Maria. That's what leaders were supposed to do. It's what Bruno would do.

"You can talk to me. Whatever it is."

"I'm fine," Maria said. "I didn't experience anything."

I couldn't give up on Maria. Something was bothering her. I took another deep breath.

"I relived the car crash where my parents died and my sister, Rebecca, disappeared. It was the worst moment of my life. But the demon made me think that I shouldn't have lived. He made me feel guilty that they were all gone. And now, I can't help wondering if I should've been the one to die. Rebecca would have been doing so many better things than me."

"I mean, you're the leader of a kingdom," Maria said. "That's pretty incredible. Look at me. I'm a failure." Maria buried her head in her hands and started crying.

"You're not a failure," I said, trying to comfort her. "You are an amazing person."

"Then why do my parents hate me?!" she shouted. "My parents are divorced, and it's all my fault. They never spoke to me, and always treated me like I wasn't family. Like a piece of dirt."

"Maria, that's just the demon's tricks. He's trying to make you feel guilty about your parents."

"No," she cut me off. "That demon might have twisted your worst memory, but he made me relive mine. He made me go back to the day when they divorced. And they took all their anger out on me. They said I ruined their relationship, and I was a burden on them. And from then on out, they never treated me the same. I never had love from my parents."

I got closer to Maria and put my arm around her shoulder. I knew what it was like to have no parents. Even though our stories were different, we had the same outcome. No parental love.

She leaned on me and cried quietly. We both sat there, watching the sun fall closer to the horizon.

One second my family was with me, and the next they were gone, and would never come back. I'd never fully come to that realization before.

A warm feeling spread through my fingers, like lava running through my veins. This was weird and new.

The sun was almost gone when light glinted off something in the sand.

Maria and I both stood up and went to the spot where the demon fell. Maria picked the thing up and examined it. The metal disc looked like a badge, or a medal. The edge of the badge was traced in red. The back read, KIMYO—BOUNTY HUNTER. It must had been the demon's. Now we knew his name was Kimyo and that he hunted creatures for a living. I didn't know how much that helped us though.

"We should take it, just in case," Maria said. I nodded in agreement as she shoved it in her pocket. "We should also head back. It's getting kind of dark."

"Are you okay?"

"Yeah. Thank you. You're the first person I have ever talked to about this. It feels like a weight has just been taken off of my head."

I smiled. I was making progress.

After what seemed like four hours, we finally approached the familiar grass lawn of the Palace. It was well past midnight, and Bruno and Angie were on the lawn, pacing, when we walked up.

"Good heavens!" Bruno explained, "Where were you this whole time? We began to worry!"

"We had trouble with a demon in the desert of Pharaoh," I said. His face turned into horror and shock as his eyes grew big and his mouth hung open.

"Yeah, we were amazing!" Maria said. "The guy swooped in and was, like, controlling our minds and stuff. We got all angry and whatnot. Then, we snapped out of it, and Leon threw the cactus berry at him. He flew away and shrieked and— Oh my gosh, we didn't even get the berry! That's literally all we needed!"

"Oh my," Bruno said as Maria handed him the badge. "You two are very fortunate to have survived. What were you doing out there in the first place?!"

"Mother Carla sent us," Maria said. "You didn't know?"

Bruno shook his head. "I'm sure she had a good reason, but right now, we have an important task, and then you two must go to bed."

Angie, Maria, Bubbles, and I followed Bruno into the Palace. He went inside this room to the right, where a couple dragons were working in some sort of mini factory. All kinds of machines were in there. Some looked deadly, like a machine that blew out fire every five seconds or so.

"I need you to melt this badge," Bruno said as he set Kimyo's badge down on a table.

"Yes, sir," one dragon said as he grabbed it and put it into the machine blowing out fire. The dragon pulled a lever, and a hiss came out of the machine. He took out the badge, and all of the outer metal was gone, leaving only a smaller piece of metal that had a picture of an orange moon.

"What does that mean?" Maria asked Bruno.

"It means we need to prepare," Bruno said in a grave voice. "The demons are planning something, but I don't know what." He walked out of the room and said to Angie, "Go get Alex. Tell him we need his assistance." Angie nodded and headed out the door.

We followed Bruno down the corridor back to the main entrance.

"Slow down!" Bubbles said. "My legs are tired. I didn't get to have my nap today." Nobody slowed down, but I picked up Bubbles and held her.

"Have Leon and Maria enrolled in the Academy. They will begin tomorrow," Bruno said to his assistant. The dragon nodded and flew out the door. Then Bruno faced us and said, "Who is ready to learn?"

CHAPTER TWELVE

I slept the rest of the day. I awoke when the sun had already begun its descent. Just as I got my bearings, a knock came at my door.

I opened it to see a dragon standing there. "Good afternoon, Leon. Whenever you're ready, please come down to the main entrance," the dragon said. His calm tone was a shock to me because last time I had no option but to rush. I smiled at the dragon and closed the door.

I didn't really have much to do except change my clothes, comb my hair, and put on some shoes, so I ended up just opening the door and following the dragon to the main entrance.

Maria was already there with Bruno, who led us out the door. We flew on his back, away from the Palace.

Bruno had told us that we were going to the Academy, which he described as a training facility for the creatures here at Strelit. We got there in no time because we were soaring through the sky.

The Academy looked exactly like a college. Not too far away, you could see Volcano Ignis, the fire kingdom, which would explain why it began to get really hot. The huge main building of the Academy had all sorts of smaller complexes nearby.

The obstacle courses, which stretched for over a mile, were on the right. On the left, there was an office building. All around the main building were different types of training grounds, like a grass field, a track field, a large lake, and a huge colosseum a little way away.

The main building itself was white and red. It was shorter than the Palace but stretched across more land. Bruno took us inside and led us around.

The color pattern followed from the outside in. Different trophies and pictures were displayed on the walls and on shelves. One picture was of Bruno receiving a medal, and a trophy next to it had the name BRUNO HIDAN etched into it. Was that Bruno's last name?

I couldn't read the rest of the trophy because Bruno hurried us down the hall. He took a right and opened one of the hundreds, if not thousands, of doors in this building.

Inside was an orange blubba gubba dressed in a green and white dress, reading a book.

"Victoria," Bruno said. "So nice to see you after such a long time."

Victoria put her book down and went to greet Bruno. "How have you been? The Academy has missed you dearly."

"I have been tremendously busy at the Palace. But now I would like to introduce you to the leader and a new council member of Strelit. Leon and Maria."

Victoria shook our hands. Her hands felt rubber and slippery, as if I were touching an eel. "Good afternoon, it's a pleasure to meet the two of you."

"Nice to meet you, Victoria," I said while shaking her hand. Maria formally greeted her as well.

We all stood there in silence as Maria and I took in the room. It looked exactly like a classroom in America, except there were no seats. There was a small desk where Victoria had been standing, and a chalkboard in the front. The wall opposite the door was lined with windows facing the track field. On the back wall, a big bull's-eye took up most of the wall.

"Are we all just gonna stare at each other?" Maria said. "Why did you bring us here, Bruno?"

She was normally polite with elders—why was she having such an attitude, especially toward someone new?

Bruno gave Maria a firm look, which made Maria look very guilty as she looked at the floor and twiddled with her thumbs. "Victoria is here to teach you two. I will let her explain. Thank you for everything, Victoria."

Bruno turned to us. "I will stay for a while, and then I will leave you two with Victoria." Bruno went to the corner of the room.

"Thank you, Bruno." She spoke with a crystal-clear voice that commanded attention. "Now, Leon, you can shoot water. So, show me." She pointed her tentacle at the bull's-eye: "Shoot water at the bull's eye."

I had never shot water on purpose before. How was I supposed to do it? I gave it my best shot and stuck my hand out and willed water to come out of it.

But I couldn't control it. A monsoon amount of water poured out and doused the entire wall.

Victoria was shaking her head. "No, that's not it. But don't worry, that is completely normal. I am here to teach you how to control your powers and use them to the best of your ability."

"I already know how to use my powers," Maria snapped back.

What was Maria doing? She was acting like a four-year-old. I twiddled with my shorts, uncomfortable in this situation.

She crossed her arms. "I've already teleported."

"Oh." Victoria looked shocked, her eyes going big and her limbs squiggling around frantically. She looked at Bruno, and they hesitated for a moment. Was Maria not supposed to teleport? "W-w-well, we didn't know you had the ability. That is a—a very r-rare talent, so let's put that to the side."

"Well, I can do rare stuff," Maria answered back.

Victoria was still looking at Bruno, but now worry and concern were on both of their faces. Was their unease still about the teleporting thing?

"I must leave now. Thank you, Victoria. I will leave you to it," Bruno said. He left, and we were alone with Victoria.

"Let's work on the fundamentals, okay?" Victoria said. "Try to shoot fire at the target, Maria."

Maria rolled her eyes and put out her hand, but nothing happened. She stuck out her hand and moved it all around, but no fire shot out. "Why aren't my powers working?!" Maria shouted in frustration. She was getting ready to try again when Victoria lowered her hand.

"See, you two need to learn how to control and use your powers to help others, and at the very least, not cause destruction," Victoria said. "I'm here to help with that."

"How are you going to help us with that?" Maria said in a snarky voice.

"Maria, stop," I whispered to her. "I'm sorry, Victoria. We appreciate you helping us."

Victoria gave me a smile and then stuck out her tentacle, making fire dance in her hand. She lifted another tentacle and made water dance. And then she did the same with two other tentacles with air and light.

Maria and I were in awe. "How—what—is that?" Maria couldn't find any words to express her thoughts. I couldn't find any words either. Weren't blubba gubbas only able to transform into different things?

"Blubba gubbas are related to dragons, and so we can have the same powers, but it takes an incredible amount of precision, skill, work, experience, and time to be able to do this as a blubba gubba. Not many of us have been able to do it. So, I do have a lot I can teach you, Maria. And you too, Leon."

We both nodded, Maria a bit begrudgingly.

"Now, we do have to get to learning," Victoria said. "I will work with each of you one-on-one for an hour, and then we will do another hour together."

"But it's already seven at night!" Maria whined. "That means we would be finishing at ten!"

"I'm well aware of the time now, and in three hours. You are welcome to leave early if that's what you want," Victoria said with a hint of attitude. Maria rolled her eyes. "Now, Maria. Will you please step out of the room while I start with Leon?" Maria crossed her arms and shuffled to the door, still upset.

Once Maria was out of the room, Victoria spoke again, "Okay, then. The first thing you need to learn is precision. I want you to learn how to control the amount of energy you use. Start by trying to form enough water to just wet your hand. As small as possible."

I nodded, and then closed my eyes. I willed my hand to summon a small amount of water, but when I opened my eyes, I was standing in a puddle.

"No, no." Victoria shook her head, and doused the room with air and dried the water. "You need to focus on not the whole room, but just on the specific target."

I nodded and tried again. This time, I focused on the palm of my hand.

Water still sloshed around me. But this time, it seemed like a smaller amount.

Victoria smiled for the first time since we got here. "Much better, but you still have a tremendous amount of work to do. Continue focusing on that specific target."

She sat at her desk while I kept trying. I only focused on the middle of my hand and was actually able to control the water so it didn't douse everything around me, just my arm. I continued to do that until Victoria stopped me.

"Leon," she started, "we should now move on to a different part of controlling your powers. You need to work on your flying skills. Let's first start by hovering. Try for twenty-four inches off the ground. Gently blast air out of your hands to maintain an even balance."

I put my hands down to my sides and blasted wind out of them, but I went crashing into the roof. I banged my head and fell down.

"Are you okay, Leon?" Victoria asked.

"I'm okay," I answered.

Victoria helped me back up. "You need to work on this a lot. This tends to take more time to learn than controlling your powers. One trick that will help tremendously is to point your toes at a ninety-degree angle with your feet. That way you don't use too much of your energy. And also imagine yourself in the air exactly where you want to be. Try it again."

I nodded and closed my eyes for what felt like the millionth time since we'd gotten here. I envisioned myself lifting specifically two feet off the ground, with my feet perpendicular to my body. I cautiously lifted off the ground, but I still hit the ceiling. The impact was a little less powerful, but it still hurt.

"Try again," Victoria said.

I tried again and again, for what felt like another four hours. When she stopped me again, I had just managed to not hit the ceiling.

"Even though we have a lot to work on, it is time for you to rest now. Please call Maria inside when you go out. Thank you for allowing me to help you on your journey."

"Thank you, Victoria."

Outside of the classroom, Maria and Bubbles were both sleeping on the ground.

I tapped Maria on the shoulder, and she jolted up in surprise. "I didn't take the last Pop-Tart!" she yelled. "Oh, sorry, Leon. Is it my turn?"

I nodded, and she went in. I took Maria's spot next to Bubbles and waited.

Halfway through the lesson, I looked through the small window into the classroom. Surprisingly, Maria seemed a lot less aggravated. She was taking the criticism really well, like she wanted to get better. And she was.

Maria had already surpassed my level and was improving a lot faster as well. She was able to shoot fire at the bull's eye and hover with ease.

Should I have been improving faster, though, because I was the leader? Would Bruno make her the leader if she transcended me?

I fell asleep with that doubt pervading my head.

I was woken up by Maria and Victoria staring at me from above. "Are you guys done?" I asked. They both nodded.

"I think we should call it a day for now," Victoria said. "You two seem tired. I will see you in the near future."

"Thank you, Victoria," Maria said kindly. "You helped me a lot." Victoria smiled back.

I was shocked. Didn't Maria just want her to *not* help us, not too long ago?

"Bye!" Maria said as she turned back toward the exit.

I waved bye to Victoria and followed Maria out. She held the door for me, which was a first. I nearly stumbled over in surprise. "Th-thank you."

Was she okay? She was like an entirely different person.

Maria smiled, and we walked in silence. She was skipping along, not shuffling her feet like she usually did.

"Are you okay?" I asked. "You don't seem like your usual self."

"Yeah, I'm fine," she answered in a calm tone. "She helped me and supported me. I never have really felt that. She humbled me a bit."

A bit?" I questioned. She giggled.

As we walked toward the Palace, we heard a creature shout: "Help, help!"

Maria and I raced to the sound and found a child dragon next to a tree. He was staring intently at the tree, never breaking eye contact.

"What's wrong?" Maria asked.

"My toy is stuck in the tree," the boy said. "Can you get it down, please?"

Maria groaned and put her hand on her face. "You don't scream for help because your toy is stuck. That's not an emergency."

"Well, I needed help getting it down. So, I asked for help," the kid said in the most innocent voice one could imagine.

Maria gave me a look, and I shrugged. "You did say you were humbled."

She rolled her eyes and climbed the tree to get the toy. It was a small blue rubber ball a bit bigger than my hand.

She pulled the ball out of the branch and tossed it to the kid. Immediately, his eyes lit up. He had the biggest smile I had ever seen.

"Thank you! Thank you!" he said and started flying around the tree with the ball in his claws.

"You're welcome," Maria said, who was now also smiling. "What's your name?"

The boy stopped flying for just enough time to answer. "Kienan." He resumed playing.

"Well, I'll see you around, Kienan," she answered, and we walked away.

That whole interaction surprised me. Maria was *nice,* and not because anyone was forcing her to.

"I never knew you were good with kids."

"I'm not," she answered, but she was smiling.

Maybe she was changing.

At the Palace, we were greeted by two dragons as we headed up to our bedrooms. We said good night to each other, and we headed inside our rooms.

I got dressed and flopped on the bed next to Bubbles. "I can't believe Maria," I said out loud. "Maybe she's changing."

"People can change."

"Good night," I said.

The only response I got was her snoring. I wasn't the only one who was tired today.

CHAPTER THIRTEEN

I awoke to Maria bursting through my room.

"We're going to the ice kingdom today!" she shouted.

"You know, I think if you yell a little louder, my aunt back in Hawaii will be able to hear you," I said, yawning.

"Sorry, it's just that I'm super excited to go and see it! I mean, aren't you excited? It is your element, after all."

"Yeah, it is." I sat up in bed. "I'm confused why you're so excited, though. Aren't you a fire type, the opposite of ice?"

"Yeah, but who cares?" she said in a nonchalant tone. "I want to see it so bad."

I stared at her, my mouth open and my eyes wide. Did she not know what could happen?

"Maria, you could get really sick. Many fire dragons have been severely hurt, and some have died, because the ice powers affect their immunity."

"Well, lucky for me. I have a strong immunity." She was on her way out the door. "Now, come on, you're already behind!"

"What was she yapping about?" Bubbles asked.

I got out of bed and got dressed. "We're going to the ice kingdom today," I told her. "Maria's really happy, but she's a fire type."

"She's so dumb," Bubbles sighed. "Anyways, let's get ready to go." Bubbles headed toward the bathroom.

"I'm ready to go," I said to her, confused as to why she was going to the bathroom. She didn't need to do anything special with her fur, right?

"Well, clearly, I'm not!" she yelled into the mirror. "My hair is a mess, it's all matted. I smell like I rolled in a pile of mud. My nails are dirty." She paused and looked at me. "I need at least thirty minutes."

"Thirty minutes?!" I yelled. "We don't have thirty minutes. We're supposed to be leaving soon."

"Okay, so, the longer you talk to me, the longer it's gonna take." She closed the door.

I went out to get some food. I would be back before she was done getting ready.

Maria, Bruno, and a dragon I didn't recognize were in the Grand

Room. "Are you ready?" Bruno asked me.

"I am, but Bubbles isn't yet."

Bruno chuckled softly to himself after hearing this. "Oh, Bubbles," he said, "ever since she was a little girl, she always took so long getting herself ready. I guess some things never change."

Maria and I were shocked. "Little girl?" Maria said. "She's all but two!"

"Bubbles may look young, but she's two thousand three hundred eighty-four years old," Bruno said. Our jaws dropped to the floor.

Bubbles walked down the stairs. "Who would have thought that it would only take me ten minutes to get ready!" She looked at us with confusion. "Did you guys see the ghost too? I knew I wasn't the only one!" she yelled.

"You're two thousand three hundred eighty-four years old!" I exclaimed.

"Oh, yeah," Bubbles said, "but did you see the ghost?" I shook my head, still in shock.

"Oh, Bubbles, you know there's no ghost. Don't scare them," Bruno said. "She's only joking."

"You look so young!" Maria shouted. Bubbles, who took it as a compliment, smiled at Maria.

"I know, right? I've been using this mud that comes from near Yggdrasil. It works like a charm!"

"Okay, okay!" Bruno stopped her. "Enough talk about mud. Damian is waiting to take you three to Crystel, the ice kingdom. Damian is the groundskeeper of Crystel, but he does so much more than that. Now come on, don't keep him waiting, Leon, there is some breakfast in the cafeteria for you. Please do not take more than five minutes."

I headed to the cafeteria and ate a bowl of something that tasted like quinoa. Three minutes later, I came back out, but Bruno wasn't there anymore. He must have gone to do some things.

Damian stood there, glowering at Maria and me like we'd done something bad. He turned toward the door and started flying to Crystel.

Maria mouthed to me, "What's his problem?" I shrugged. He gave me the chills, but I picked up Bubbles and flew out behind him anyway.

The first thing I noticed was that my ability to fly was a lot stronger. All that training yesterday must've worked. Maria and I caught up to Damian in a short time.

"So, have you always lived in Crystel?" Maria said, trying to create conversation and lighten the mood.

Damian, however, seemed to want nothing to do with us, and sped off. This guy was not to be messed with. We made no other attempts at talking to him, and instead focused on following him.

Damian was the fastest flier we had encountered during our time here, and it didn't look like he had any intention of slowing down.

We kept chasing after him for what seemed like forever, until a huge castle loomed in front of us.

The castle was bigger than the Palace! It was at least ten stories high and completely made out of different colors of ice, but mainly blue and crystal-white. When we got closer, I could see that the ice had an intricate pattern of swirls etched into it.

Snow was falling, completely covering the ground. We landed pretty hard and Maria and I both took a tumble, but we got up and followed Damian to the castle. Snow seeped into my shoes with every step, but I hardly felt it. Maria, however, could definitely feel it.

"Since when did snow get so cold?!" she yelled, "Oh my gosh, it's, like, really cold!" We all ignored her.

When we reached what seemed to be the center of the kingdom, ice dragons were everywhere. Some were doing different chores and others seemed to be just walking around. Their scales looked like icicles, and probably were just as sharp. Their eyes were a mix of white and blue. Wherever they stepped, the ground turned from snow to ice.

They all seemed equally as rude as Damian. They gave us side-eye and mean looks and moved away the second they saw us. Maybe that was just how ice dragons were?

"Why is everybody so angry?" Bubbles said as I held her in my arms. "You would think since it's my first time here, I would get a warmer welcome.

You guys, the sun is still shining!" she yelled to the ice dragons. They all looked at her, and then carried on with what they were doing.

When we got to the castle, another ice dragon came to greet us. "Hello, welcome to the Castle of Crystel." The dragon talked in an unenthusiastic, gloomy, flat voice. He seemed extremely grumpy and sad. "Please follow me into the castle. Thank you, Damian." Damian flew off into the distance as we entered the castle.

The castle was breathtaking. Everything inside was made out of ice as well. The stairs spiraled around the walls in what seemed like an infinite loop. A crystal-looking chandelier hanging from the first floor looked like the slightest breath would send it crashing. The floor was solid ice but wasn't slippery.

"My name is Julian," the dragon said. "If you have any questions, please don't be afraid to ask."

"I have a question," Maria said. Her teeth were chattering, and her whole body was shaking. "Do you guys not have a heater?!" Julian ignored her and continued on with the tour.

He took a right from the main entrance to a café-like restaurant. Another sullen ice dragon was tending the restaurant.

"What can I get for you?" the ice dragon said. He had the same voice as Julian did, sad and gloomy.

"Three icicles," Julian said. The other dragon grabbed three packages from a shelf and handed them to him.

Julian gave a package to each of us, but Maria refused hers. "I'm good, thanks," Maria said. "I'm a fire type." Julian shrugged and kept the other two.

Inside my package was a straight-up icicle. There was nothing on top of it, around it, inside of it. It was just an icicle. I'd thought *icicle* was, like, a name for some sort of food. Turns out, the food was just as bland as the people. I took a lick, and the icicle was just water. Julian was chomping on his, and soon he had finished both of them!

"That was Crystel Café," Julian said. "They have a large variety of foods, such as water, icicles, snow cones, and ice cubes." We walked back to the main entrance and then up the stairs. The stairs seemed to go on forever, but we finally got up to the second floor.

There was no noise coming from this floor. All around us, dragons were playing some sort of game. I stepped closer and saw that the game was chess. But the pieces were moving around on their own and hitting each other, knocking one another onto the icy ground.

"This is dragon's chess," Julian said in a more hushed tone.

"This looks really cool. How do you play?" Maria said. Instantly, all the other dragons turned and glowered at her.

"Be quiet," Julian said. "They need to concentrate while playing; they cannot be disturbed."

"Okay!" Maria yelled. "Don't EVER tell me to be quiet!" She wagged her finger side to side. "Matter of fact, don't ever tell ANYONE to be quiet!"

That outburst was a lot. Maybe she had a weak spot for people shushing her? Maria's temper wasn't anything new, but this seemed like a bit much. Maybe the bitter cold was getting to her?

"Shall we move on with the tour?" Julian said, bored, as if he hadn't heard a word Maria had shouted.

"Only cuz I could probably blow this place up," Maria grumbled. We moved away from the dragon's chess matches and back up the stairs.

"On the third floor, we have dormitories for some ice dragons who work in the Castle of Crystel," Julian continued. "And on the fourth floor, we have offices for those dragons who work here."

"So, dragons actually work in this castle?" I asked him. This was new to me. "Do all the different kingdoms do this?"

"Yes to both of your questions," he answered. "Some of the work that doesn't need to be done outside or hands-on is done here. Such as making designs for different gear, proposing new laws, etcetera."

"Don't you have anything interesting here?" Maria said, her body still shivering. Julian looked at Maria and blinked in exasperation, and then turned back to the stairs.

"Come with me, then," Julian said. This was the first time he had acknowledged any of her words. He kept going up the stairs until we reached the ninth floor.

Nothing was on this level except pieces of ice sprawled along the floor. "This is Crystel's most recent invention. It is dragon armor made of ice. It is still in testing, but it will be able to withstand virtually anything." He said this with a little more enthusiasm, but he was still as unenergetic as a sloth.

"That's it?" Maria said with disappointment. "This is your"—she used air quotes— "*interesting thing?*"

All of a sudden, a dragon yelled from the first floor, his voice echoing all the way up to us, "Medius is about to speak!" Everyone started moving, running, flying in a frenzy toward the main door on the first floor. They all were instantly so happy and excited. Who was Medius, and why was everyone so interested in hearing him speak?

Julian sped off to the door, leaving Maria and me on the ninth floor, alone. We rushed down the stairs, where we met the traffic of dragons trying to bust through the doors.

A dragon said, "I'm not waiting in this line!" The dragon flew up to the roof and literally crashed through the castle, leaving a hole! Many other dragons followed him, and Maria and I did too. I grabbed onto Bubbles and flew out the roof.

Outside, hundreds of ice dragons crowded on the snowy grounds, stampeding toward the back of the castle. We followed the dragons all the way to the outskirts of Crystel, where the snow ended and turned into dirt.

Right on the edge of the snow stood a stone statue of a dragon. It was the only thing that wasn't made of ice in this whole place. The dragons huddled around this life-size effigy, everybody chatting with one another.

"Isn't this exciting!" Damian, who had escorted us to Crystel, said to us in a cheery voice. "I forgot, you two are humans. Let me fill you in. Medius was our leader. He was the best leader we ever had! But then he was killed, and before he passed, he said that one day, when the time was right, he would tell us a message that would be important to us all. Someone said they heard the statue starting to mutter something. That must be a sign that he will deliver his message!"

Everybody looked up at Medius, waiting for something to happen. When he finally opened his mouth, all the dragons hushed. Nobody spoke a word.

"The humans are nice." His assertive voice boomed. "The sun shines at night." When he said that last part though, everybody except me cried in agony, trying to cover their ears.

"Why did he speak in the scarred tongue?!" Damian howled. "The shrilling is unbearable!"

What shrilling?

"I didn't hear any shrilling," I said to Damian. Apparently, everyone heard me say this, because they all gasped in shock.

"Y-y-you could understand that?" Damian stuttered. I nodded, generating another round of gasps.

"I knew it!" a dragon yelled. "You're one of them!" Everybody started hollering and charging after me. I grabbed Bubbles and Maria, and we flew away as fast as we could. Ice dragons started flying after us, but we were able to escape them.

We left Crystel and headed toward the Palace. The yells of the ice dragons grew softer as we flew farther and farther away.

"What was that all about?" Maria asked. "And why was that the same shrill as the one when Kimyo attacked us in the desert."

"I guess Medius spoke in the scarred tongue, but I was able to understand it. I guess?" I worried about what had happened with the shrill as we flew past some roads. And since that was the same noise as the desert incident, did that mean that Kimyo was speaking in the scarred tongue there as well? "Did you understand it?" I asked Maria.

Maria shook her head. "What did he say? I just understood up until 'the humans are nice.'"

"He said, 'The sun shines at night.'"

Maria cocked her head to the side like a dog.

"I don't know what that means either."

"Do you know what the scarred tongue is?" Bubbles said. I shook my head. "Do you know who Medius is?" Again, I shook my head. "Oof, I better leave it for Bruno to explain to you. It's a deep story."

We rode in silence the rest of the way, each of us pondering what had just happened.

We arrived at the Palace and stepped inside. Simon, who we hadn't seen for a long time, was at the front.

"Good afternoon, Sir Leon, Lady Maria, and …" He trailed off when he saw Bubbles. "That thing," he said with disgust.

"My name is Bubbles, for your information."

Simon ignored what Bubbles said and opened the door to the Palace.

"Do you know where Bruno is?" I asked Simon.

"He is at home. He lives in the third house on Calidi Circle, near the volcano." We thanked him and took off to the volcano. I didn't know where Calidi Circle was, but we would have to find it somehow.

We flew across the sky to the right of the Palace. The volcano wasn't too far, and we shortly felt the heat coming from it. I scanned the area for Calidi Circle. There were at least fifty communities, and hundreds of houses in total. How were we going to find the right one?

Just as my hope diminished, we saw Bruno on the street. He seemed to be carrying something as he headed toward his home.

"Let's go catch up to him," Maria said. We dove down, gaining speed fast. A little too fast. We lost control and tumbled into the dirt off the side of the street.

"Are you nuts?!" Bubbles yelled. "You're nuts!"

Bruno turned around at the sound of the crash and Bubbles's voice.

"Oh!" Bruno said. "You scared the wits out of me." Maria and I were panting, our hands on our knees. "Is there something I can do for you?"

"What is the scarred tongue?" I asked, trying to catch my breath.

He stumbled back, startled. "How do you know about the scarred tongue?" he asked, a worried tone in his voice.

"I can understand it." His eyes widened, and he nearly lost his balance. "What does that mean?" I asked.

"Well," he said, looking worried, "it means that you are a demon."

CHAPTER FOURTEEN

Bruno invited us into his home and poured us each a cup of tea. He kept pacing around the kitchen, pondering something.

"You understood the scarred tongue?" Bruno asked. I nodded.

"What do you mean, he's a demon?" Maria said. We were both confused, but Bruno hadn't said anything yet. Instead, he kept muttering to himself, thinking out loud.

"Let's start from the beginning," he said. He stopped pacing and looked at us. "Roughly two hundred years ago, I became appointed the leader of Strelit. Back then, I was young. I was naïve. I had no experience being a leader of anything whatsoever. And back then, the demons used to live in synergy with dragons. We had our side of Strelit, and they had theirs. We lived in harmony together. Until one day, the demons became selfish. They wanted more. More power. More food. More finance. And so, they planned to overthrow the leader, which was me. They charged in waves of hundreds, wreaking havoc in the streets and homes. Creatures were frightened, injured, and killed."

The sun glinted through the window, illuminating the rock walls and Bruno's face as he told his story.

"The demons knocked down the doors of the Palace and raided it. They went looking for me all over. Soon, they found me, but I was not alone. I was with a … a witch, the only thing known to be able to hurt a demon without touching them. And so, I had them banished to the forest, where they were put under the Curse of Niflheim. The sun would not touch upon their earth, and no crops would be able to grow. And the demon tongue was called the *scarred tongue* after what happened," Bruno concluded, and looked at us.

We were both speechless. I couldn't imagine the demons living in harmony with dragons. After our encounter with one, it seemed as if they don't live in harmony even among themselves. I didn't know there were witches in Strelit either.

"Who are the witches?" Maria asked, wondering the same thing.

Bruno began stammering over his words. "Oh, um, well. The witches are a-a species that doesn't exist anymore, so you don't need to worry or know about them right now."

That was a bit odd. Why would Bruno hide an entire species from us? I had bigger things to focus on at the moment though.

"So why does that mean I'm a demon, then?" I asked, still confused. Bruno took a deep breath, like he was about to give some bad news.

"The scarred tongue was banished," he said. "It was not taught by schools, by parents, or by anyone, for that matter. And so many creatures forgot how to speak and understand it. However, you are able to understand it and, perhaps, speak it. There is only one possible explanation for this since you are not a demon."

He paused and took a shaky breath. The chirping of the bird outside stopped as we waited for what he would say.

"You are, in some way, related to a demon." Maria and I gasped. "Theoretically, if a bond between two creatures is strong enough, then those two creatures should be able to understand, process, and replicate the other creature's thoughts. And the stronger the bond, the farther away the two creatures can be and still be telepathically connected."

I was in shock. My body went numb and I was struggling to breathe. How could I have a bond with a demon? Who could that demon even be? I'd only just started encountering them!

Angie overheard our conversation as she walked to the kitchen. "But this bond could be with a different creature?" she asked Bruno. "If another creature was able to speak the scarred tongue, then it could mean it isn't a demon."

"That is possible," Bruno replied. "But the language was forgotten by everyone except the demons themselves." He thought for a moment. "How did you find out that you were able to understand the scarred tongue?"

"When we went to Crystel," I told him, "this statue of a dragon named Medius spoke. It said 'The humans are nice' normally, and then said 'The sun shines at night' in the scarred tongue. At first, I thought he'd spoken normally, but then I found out that everybody else heard a shrilling."

Bruno and Angie looked at each other with worried expressions.

"What does that mean?" Maria asked in a trembling voice.

"It means the demons are planning something," Bruno said. "Medius was killed by a demon, and when he was dying, he said that one day he would give us a very special note. And now he spoke in the scarred tongue itself. Medius didn't know how to speak the scarred tongue. There are too many ties to demons to be coincidences. First with the demon attacking you in the desert, and on the beach where you're from. Now with Medius. What are the demons up to?"

"What does the note mean?" Maria asked. "You know. The whole 'sun shining at night' thing?"

"I do not know what that means yet," Bruno replied. "Perhaps it's a clue of some sort." He started pacing again. "But let's change the subject for now. How did you like Crystel and the castle?"

"Um." I struggled to find the words to put it nicely. "It was … I mean, the ice dragons were …"

"Everybody was super distant and cold and had no soul," Maria said blatantly.

"Yes, they can be like that sometimes. Especially after Medius passed away. They were full of life before. If only I had the knowledge that I do today. What would Strelit be like now? A whole lot better, that's for sure," Bruno said with a hint of guilt.

He paused for a moment. "Have you come in contact with any other demons?" I shook my head. "Are you sure about that? I need you to be completely honest with me." I shook my head again, starting to worry a little bit.

"Do you know anyone, here or in Midgard, who has ever spoken the scarred tongue?"

I shook my head again. I was getting scared and leaned back.

"I think that's enough for now," Angie said, breaking Bruno's interrogation.

He snapped back into his old self. "Ah. I apologize for acting the way I did. Where were my manners?" He opened the door for us as we got up to leave. "If you need any assistance, you know where I am. And if you think of anything that could help, come to me immediately."

I nodded. "Thank you for your time, Bruno." Maria thanked him as well.

We headed toward the Palace. The weather was nice and cool, with a slight breeze. We decided to walk back instead of fly because the weather was so nice.

"Aren't you scared?" Maria asked.

"Of what?"

She looked down at her shoes and chuckled. "Of being the new leader, of having all this responsibility suddenly put on your shoulders. You need to make plans, make changes. You have to care for hundreds of thousands of creatures that you have just met! And on top of all of that, you are now part demon, and soon the demons might attack, and you'll have to go to war!"

Ever since I got here, I actually hadn't stopped to think about all the responsibilities and risks I now had.

"Yeah," I said, "I am terrified. I'm terrified of EVERYTHING! The more I think about it, the more I want to go back to Hawaii."

"So, then, like, why not leave?" Maria said. "Do you ever think it wasn't worth the risk? I mean, we made the decision to stay in a matter of a couple of minutes."

"I'm glad I left, even if it was a scary choice to make. I didn't have a life back in Hawaii. I had no parental guidance, and I didn't have anyone I could look to for help. What about you?"

"Same for me," Maria said. "My parents were never there for me, and

I didn't have any sort of relationship with them. I was on my own. I think part of that was my fault. I used to be so cold and distant, but only because I didn't want to get too close to someone and have them leave me like my parents. Here, I have a family, and I have people who are there for me. We have each other."

We walked back to the Palace, admiring the setting sun that painted the sky with a thousand colors.

Looking back at my conversation with Maria, we did have a lot in common. We both grew up basically on our own and used Strelit as a means to start a new life. Maybe we weren't so different.

We were getting pretty close to the Palace when Maria nudged my shoulder. "Look," she whispered, pointing. Professor Henchberry, the grumpy council member who was always making mean comments, was looking pretty suspicious as he checked his surroundings and rounded the corner of the Palace.

"Let's go follow him." Maria started running after him.

"No," I yelled at her as I tried to catch up. "Are you crazy? We could get in trouble."

Maria tiptoed around the corner. "Only if we get caught," she said with a smile, and disappeared.

I sighed and hurried after her. I did not want her getting into trouble.

"She's crazy," Bubbles said. I nodded in agreement, and we ran after

Maria.

She was crouched down, pressing her hand against the wall of the Palace.

"What's wrong?" I asked.

She examined the wall. "He went through here."

"Through where?" There was nothing on the wall, but she kept pressing it.

"There was a door here that he went through." I looked at her like she was crazy. "I promise you."

"Allow me," Bubbles said as she hopped from my hands. She arrogantly walked to the spot. Her paw swiped the wall from top to bottom, and then left to right. Then, a piece of the wall turned around to reveal a hole.

I was speechless. How was there a hidden door on the back wall of the Palace?

Maria crawled through the four-foot-high, four-foot-wide hole. I gulped and went in after her.

Inside, steps led down to a tunnel. Other than the sound of a slow drip, it was completely quiet. Maria creeped down the stairs, but her footsteps echoed through the cold hallway. It smelled more of moss with each step we took.

It amazed me that there was a whole network of underground tunnels. How did I not know about this?

We gently floated above the ground, flying to avoid being heard as we sped along the path. The tunnel had few turns and no intersections. Pretty soon we heard another sound, like something squishing on the ground—which must've been Professor Henchberry. We peered around the corner and saw him walking down the hall. But then he paused and looked around, as if he thought he saw something.

Finally, he took a right at the end of the hallway. We kept following him until he went into an arched wooden door with a small glass window at the top.

We stared through the glass. Professor Henchberry was standing in the room, but I didn't see anything else.

"There's nothing else there," I said.

"Look at the ground," Maria said.

What I saw took my breath away.

On the floor, dozens of baby Schnawegians were running all around. They were about one quarter the size of Bubbles, and they were so cute! An adult Schnawegian talked to Professor Henchberry.

"The adult is my cousin Andrew!" Bubbles shouted.

Professor Henchberry whipped his head toward the door as we ducked below the glass.

I gave Bubbles a stern look, then slowly peeked back in. But he wasn't there.

"What are you doing here?" a voice said behind me, making me scream and fall to the floor. Henchberry was *outside* the door, giving me an evil look. His eyes beaded into me and his mouth twisted in all sorts of ways. How did he get past me? He must have transformed into darkness or something.

"W-w-we saw you going in here and we—" I was stammering. I couldn't get my words out, terrified of what would happen.

"Followed me?" Henchberry finished my sentence. I gulped and nodded. Beads of sweat were rolling down my face.

"The question is, what were *you* doing in there?" Maria said.

I lunged over to Maria and covered her mouth. "She was just joking. We don't need to k-know what you were doing." I gave a weak smile.

"Um, we kinda do need to know." Maria moved to the side. I went to cover her mouth again, but she grabbed my hand. "Unless, you know. We could spread the word of how you take care of little babies. Your reputation of being this big bad wolf would be replaced by being a puppy-loving blubba gubba," Maria said, taunting him.

"I wouldn't s-say anything l-like that," I said.

"Oh no, he will," Maria said again. "I'll make sure of it." She sounded so calm, like we hadn't just gotten caught spying on a member of the Council.

Professor Henchberry sighed. "I volunteer to help these Schnawegians. They lost their home and have nowhere to go. So, Andrew and I are trying to help relocate them."

"That's so sweet!" Maria exclaimed. "Let's go tell Bruno!" She had started to make her way down the tunnel when Professor Henchberry stopped her.

"No one must know about this," he said with a stern voice, "This is just something only we can know about now. I need people to respect me and fear me."

Maria crossed her arms and looked at him. "And if I do tell someone?" she said, testing him.

"Well, then. I would just have to tell everyone that the leader and his *secretary* were sneaking and following a council member." Maria was fuming, especially because he called her a secretary. "You don't want that, do you?"

"Fine," Maria said. She turned on the ball of her foot and angrily marched away. I followed her with Bubbles in my arms, making sure to not make eye contact with Henchberry.

"I told you we were going to get caught," I said as we headed out the tunnel. Even though I had been frightened for my life and had thought Henchberry might kill me, in a way, this encounter helped me not be so scared of him. Maybe he wasn't that bad.

Maria rolled her eyes at me. "We didn't get caught. Bubbles just blabbed her big mouth."

Bubbles started growling. "How 'bout I put this big mouth around your big ankle!" she shouted back. Maria was about to say something back.

"You guys, stop," I said. "Let's just focus on getting home in peace, okay? We don't want any more attention." Maria and Bubbles gave each other side-eye, but we kept walking.

"How did Henchberry get behind us, though?" I asked Bubbles. "Blubba gubbas can't teleport, right?"

"No, they can't," Bubbles answered. "But since Henchberry is black, he can turn into a shadow and blend in with it."

We continued down the tunnel and finally got out. We headed toward the front of the Palace, with me in between Bubbles and Maria, who were still glowering at each other. We finally got inside, where we were greeted by Simon again.

"Good evening," he said. We waved hello and headed to the dining room for dinner. We ate a plate of mixed vegetables and returned to our rooms. I got ready for bed, but when it came time to fall asleep, I couldn't. My mind was still racing with ideas.

How could I be connected to a demon? I'd only lived here for two months! The only demon I'd come in contact with had tried to kill us. I kept going through different possibilities, questions, and conspiracies until my eyelids drooped down.

CHAPTER FIFTEEN

It had been about two months since I found out that I was connected to a demon, but nothing had changed so far. I'd been going to the Academy four times a week, attended council meetings, and occasionally visited other kingdoms.

But today, *today* was different. And not in a good way.

I woke up to a mess. My clothing was strewn all over the floor. The bedsheets were ripped; the rest of the pillows were scattered all across the room, some torn apart. The shower curtains were thrown on the floor. My eyes widened in shock.

"What happened?!" I shouted. Bubbles, who had a towel in her mouth and was shaking it vigorously, immediately stopped and looked at me. Her eyes were filled with guilt.

"I …" she stuttered. "Well … you see. I d-don't know. I was a l-little anxious, I guess. I took it out on the pillows, and curtains, and your clothes, and part of the toilet, and the door, and—"

"Okay! Okay!" I shouted. I got out of bed. "I'm going to deal with this later." I went into the bathroom and started getting ready by brushing my hair. How could she do something like that?

I heard "I'm sorry" come from the other side of the door. I shoved my comb down on the counter, curling my hand into a fist.

"If you were sorry, you wouldn't have done it." I finished getting ready and came back out.

"Clean all of this up, quickly. We have to go n—" I froze. Out of the corner of my eye, I saw my purple hat. I rushed over to pick it up. My mom and dad gave me that hat for my fifth birthday. It was the only thing I had left to remember them by. It had slobber and smudges all over it, but thankfully, it was still intact.

I glowered at Bubbles. "You almost ruined this!" I yelled. "How could you!" I threw the hat down in frustration. "Clean it up, right now! I'll be back later!" I threw open the door.

"Wait! No, don't leave me!"

I shut the door, drowning out Bubbles's voice. Maria, who was exiting her room, looked at me with wide eyes.

"What happened in there?" Maria said. Bubbles was pawing the door and yelling at the top of her lungs.

"Don't ask," I told her. My blood was boiling.

We went downstairs and headed out the door toward the Academy. I flew in a hurry, trying to get there as fast as possible.

Bubbles was so dumb. She knew not to do this stuff. She'd almost ruined the only thing I had left of my parents!

"Okay, what happened!" Maria shouted. "You never fly fast."

I rolled my eyes. Did she really need to know? "I got mad at Bubbles," I said. Maria looked at me, leaning in and nodding encouragingly like she wanted to know more. "She tore my whole room up."

Maria's mouth stood agape. "Seriously?!" she exclaimed. I nodded and looked away. "That's nothing, though. One time, my dog chewed my entire bed into shreds. And my blanket, my slippers, and basically everything else. It was a nightmare."

"I don't care about your dog!" I yelled. "Bubbles ruined the only thing I had left of my parents. A hat they gave me for my birthday. Now it's practically ruined."

"I mean, she is an animal, and they do have that animal instinct. That was just her instinct. I know it must be hard getting the hat ruined, but you can't be too mad at her. Besides, you don't need a hat to remember your parents."

I made sure I looked angry on the outside, but inside, I was thinking about what she said.

I knew the destruction was Bubbles's animal instincts, but that didn't make it okay, right? Had I been a little too harsh? I wanted to apologize as soon as I got back to the Palace. But for now, guilt knotted in my stomach.

We headed directly to the big field in the back of the Academy. Today was supposed to be an important day in our training. Last week, our coach, Coach Carl, told us specifically, "You better be here on time! And I don't want no excuses!" Carl tended to yell a lot.

We were the first students on the field. It was completely empty except for us and Carl. The others started showing up one by one. Sam, this really big and muscular ice dragon, made a grand entrance by nose-diving onto the field, missing the ground by an inch, then gracefully landing. Heather, a shy light dragon, peeked out from behind a tree and slowly made her way to the field, her eyes locked onto the ground. Other students poured onto the field until there were fifteen of us.

I was the odd one out of the group, though. Everyone here was a crucial member of the team. They were either the best fighters in the Academy, or the smartest, the fastest, the stealthiest. I was probably the worst one in the whole Academy. What was I doing here?

"Now!" Carl barked. "The fifteen of you have been chosen, by the Council of the Academy and the Council of the Palace, to represent Strelit in the Wohna Games." Everyone started shouting and whooping in excitement.

Maria and I sat there, confused. What was the Wohna Games, again? I barely remembered Angie mentioning it when we first came to Strelit. Why was this such a big deal?

Carl looked at us. "Leon and Maria. I suspect you two don't know a lot about this?" We shook our heads. "Well, the Wohna Games is a tournament. It has been held every year in different parts of Wohna for over a hundred thousand years. It is a series of events where fifteen participants from each world compete for the Trophy of Wohna."

Only fifteen! That was crazy! And I had been chosen!

"Wait," I said. "Why was I chosen?" They could have found fifteen *thousand* better creatures to replace me.

"Cuz you are the cream of the cream of the crop," Carl said, making my mouth drop to the floor. "All of you are."

I felt as though I was in a dream! I was speechless. I couldn't believe it. This was amazing. I had really never been chosen for a team, I was always the last one to get picked. And now I was being called the best at a sport? This was insane!

"Now, let's get to working!" Carl said. He moved us away from the main building, taking a different route to a smaller side building.

What were we doing here?

He walked through the back entrance of the side building and up a set of steel stairs. Once on the second floor, he went through a room filled with all sorts of posters, maps, 3D models, diagrams, and pictures.

This must be the room where we study for the games. Everything about them was in this room.

"Let's break off into teams, and each team will learn a specific game. Team One is Sam, Heather, and Leon. You will take on this game." He pointed to a picture on a chalkboard. "This is called Capture the Horn."

I gulped.

"Wait, can we get hurt in these games?" I shouted. All of a sudden, I didn't want to do the Wohna Games anymore. I didn't want to get hurt.

"Well, yes. That's kind of the point." Carl said.

I rushed to the door, wanting to leave at this very moment. Carl stepped in front of me, blocking my exit.

"Leon, you are the strongest person here. Your powers are far beyond anything I have ever seen before. And you have super healing, so there is a less chance of you getting hurt. This is a big deal, and Strelit needs you."

I thought for a second. I wasn't going to chicken out of this, especially in front of everyone. I nodded and came back.

"Now, back to what I was saying. You three group together in the back corner."

We headed to the back as Carl assigned more groups and games. Sam, Heather, and I sat down and awkwardly waited in silence. Once he was all done, Carl commanded our attention to the chalkboard at the front.

"Okay!" His voice boomed through the room. "We will be here for an hour. After that, you are free to go. Today will be a short day. But you must study as much as you can about the game. Begin!"

Some groups started grabbing stuff off the board, shelves, and the floor. Others stayed in their groups and talked. We stayed in our group.

"Um, I know a lot about this game," Heather said. "I can tell you guys what it's about in more detail?" Sam and I nodded and waited. "Okay, so, um. This game is played in the forest. First, one player of each team goes into the forest and hides a unicorn horn for their team. Unicorn horns are used because, when hit, they make a vibrating sound that can echo for miles. So, once the players come back from hiding the horn, the game starts and in order to win, the teams must find the other horn and clash it with their own horn to make the vibrating sound. Anything is allowed, even hurting the other team."

"Okay," Sam said in his deep voice. "And I'm assuming it's just played in a section of the forest, correct?"

"No, it's played in the entire forest," she answered back.

I was shocked. The forest was huge! How were we ever going to find one silly little horn?

"It'll take ages to find it," Sam complained. "But don't they shine?" Heather and I nodded. "At least that helps." He grumbled as we started reading about the rules, studying maps of the forest, and going through certain scenarios at the end.

The hour went by so quickly, it felt like we had just started.

"Okay, everyone!" Coach Carl said. "That's it for today! Everybody go home, and we'll continue next time!"

We all shuffled to the door, thanking Carl as we left. Maria caught up to me on the stairs.

"Hey!" she said. "I got to learn about skyball. It's like soccer but you play it in the air. It sounds so cool!"

We headed toward the Palace, Maria talking about the game she'd learned. "Apparently, this one time, the weather was too bad, so they had to play it on the ground. It got brutal."

I gulped. I started fiddling with my fingers. I could die playing these Wohna Games. I didn't want to die.

"Leon!" Carl called from behind me. "I need to speak with you for a moment." I turned back around and flew to him.

"Look," he said. "I know you're feeling scared and nervous about these games. It's written all over your face. But you have nothing to worry about. You have speed healing and all the powers in the world to protect yourself."

I shifted my feet as he talked to me. "Thank you for that, but there are stronger creatures out there to be on the team. I'm just going to bring the team down."

"You're wrong." I looked up from the ground at him. "You are the strongest person here. Your powers are far beyond anything I've ever seen before. And you're just getting used to them. The truth is, Strelit needs you to win the Wohna Games."

Hearing that was a shock. Carl was usually a very serious person who gave little to no compliments. Hearing this from him lifted my spirits, but that didn't mean I would be safe. I could still die just as easily.

"Thank you," I said. "I'll try my hardest to make Strelit proud." Carl smiled at

me as I flew back to Maria.

Once we got home to the Palace, I felt at peace. I was now back in my comfort zone and could relax. But first, I had to make amends with Bubbles.

"See you later!" Maria said as I slipped into my room. I waved bye and closed the door.

My room was spotless. Everything was back where it should be. My clothes were neatly put away, the pillows were replaced. The place was as good as new.

"Bubbles," I called out, but there was no answer. "I'm sorry for the way I acted earlier." I searched around the room, looking for her. "I shouldn't have lashed out at you. It was just your animal instincts. Can you forgive me?"

Where was she?

I entered the bathroom, and my heart sank. On the ground lay Bubbles, motionless.

She quivered like she was freezing. Most of her fur had fallen out and was strewn around her. Her paws were limp and her mouth was partially open, her tongue resting on the ground.

"Bubbles!" I yelled. I picked her up and frantically searched for a pulse. I finally felt a faint and slow one. Her eyes were hardly open.

"Help me," she said in a hoarse and barely audible voice.

CHAPTER SIXTEEN

My heart pounded in my chest, and my stomach churned. My face was buried in my hands, and I was sobbing, shaking.

I had taken Bubbles directly to the hospital, and she was rushed straight to a room. Now I was in the lobby, as I wasn't allowed to be with her while the doctors were there.

How could I have let this happen? One of the doctors told me that Bubbles was in terrible condition. I couldn't do anything except sit with my guilt and hope. I ended up sleeping at the hospital with horrible thoughts crowding my head.

I was woken up by the nurse who took Bubbles in. "Good morning, Leon." Her voice had a calming effect on me. "Bubbles is allowed to see visitors now. Would you like to go visit her?"

I jumped up out of my seat. "Yes, I want to go see her."

The dragon nodded. "Please follow me."

She walked down the hall, rooms lining each side. Behind the closed doors, I could hear commotion in some rooms, steady beeps in others, but some were dead silent. I started fidgeting with my fingers and kept my head down.

"What's wrong with Bubbles?" I asked in a hushed voice.

She slowed her pace to walk alongside me. "When a Schnawegian and another creature bond to a certain degree, they experience what is called *emotional symbiosis*. It is where the two creatures are so connected emotionally that they feed off of each other. When the connection is strong, each creature gets stronger. Some pairs have been so strongly connected that they are able to read each other's minds. But when the connection is weak, the creatures are more prone to fall ill. And that is what happened with Bubbles."

The knot in my stomach came back, and I felt like I was going to throw up. This was all my fault.

"Will she be okay?" I asked.

She grimaced. "I'm not sure. She was having heart problems, and she still has a very high fever. It was a blessing she lived through the night."

The knot was pulled as hard as it could be.

"You must take much better care of her. They are very fragile creatures."

I nodded. I could barely walk. Finally, we got to Bubbles's room. The nurse opened the door, and I ran to the bed. Bubbles was there, her eyes slightly open.

"Hey, Bubbles," I said. She smiled weakly. "How are you feeling?" I patted her forehead. Her tail was slowly wagging.

"Tell them to not feed me that disgusting pudding," she said slowly.

I chuckled softly. "I'm sorry. This is all my fault. I should've known better. Now you're in a terrible position because of me." I started crying.

"It's fine. I forgive you. I am so lucky to have met someone as amazing as you. Back at home, there aren't many people as nice as you."

I smiled. "Where is home for you?" She had never talked about where she used to live.

"Us Schnawegians live in a section of the forest called Hidden Meadows. It's not very nice. We live in two-foot-high huts that are built out of sticks. We eat whatever we grow. Everybody is always on their toes. You don't know if you're going to wake up tomorrow and have your house gone, or all your food supply robbed."

"What's your family like?"

"My family was the best. I lived with my mom, dad, older brother, and younger sister. We were so happy together. My dad always made us laugh, even through rough times. My mom made the best vegetable stew. My siblings and I used to play in the yard all day until it grew dark." She teared up. "They were killed by a demon who robbed our house. I was only forty when it happened. That's how I wound up at the Palace. I worked as a messenger before I met you. I would deliver letters or messages to people all across Strelit. I hated it. Now, I have the best life I could ever imagine."

I smiled as I sat there with Bubbles.

"What about your life before you came here?" she asked. "What was it like?"

"It was awful. Before I was in Hawaii, I had an amazing life. I lived with my parents and my older sister in Boston. I loved them so much." I choked up. "But they died in a car accident. Well, my parents died, but my sister disappeared."

"What do you mean, she disappeared?"

"Well, the car rolled down a ditch and hit a tree. There was some sort of oil leak in the car, which set it on fire. My sister was able to get me out of the car before it burned. But when the fire was put out, there were only two bodies. My mom and my dad. My sister was nowhere to be found."

"And did you tell this to anybody?"

"Yeah, but no one believes me. They all think I'm making it up. I saw what I saw, though. I'm telling the truth."

"I believe you."

I smiled. Mom and Dad had always made me feel like I could do anything. And Rebecca was my best friend. She had always stayed with me after school while my parents were out working. She would help me do my homework. We would make hot chocolate together on the cold days, and she would take me to the beach in the summer. I missed her so much.

Maybe she wasn't in Strelit after all. I had gotten my hopes up, but I had had no luck so far.

"After that, I lived with my aunt," I continued. "I hate her. She always made me feel like I was worth nothing and I was deranged. It seemed like everyone thought that about me. And then one day, I met Maria at a fast-food restaurant."

"What's fast food?" Bubbles interrupted. I laughed, confusing Bubbles.

"I forgot that there isn't any of that here. Fast food is food that is pre-made. So it's made really fast and served in, like, a minute."

"Is it fresh?"

"Well, no."

"That's disgusting."

"Yeah, but it tastes good," I said. "Anyways, that's where I met Maria, and we found the tail of an ice dragon together. After that, Bruno found us."

"What was your sister's name?" Bubbles asked me. "My sister's name was Peach."

What kind of name was Peach? "My sister's name is Rebecca—"

Bubbles howled in pain. I jumped out of my seat.

"What's wrong?" I said, alarmed.

"You spoke in the scarred tongue," she said. "You said her name in the scarred tongue."

I sat back down, perplexed, my brain trying to make sense of this. "But I don't even know the language." I said.

Why was this happening to me?

We sat there in silence for a while, listening to the steady beat of the machines working.

* * *

The day passed by slowly. I comforted Bubbles as she recovered, staying with her the whole time. Maria came at around one o'clock and brought us food. She stayed with us, and pretty soon it was nine at night.

The doctor came into the room. "Bubbles, it looks like you're healed!" he shouted. Maria and I clapped and cheered. "Having Leon with you sped up the process tremendously. You are ready to go home."

The doctor removed some needles from Bubbles, and then she hopped out of the bed. "Finally!" Bubbles shouted. "Now, let's get out of here."

I chuckled as I carried Bubbles out the room and down the hallway. "Thank you for being there for me," Bubbles said.

"Always," I answered.

We stepped outside and walked back to the Palace. The sun had already set and the sky was pitch-black. The only lights we had were streetlamps and a light dragon that we passed every so often.

The night seemed eerily quiet, though, like the world was holding its breath.

Simon greeted us at the door. We ate a quick dinner, then headed up to our rooms.

I flopped onto the bed, relieved Bubbles was okay. I promised myself I would never neglect her again.

"Something doesn't feel right," Bubbles said, worried.

I looked at her, concerned. The doctor had said she was fine. "Should we go back to the hospital?"

"No, I feel fine after what happened. It's something else. It's like a feeling in my gut." We sat there in silence for a while.

"Eh, it's probably the pudding," she said, allowing the tension inside of me to release. She hopped onto the bed, and I fell asleep.

* * *

A siren rang through my room. I awoke, startled.

"What's wrong?" Bubbles yelled. The siren was wailing all throughout the Palace.

"I don't know!" I got out of the bed and peered out my door.

All the guards were flying past the hallway and up the set of stairs in the back, their suits of armor clanging as they made their way.

"What's happening?" I asked, hoping someone would answer me.

"There's been an intrusion in the safe. Please stay in your room," a guard said. The guards passed, and all that was left was the ringing siren flooding the hallways.

Maria's door flung open. She stood there in her pajamas and pink poofy slippers. Her hair was all over the place, and her eyes were wide with excitement and craziness. Whatever she was about to say wasn't going to be good.

"We should go stop the intruder!" Maria yelled.

Did I hear her right? We could get hurt!

"Are you crazy?!" I shouted.

Maria ran across the hall to my room. "They might get away. We can stop them with our powers." She turned to go after the guards.

"No!" I shouted, grabbing her wrist. "It's too dangerous. We don't even have protection!" She rolled her eyes. "We have speed healing!"

"Shh!" Bubbles yelled. We both stopped shouting.

"Under the bed," she whispered. "Quickly." We all ducked underneath my bed, panicked. "The intruders are coming."

CHAPTER SEVENTEEN

The intruder slowly walked along the floor of my bedroom. The floorboards creaked with each step. Its breath was raspy and guttural, like it was snarling.

The feet of the intruder were black and scaly. *Very* scaly. The cracks between each scale were glowing red.

And that walk. I'd recognize that walk from anywhere. The limp and the dragging feet.

It was a demon.

We were going to die here. I held my breath, hoping he would go away soon. My heart pulsated as I lay on my stomach.

Maria's eyes and mouth were wide open. She was forming a ball of fire in her hand in case we needed to fight.

The demon dragged its feet along the floor like a zombie in a hurry. It rummaged through stuff in my room as if it were looking for something. Books and clothes rained on the floor as the demon tossed them in his search.

And then, the demon turned toward the bed.

My breath quickened and was so loud I felt as though he would hear it. I covered my mouth with one hand and formed an icicle in the other.

The demon walked around the bed and then froze, standing a few inches away from my head.

The world seemed to stop as I waited for his next move. Was he going to find us? Would he throw the bed over?

And then, he walked toward the door. I exhaled.

But right before the demon left the room, I bumped my head against the bed.

Great.

The demon turned around as we backed up against the wall in terror. He threw the bed against the wall, metal bars and shards of wood showering down on us as we scrambled to face him.

"What a pleasant surprise," the demon seethed, drool dripping from its teeth.

The voice sounded like the demon we'd met in the desert, Kimyo. Was it him?

He lunged after me, his claws barely missing me as I stepped out of the way. "I've been waiting for my revenge!"

It *was* Kimyo! I blasted water out my hands directly at him, but he dodged it with ease. He blew fire from his mouth, almost hitting Maria before she teleported away.

When had she been practicing teleportation?

She reappeared behind him as she grabbed a book and smashed it over his head. He stumbled forward, his claws clinging to his head.

"Y-you huldra!" Kimyo yelled at Maria. What was he saying? What was a huldra?

Maria opened a blue and purple portal underneath Bubbles and then she was gone, teleported away from the fight. I nodded at Maria, saying thank-you.

She then blasted Kimyo with fire, but he just consumed it, his veins glowing bolder. Demons must be immune to fire.

Maria must've been thinking the same thing because she picked up a metal rod from the broken bed and started swinging it maniacally, but he dodged every blow.

Kimyo swatted at Maria, sending her crashing into the wall. Maria crumpled to the ground, going in and out of consciousness.

The demon flew at racing speed toward me and lunged at my throat. He pinned me to the wall and wrapped his scaly talons around my neck, making me gasp for air.

My lungs were going to bend and shatter in his claws.

His grip got tighter and tighter. He cackled as my vision went dark, and spots started dancing before my eyes.

Then, Maria grabbed the metal rod and banged it on the top of his head again. He let go of me, and I took huge breaths of air as I recovered.

Maria tried to teleport the demon away. He dodged the portal, but this gave me a chance to defend myself. I blasted him with water, which sent him howling in pain, and let me catch my breath.

He seemed to disintegrate a little with the blast of water, as steam started coming off of him. That must be his weakness. My mind raced with an idea. I kept shooting water at him while I figured out how to put my plan into action.

Then it came to me. I knew what I had to do.

I blasted water at Kimyo and trapped him against the wall. "Teleport him to the shower!" I yelled to Maria.

Now that the demon was still, she was able to teleport him. When he was gone, I blasted water at the knob of the shower to turn it on. He howled in pain for a while, and I thought we had him.

But then his cries of pain stopped.

The crackle of flames could be heard now. The shower head burst off and flew toward me. I ducked just in time for it to indent the wall.

The demon came out of the shower, flames surrounding him rising five feet high. He cackled like an evil witch.

But he didn't attack. Instead, he turned to the nearest wall, which happened to be the shower, and flew through it at full speed, leaving a demon-shaped hole.

Maria and I ran to the wall as he flew off into the distance. We were lucky, because we didn't stand a chance with him wielding fire like that.

The click-clack of the guards' uniforms could be heard down my hall. The guards came into my room and stared at the broken wall exactly how we did.

"The demons ransacked every room they went in," one of the guards said to me as they examined the hole in the wall.

"There were multiple demons?!" I shouted. He nodded back.

What were they doing here?

"Was anybody hurt?" I asked. He shook his head. "Did they take anything?"

"We're waiting for Lieutenant Rick to come back," he said. "He's making sure nothing was stolen."

I nodded as I thought of all that had just happened. They must have been looking for something. Why else would a bunch of demons break in? Were they sending some sort of message?

I went up to Maria. "How did you know how to teleport?"

"I've been practicing in my room. And now I think I'm pretty good at it."

"So, how do you teleport? Sometimes you open portals, but then sometimes it looks like you just disappear."

"I always open portals. But when I do it to myself, it's like I open a portal right on me, which makes it hard to see it. I don't fully understand it either, but I can do it, at least."

"Oh." I couldn't believe she had been practicing. It probably saved our lives today.

Rick came into the room, followed by three other guards. Rick was a huge ice dragon with eyes so blue, they were almost white. "The dragons stole one thing, from what we can tell so far. The badge that the demon dropped when you fought him in the desert."

I gasped. They stole the one thing we had to connect to them. Now, not only had we lost the little leverage we had, but we also knew they could break into the Strelit safe.

The safe was a heavily guarded room in the Palace that stored precious and valuable things. Two guards stood outside of it, and the door required the answer to a question that I had made.

How was someone able to know my friend's cousin's dog's name? (And his name was Rooftop.) They must have had some sort of technology that could hack into the door.

Rick took us to the safe, and I put in the answer. The two guards pushed open one of the heavy doors, and Maria, Rick, and I stepped inside.

I went over to Maria. "Where did you put Bubbles?"

"In the hospital lobby. I thought she'd be safe there."

I nodded. "Thank you. Also, do you know what the demon meant when he said you were a huldra?"

She shrugged. "Maybe it was supposed to be an insult or something?"

"Maybe."

The safe was about thirty feet wide, and it stretched about fifty feet. The space almost looked like a museum. A bunch of precious and special artifacts were inside, such as a sword that was a million years old, and an ancient teapot from the first leader of Strelit. Stuff like that. And the newest addition had been the badge, but all that stood in its place was the empty pedestal.

"And for this to happen on today, of all days," the guard said.

"Wait, what's today?" I asked.

"Today is the Grand Festival, sir," he answered. I had completely forgotten about it. "But going back to the matter at hand, that's all we know for now. I will get in touch if we have more information about the break in."

"Thank you, Rick."

My mind raced. Why just steal one thing? There were at least thirty more valuable things in this room alone. And all that was on the badge was a picture of a sun (Or was it an orange moon?). Was the creature who stole the badge the same one who'd come into my room? I had so many questions right now.

The guard left, leaving the two of us alone.

"Why would they steal that?" Maria asked.

"Maybe the demons know there's something important on that badge, and they don't want us to know. There was too much to risk to steal a badge if it was useless."

Maria nodded. "We should start looking into it right away. Do you think the picture of the badge has anything to do with the saying Medius said? The whole 'sun shines at night' thing?"

"I mean, maybe," I answered with a shrug. "It can't hurt to see if there's a connection. Especially with nighttime being a theme with the moon on the badge, and in the saying."

Bruno emerged into the safe, panting. "Is everyone all right?" We said yes and caught him up on what was happening. "Hmm, I can't think of any connection right now between the badge and the saying, but it is a good idea to start looking into it. Who knows when the demons will strike again."

"Thank you," I said. "There is also one thing that I want to ask you. When we were fighting the demon, he looked at Maria and said she was a huldra. What does that mean?"

Bruno seemed at a loss for words. "Well, it's a certain type of creature that used to live here in Strelit. B-but I'll tell you more about that when the time is right. Okay?"

That was odd. What was so secret about a huldra? Did it have something to do with teleportation, and Maria being able to do it?

We exited the safe and went down to the Grand Room, picking up Bubbles from the kitchen on the way. Then, we flew to the Tower of Magic, which was the library in Pharaoh.

Once we got there, we went inside and sat down at a table. Maria grabbed a loose piece of paper and wrote down the saying that Medius had told us.

"*The sun shines at night*," Maria said. "So, now what do we do?"

I thought in silence. We didn't have much to go off of. So, I tried to find the best way to use our time. "There isn't much we can do. We have no new evidence, so the only thing we can do is find the meaning of the words, or the orange moon from the badge." Maria nodded.

We worked on finding something related to either the moon or the saying Medius told us. With the small amount of knowledge we had about the saying or the picture on the badge it could be anything.

We deciphered this mystery for what felt like hours, trying to find some sort of hint of what the moon and saying meant. We looked through old books, papers, scrolls, poems, everything we could find in that place.

"Uh!" Maria threw down a book in frustration. "This is useless!" She groaned. "We've been here for two hours and haven't found anything." She headed toward the door. "I'm getting something to eat."

"Wait, I think I found something!" I exclaimed. Maria teleported to me and leaned over my shoulder.

I held a thick leather book that looked older than Bruno. "Look." I pointed toward a picture of a full moon shining down on a forest. "It says here that 'A Sun in the Sky' is a famous poem, and one of the lines is 'The sun shines at night.' That line refers to a time when the moon shone so bright that the creatures thought it was the sun. It was written by Kujo Monche over a million years ago. It says the original scroll is the only copy ever made, and it's stored in Crystel."

"And that's the same moon that was on the badge!" Maria shouted. "There must be something in the poem that has something to do with what the demons are planning. But how are we going to get it? The ice dragons didn't seem to like us. And besides, it's locked today because of the festival. We need to get to it before the demons do. They might try to steal it to cover all of their tracks."

"I think I know how we can get it. It also says that the poem is brought out at every Grand Festival to show the history of Strelit. We can keep an eye on it there, and then tomorrow we can take a look."

"In that case," Maria said, "we have a party to attend."

CHAPTER EIGHTEEN

We went back to the Palace to get ready for the Grand Festival. I put on the nicest pair of pants I had, and a shirt that I had lying around.

"Did you prepare your speech?" Bubbles asked. I groaned. I'd completely forgotten about that too! I hadn't prepared at all! "I don't have anything!" I shouted.

I had to prepare a speech to give at the Grand Festival, in front of everyone. What was I going to do?

"Oof," she said. "It's like a whole, long, powerful talk about Strelit."

I started hyperventilating. I had about an hour left to come up with it. But I had no idea where to start.

"I can help you, though," Bubbles said. "I can come up with the words.

All you have to do is talk."

"How are we going to do that?" I was a nervous wreck. I paced the room, biting my nails. Every once in a while, I felt like I would faint. I was already terrified of public speaking, and now I would have to go up on stage with nothing prepared.

"Relax," she said. "You're going to read my mind. I have a friend who will help us with that." She smiled at me. I put my faith into Bubbles, hoping she could come through.

The hour went by too fast, giving me no time at all to finish my speech. All I had was one line that read, "Fellow citizens of Strelit." That wasn't going to cut it.

A knock came at my door. I opened it to see Simon there.

"Good afternoon, Sir Leon. We shall go to the Grand Festival now. Are you ready?" I nodded, not knowing what else to do.

Bubbles followed me out as Simon knocked on Maria's door. She came out, wearing a tangerine-colored dress with swirls of yellow. Her brown hair flowed down her back in light curls.

"Wow, you look beautiful," I said.

"Thank you," Maria said, doing a little curtsy. "And you look … very comfortable." She eyed me up and down, her face twisted in disgust.

"I don't have a suit. Are you ready?" She nodded. We walked down the stairs to the Grand Room.

"At the party, we should keep a lookout for any demons," Maria said. "They might try to steal the poem since it's outside of Crystel today."

I nodded. "Yeah, that's a good idea. We'll need to be watching out."

A dragon with a carriage was waiting for us outside. Bubbles, Maria, and I hopped in, and the dragon flew all the way to Pharaoh.

About thirty minutes later, we arrived. The dragon stopped at the entrance, a grand archway covered in a beautiful arrangement of vibrant flowers. The fountain that I had seen someone carry when I visited last was now in the middle of the walkway, flowing gracefully with crystal-clear water. The ground was not dirt anymore, but instead a red carpet. We thanked the dragon and walked up to the archway.

Two dragons greeted us and gave us each a headband with all sorts of feathers and flowers on it. "Welcome to the Grand Festival!" one of them said. "These headbands are part of the green theme of this year. Please enjoy everything Pharaoh has to offer!"

We passed through the large flower arrangements and down the path.

Pharaoh was nothing like it was before. All of the buildings were covered with all sorts of plants as bright as the sun. We walked down a corridor, statues of creatures lining both sides. They must have been past leaders because I saw Bruno.

Oh look, there *I* was! My arms were crossed, and I looked off into the distance. My back arched down, and my shoulders slumped. My face had a queasy look, like I had just fainted.

"You look like you just threw up fifty times after being strapped to a roller coaster for three hours," Maria said, trying to stifle her laughter.

"What was the inspiration for this sculpture?" I asked the lady who had just brought us in, ignoring Maria. I tried to sound intrigued, but I was really upset by the statue. My eyes were even closed.

"Why, it was your entrance into Strelit!" she answered. "Thankfully, we were able to capture all the emotion you showed in just one statue. You really were the perfect model. This statue will be the talk of the town!"

"That's for sure," Maria said as she giggled.

We got to the heart of the party. Creatures gathered around, chatting, laughing, and eating. But as soon as I came in, some of them gave me a little side-eye or wary looks. Were they whispering about me as well?

In a seven-foot-tall clear box on a pedestal was the poem. The ends of the paper curled up, and the page itself had a yellow tint. I couldn't let it out of my sight.

Maria and I sat down at a table next to some of the creatures who trained with us at the Academy, but as soon as we sat, a bunch of them groaned and left.

Why was everyone so angry with me?

One looked over their shoulder and said, "Learn how to run this kingdom."

Was I doing something wrong?

To the left, I could see a show. A couple of dragons were soaring in the sky and doing all kinds of tricks. Up ahead, there was a concert of some sort, with singing and instruments. To the right was a gate, and a sign that read Employees Only. Some small restaurant carts with little appetizers were scattered about the grounds. One cart had what looked like a taco. Another had ice cream. One even had full meals! This party was nice!

A dragon came up to us. She was covered head to toe in a mixture of green and purple feathers. She also had a mask that basically covered her face.

Now that I realized it, almost everyone had a mask, and feathers covering their body. How were we going to keep track of the scroll of the poem now? Anyone could take it at any time and we wouldn't know who took it!

"HELLO!" the dragon said. "I'M SO GLAD YOU COULD MAKE IT!" Even though she was yelling, her voice almost got lost in the loud crowd. But somehow, I still recognized the voice.

"EMILY?" I asked. She nodded. She *was* the leader of Pharaoh. "OH, I THOUGHT IT WAS YOU! THE PARTY IS AMAZING!"

She nodded again and smiled. "HERE!" she said, handing us both a mask. "WEAR THESE!"

Maria and I nodded back and put them on. I could hardly see through the mask. I put one on Bubbles, but she instantly shook it off. We waved goodbye to Emily, and she merged back into the crowd. Soon enough, she was engulfed, and I couldn't spot her.

*　*　*

"Okay," I started as we sat back down with some food. "We're going to need a strategy if we're going to look for demons and keep the poem safe."

"Can't we just start looking?" Maria asked.

"Have you not seen what everyone is wearing?" Bubbles said. She looked around at the different creatures.

"Oh," Maria said. Bubbles rolled her eyes and turned to me.

"So, we will need to find the demons by their walk," I said. "That's probably the easiest way." Maria nodded. "They drag their feet on the ground and have a limp. I saw that Kimyo had one, maybe they all do?" I looked back at the crowd and gulped. This was going to be hard, but I had an idea.

"Bubbles," I said, "you said you have a plan for my speech?"

"Yes, I do!" she shouted, and jumped off the table. "Follow me."

She walked in a hurry. I scrambled after her, with Maria behind me. She zigzagged through the legs of dragons, but Maria and I made our way by pushing past creatures and dodging many tails and wings.

Bubbles came to a stop at a small tent. It looked like it would collapse any second. The top was sagging so much that, when we stepped inside, Maria and I had to crouch.

Inside, some Schnawegians were engaged in some serious activity.

Two of them talked in low voices without any emotion. Another two were going over some scrolls, and then there was one who just stood there, waiting.

Bubbles went up to the Schnawegian just standing there. The Schnawegians turned to her, stared at her, and then they all started shouting and laughing.

"Bubbles! You came! So nice to see you!" They all welcomed her and went over.

"How have you been?" the one who stood by himself said.

He was a little larger than Bubbles, and his hair was straighter and more wiry. His fur was gray mixed with light browns, and his eyes were gray.

That was strange. I looked at everyone else's eyes, but none of them were gray.

"Good, Uncle Hugo," Bubbles said. "How is everyone at home doing? Are Mona and Wallow getting along yet?"

"You know those two will always be at each other's tails," he answered. Hugo had a soft voice, so tender it almost melted any nervousness I had.

Maria was more relaxed also. She was as relaxed as a dog taking a nap on a porch. She was smiling and laughing. It was a shock seeing her like this, but also nice.

After he and Bubbles talked for a while, Hugo turned to me.

"Now, Bubbles has told me you would like my assistance?" I nodded but didn't say anything. I didn't know what Bubbles had in store, so I motioned toward her.

"I need you to connect his mind to mine," Bubbles said. "Can you use your powers as a mind-bender?" Her uncle nodded and then turned to me.

"Wait, wait, wait!" I said, backing up a couple of steps. "What are you going to do to me? Are you going to hurt me?" I started hyperventilating.

"I will not harm you in any way," he said in his soothing voice. My breath slowed, and I loosened up again. "Some Schnawegians, like me, are mind-benders. We are able to connect into someone's mind, connect two minds, and also alter someone's mind. Hence the name *mind-benders*. Fear not, I will only be connecting your mind to Bubbles, so then you'll be able to read her mind."

"Okay," I said, thinking about the process. "Wait, but how will that help me with my speech?"

"Because I," Bubbles started, "have prepared your speech."

My mouth gaped. "When did you prepare it?" I said in awe. Maria and I had been pretty busy lately, and Bubbles went wherever we did.

"Well." Bubbles cleared her throat. "I haven't come up with it yet."

"Wait, so you're just going to make it up as you go?" Maria asked. Bubbles nodded. "Well, this is a disaster."

"Relax, I can do this," Bubbles said, trying to copy Hugo's voice, but her attempt to calm me down wasn't working.

First the statue, now this! There was no way I would be respected now.

But did I really have a choice? I mean, either I made something up on the spot or Bubbles did, and she was a way better speaker.

What was the worst that could happen?

I took a shaky breath and stepped forward. "Okay, I trust you, Bubbles." I gulped and waited for instructions.

"Okay, get ready," Hugo said.

"Wait, that's it?" I asked. Bubbles and her uncle looked at me, confused, with their heads tilted. "Like I don't need to do anything?" They both shook their heads.

I shrugged and stared into Bubbles's eyes. I tried to do what I'd seen in the movies, where the actors seem to stare into each other's souls. Bubbles had her eyes pointed down, but then she looked at me.

"What are you doing?" she asked, confused.

"Um," I started, "I thought that's what you had to do. Like, you know, look intently into someone's eyes."

"That's not a thing," Bubbles said. "I mean, I've never heard of it. Have you heard of that?" she asked Hugo, who shook his head. The Schnawegians all went around asking each other the same thing.

"Okay, I get it," I said. "Can we continue?"

Bubbles and Hugo refocused, and we all stood quietly. Nothing happened. Nobody moved, nobody spoke. It was as if a silent wind had sucked the breath out of the tent. There didn't even seem to be commotion outside.

All of a sudden, I smelled something. Was it sugar? Or something burning? No, wait, it was … a churro? And then, something spoke to me.

Why does it smell like someone ate a whole bag of sugar?!

I laughed. I was in Bubbles's head all right.

Wait, so she could read my mind now?

You know I can.

It was weird hearing her voice even though she wasn't talking. I could even hear the tones and uniqueness of her personality.

"Okay," I said out loud. "Are we ready?"

Simon peeked his head in the tent. It was as if someone had read my mind. Well, other than Bubbles.

"Sir Leon, it's time for your speech," he said. And then, a bunch of creatures stormed inside, surrounding me, Maria, Bubbles, and Hugo. We were ushered outside, where they directed us through the party.

Hugo yelled over the crowd. "If you ever want to disconnect, think about only your memories, and block Bubbles's. But you must solely think about yours. If not, it can cause problems."

I gulped. Well, that was reassuring. My palms were sweating, my knees became weak, and my arms felt heavy.

You got this, Bubbles said in my head. *You just have to talk. That's it. And if it makes you feel any better, Bruno threw up at his first Grand Festival speech.*

I chuckled a bit. I felt a little better, but not a lot.

Soon, I found myself next to the podium. Well, more like underneath it. About twenty feet above the floor was a floating stand where I would speak. This location would make my plan to look for demons even easier.

So, what is your plan?

I'm going to look for the demon during my speech, I said in my mind. *Everyone will be gathered around, and it'll be a lot easier. And now I have a higher viewpoint.*

Oh, that's smart.

Bruno met me before I went up. "Are you ready?" I nodded. "Okay. There is no need to be nervous. You will do fantastic. Just speak from the heart. People already love you and that statue of yours."

Did they not know that the statue looked completely ridiculous?

He walked away, and I was by myself again. I closed my eyes and tried to relax. I pictured the calm waves back in Hawaii. The warm sand crunching underneath my toes. I pictured the sky that looked like a painting, with swirls of white clouds. And then, my voice was called.

"Please welcome the leader of Strelit, Leon!"

The dragons shouted and hollered as I floated up to the podium. I gulped.

Fellow citizens of Strelit, Bubbles said to me. I repeated it back to everyone. *First of all, is everyone having a great time?* These words generated another round of whoops.

But the speech didn't sound like me. And as it continued, none of it sounded like I was speaking from my heart. But at least it was a speech, and it wasn't going wrong.

It was like I jinxed myself. Because as soon as I thought that, the speech went wrong. A word came into my head: *cookies.*

"Cookies?" I said out to the crowd. The creatures shared confused looks.

Bubbles, focus, I said mentally.

Sorry, I love cookies, and a cart passed, but it's okay, I've got this. The next line is 'Strelit has given me a home.'

I put on a confident face for the crowd and said the next line, but inside, I was praying Bubbles didn't get distracted again.

The speech was going well for the next two lines and then—

Chocolate.

"Chocolate," I said before I could realize what I had just heard.

Chewy. Soft. Yummy. Ohhhh, I have to go get one.

I saw Bubbles follow a cart down a path, and my heart sank to the ground. Maria shrugged, and then gave me a thumbs-up, trying to raise my spirits. I smiled weakly.

What was I going to do? I took a deep breath and remembered what Bruno had told me. I had to speak from the heart.

"Strelit has given me a place that I can forever be at peace," I said, without Bubbles telling me to. "And all the citizens have become my family. And as I learn and gain experience, I hope to become the same for each and every one of you. I have been handed down this amazing torch that I will keep burning for as long as I am the leader!"

The crowd went into a frenzy, and the shouts were three times as loud as before. Bubbles had come back and was smiling.

Wow, you did it, Bubbles said.

Well, what was I supposed to do? You left me there.

I might have left you, but I did find a demon. Look by the concert. And I checked to see if the poem was there. It was gone. They probably have it.

To the right, I saw two creatures with red cracks glowing in their skin. I then looked at the box that had the poem.

It was empty.

I stepped down from the podium and raced toward the outskirts of the party. Creatures swarmed me from every direction, congratulating me, asking me all sorts of questions, commenting on my speech. As much as I loved and appreciated the attention, I couldn't let the demons get away. But I had no idea how to get out of there.

By some miracle, Maria and Bubbles found me in the monsoon of people.

"What do we do?" I asked. Every second that went by, more creatures suffocated me.

"I have an idea," Maria said. She cupped her mouth and yelled, "OH MY GOSH, WHAT IS THAT?!" All of a sudden, the attention shifted to where Maria was pointing.

The dragons flew over to see what Maria had found. Her distraction gave us time to slip away and fly to the demons.

I went to scoop Bubbles up, but she stopped me. "I'm gonna slow you guys down," she said. "Go stop them!" I nodded, and Maria and I zoomed after them.

The demons were flying away, thinking they had gotten away with the poem without anyone noticing. But as soon as they saw us, they sped up.

Soon enough, Maria and I were in a chase through the desert, and neither of us had any intention of slowing down. The cacti turned into green blurs that we dodged with ease. The sand blew around us as we sloped over the dunes.

The demons kept trying to shake us off their trail by getting us to hit a rock or knock into a cactus. But we kept up with them.

I gingerly lifted my hand from my side and steadied it out in front. I blasted water out of my palm, aiming for the demons. Two of my shots missed and nearly sent me barreling into a sand dune.

My third shot managed to clip the wing of one of the demons, which made him crash into his partner, sending them both tumbling to the ground.

I blasted both of them with water, and Maria teleported a cactus onto their heads. I guessed that would work. Soon, they were unconscious.

They both carried a satchel, so we searched them. We found their badges and took them just in case we ever needed them. But there were no scrolls inside.

Where was the poem?

CHAPTER NINETEEN

I went frantic. What were we going to do? My head felt like it was going to explode. My palms were sweating.

We had no poem, and whoever had it was probably long gone. I had lost the poem. I was going to be known as the worst leader in history!

"We have to start looking," Maria said, in equal panic. She flew into the sky and I followed after her.

We took off high and looked around the desert, then went back to the Grand Festival. I felt weightless as I zoomed in the air. The pressure on my feet released, and I felt more agile.

I searched and searched around the mix of the yellow sand and the spots of green bushes, but couldn't find any other demon. All I saw were regular dragons and other creatures of Strelit.

"I found him!" Maria shouted. "He's heading to the forest!"

Without a second to waste, Maria dove down and I followed her. The stinging wind whipped against my face like an ocean wave. My eyes watered, but the tears were brushed off into the air. My hair was blown straight back and flew behind me as we chased after him.

Slowly, the demon came into view. He was a lot bigger than the other demons I'd seen. He made it into the dense forest, and we followed him in. The demon swerved through the trees and boulders like a pro, dodging everything in his path.

But so did we. Our flying had gotten drastically better ever since our training with Victoria.

The trees swayed with the wind we created as we flew, and the leaves on the ground rustled. Different creatures could be heard flying and chirping around us. It was raining a little, causing the air to be cool and moist.

The demon kept throwing rocks at us and would sometimes whip branches down. Thankfully, he never hit us. But I felt like I was going to get hurt any second now.

Then, by some miracle, rain started pouring down. Demons were weak against water, so he would be slowed down enough so we could catch up to him.

But Maria was also weak against water because she was a fire type. I looked at her, and she nodded, saying she would keep going.

The demon slowed gradually, like a car going empty on fuel. He sluggishly made turns and ended up knocking into multiple rocks and trees.

Maria made one big boost and tackled the demon to the ground. Maria grunted as they rolled on the slick mud. The demon kicked Maria and knocked her into a tree.

I blasted water at the demon, which sent him sprawling in pain. Maria went over to kick him and teleport rocks onto him.

And then, out of nowhere, the demon got up and tackled Maria to the ground.

"Aaaah!" she shouted as she slid into the mud. The demon got a hold of her neck, and Maria was trying to wrench free—and they were headed straight to a boulder the size of a pickup truck.

My heart sank to my feet. She was going to get hurt, she could die. What was going to happen? If I'd thought my heart had been beating fast before, now it was leaping. I held my breath as they approached the boulder.

Thankfully, Maria noticed it and teleported just in time.

But the demon couldn't do anything. He bashed into the boulder, creating a skull-rattling *THUD*. The boulder split as the demon slid down, unconscious. My heart slowed down, and my breath came back. Maria was safe.

I gingerly went over to the demon. Was he still awake? I stepped up to him and carefully watched for any sign of movement. There was none.

An eerie silence filled the forest. It wasn't raining anymore, but it almost seemed like a dark cloud above us would storm any second. Even the wind seemed to hold its breath.

The demon had a satchel, and we searched it. While we were looking, a piece of paper fell out into the mud. I gasped and quickly snatched it. I unrolled it and examined it. It was the poem. All I had needed to see was the shining moon to recognize it.

"Okay, let's go," I said, and started to fly out.

"Wait, look," Maria said. She pointed to something in front of her. It looked like a castle.

Was that the demon kingdom?

All of a sudden, the wind picked up. Viciously. The castle was a looming figure that reached the top of the trees. And all of the trees around it were dead.

The castle was all black and hideous. It leaned to the left, with five different segments building on top of each other. The castle seemed to be looking at me: each segment had a balcony that wrapped around it entirely, almost like a lookout, and each balcony was occupied by several black birds with beady red eyes that stared at me.

Wilted vines crept up the building like the nerves up my back. I had goosebumps from head to toe.

"Look at the top," Maria whispered.

At the very top lookout stood two creatures. One was a demon: I could tell by the glowing red scales. But the other was something I'd never seen here before. It stood on two feet and didn't have a hunched back like a normal demon.

I was frozen in terror. Were they watching us? Did they see what happened just now with the other demon? They didn't seem to notice us. But I just stood there in fear. I couldn't move. Something about the place and these creatures made my back feel like it was crawling with tarantulas. Maria had to pull me by my shirt to snap me out of my trance.

"That was crazy," Maria said on our way back. "What were you doing back there?

"I don't know." What *was* I doing? "Can you just teleport us out? It will take us forever to get out of here." Maria agreed and teleported us to Pharaoh to pick up Bubbles.

I landed on the red carpet of the Grand Festival, feeling slightly woozy. But my wooziness was nothing compared to how Maria felt. She looked as pale as a ghost, and her arms were limp at her sides.

"Are you okay?" I asked.

"Yeah, I think I'm just wiped out from the rain and using my powers."

We had landed next to the glass case that had held the poem. The festival had ended, and Pharaoh was vacant for the most part, so it was easy to find Bubbles. She was sitting at a table with someone I didn't recognize.

"I mean, I just don't know what to do with myself," Bubbles said, getting worked up. "Is he okay? Did he get hurt? And it's just so hard on me right now. And I— Are you even listening?" she asked the stranger, who didn't pay her any attention.

Bubbles spotted me, and she gasped and ran over. "I'm so glad you are okay!" she exclaimed. "Did you get the scroll?" I held it up, and she squealed with excitement. "Okay, now let's go. I'm hungry." I laughed as we headed out of Pharaoh.

We hailed a dragon carriage with ease, as there were many of them but only a handful of people. The carriage glided through the air gently and flew past the sandy dunes of Pharaoh, into the streets.

On the way back home, my mind was crowded with thoughts. The most prominent one being, *What's next?* Okay, we had the scroll, and we could find whatever it was we needed to find, but what would we do after? What would *I* do after? I was swimming in my fears, with no air to breathe.

We finally got back to the Palace. We headed up to the office, which was really a meeting room on the third floor. The walls were frosted glass so you couldn't see from the outside in. Other than a long table, there wasn't really much to the room.

Maria and I sat in two chairs, side by side, and Bubbles stood on the table. I rolled the scroll open, and we examined it.

"So, what are we exactly looking for?" Maria said.

"I don't know," I answered. "I guess we will just read it and see?"

We both read silently to ourselves. Nothing really stood out to me at the beginning of the poem. But then, there was an interesting line at the end. It read: 'The havoc will shower when the wind blows a cry from afar." I pointed it out to Maria.

"Do you think that's when they will attack?" she asked.

I shrugged. This whole thing about the war coming was an entire mystery, and the best I could do was guess. "I mean, it could be a red herring. Like them trying to throw us off. Or it could be something else that they have planned. Or it could be the actual date that they are going to attack. Or—"

"You're overthinking this!" she shouted. "You have to focus. If you lose your head, the citizens will as well."

What she'd said made sense. I was a mess. And what message did that convey to other creatures in Strelit?

But how was I *not* supposed to be a mess? I mean, there was so much going on right now. It felt like I was being hit by a semi-truck with all the work they relied on me to do. These past few days, I'd been doubting every move I made. I couldn't make a decision without questioning my every move. I needed to at least try to be better about being decisive and focused.

"Okay," I started, "so what do you think it is?"

"I think it's as simple as when they're going to attack," she said. "'The havoc will shower' is talking about the war. And the 'whole wind from afar' thing is the date. But it's not an actual time date. It's, like, a vague date. So, I don't really know how that helps."

"Well, it's what we have. And we are going to have to work with it until we find something else."

I got up and headed to the door. I held it open, but Maria didn't get up.

"Are you coming?" I asked.

"I'm just going to look this through one more time."

I nodded and closed the door. I went up to my room and shut the door. Bubbles laid down on my bed, and I was going to relax as well, but I changed my mind and headed out the door again. I couldn't be wasting time being lazy. I had to show everyone that I could keep up.

"Where are you going?" Bubbles asked.

"To the Academy. I'm going to go practice."

"Well, then, I'm coming with you." Bubbles hopped off the bed and followed me out.

All the hardships we'd endured together had brought Bubbles and me closer. Sometimes, I could almost sense what she was feeling. That might just have been me guessing, though.

I went outside and started flying, with Bubbles inside my backpack. I let the wind of the cool night wash over me as I rode it like a wave. I needed to get my thoughts out and let go. And the best way to do that would be to practice.

We got to the Academy. I went inside one of the training rooms, and Bubbles found a spot in the back corner. She curled up and fell asleep.

The wall was lined with all kinds of weapons: swords, nunchucks, throwing stars, escrima, and more. There were a lot of punching dummies as well. I grabbed one of them and started hitting it with a sword.

As I kept hitting it over and over, my thoughts rose up. But I was getting angry. My shots got harder and my grunts louder.

I kept failing this kingdom and wasn't doing enough. I should have already stopped the demons. Everyone should love me already and be by my side. But it seemed like I had more enemies than allies! And there was also this whole war coming, and I didn't know what to do. I shouldn't even be the leader!

Not to mention, I hadn't even found Rebecca yet. She was a big reason I had decided to stay in Strelit, and now there was no sign of her. The dream I had when I was still in Hawaii was useless!

I hit the neck of the dummy with all my anger, and the head soared off and hit the wall. The head rolled back, and it seemed to watch me with a look of disgust.

CHAPTER TWENTY

Bubbles's head perked up as the dummy head rolled along the floor. I grabbed my backpack and stormed toward the door.

"Let's go," I said to Bubbles. My voice was angry and gravelly. I wanted to get out of the room and forget this training session ever happened.

"But you have to deal with your emotions."

"No, I don't," I said in a gruff voice. "Let's just go."

Bubbles slowly followed me out the door. She hopped in the backpack, and I put it on and started flying home.

I tried to not think about what had happened just now. Right then, I didn't want to fill my head with anything remotely related to me being the leader.

"You know you can talk to me, right?" Bubbles said in a soft and gentle voice.

"I'm fine!" I shouted at her. "There's nothing to talk about." I was angry, but I wasn't doing anything about it. I wanted to shut this experience in a closet and lock it tight.

I raced past the trees, nearly hitting some branches. I made the grass underneath us whip up and fly in my draft. The sun had barely set when we got to the Palace.

"Have a good night, Mr.—" Simon said, but I closed the door before he could finish. I stomped upstairs and slammed the door to my room. I changed my clothes and got in bed.

That night, I dreamed of the dummy head endlessly rolling, its eyes never wavering away from me.

* * *

A couple of days went by, and I was in the same grumpy mood. People around me noticed as well. I was angry all the time. And it only seemed to get worse from there.

Hundreds of creatures came by my office daily. Whether to ask for a new law or to complain about their neighbor. I got all kinds of complaints. And with each day, the complaints and pressure seemed to pile up even more.

I was carrying the weight of every citizen of Strelit. And their anger too. Over half of the creatures seemed to hate me, and I had no idea why.

Today was the Council's meeting. I headed toward the office, my feet shuffling along the floor. Maria was already there.

"Good morning," I mumbled.

She looked up from a book she was reading, which shocked me. I'd noticed she'd been reading a lot more recently, which was a new trait for her. "Good morning," she said in a cheerful tone. "You look like you need a cup of coffee. You look beat."

I plopped down on one of the chairs and rested my head on the table. Slowly, the different members of the Council joined us. First, Bruno came. And then Chip, the small dragon that leads the fire kingdom, and Violet, the unicorn, joined us. And finally, Henchberry, who always seemed to be late. Couldn't he just show up on time like everyone else?

I got up and made my way to the front of the table.

"Good morning, members of the Council," I groaned. "Any suggestions on what to do differently?" Maria raised her hand and spoke.

"Um, a lot of people are complaining about the war coming up. They're asking what type of protection they have against them," Maria said.

I started to get angry. This war was just another huge problem piled on top of this mountain of issues.

"Yes," I started, "that is a big issue we need to fix." I paced the room while everyone thought about it. And then, the solution hit me.

"We can build small dividers that separate each kingdom," I said with the most joy I'd had all week. "That way, if the demons come, it'll slow them down." I saw mixed emotions around the room. Some people, like Maria and Chip, liked this idea. Bruno, Violet, and Henchberry hated it.

"That's the dumbest thing I've ever heard," Henchberry scoffed.

I got upset. How was my idea dumb? It made perfect sense.

"What you're saying is a bit … different," Bruno said.

Well, wasn't that the point of a new law?

"This would hurt the kingdoms who are under attack," he continued.

"Yes," Violet said, "I agree with Bruno on this one. They would have no support from allies."

Why was this decision so hard for everyone to make?

"This would buy time for the other kingdoms, though," Maria said. "And these kingdoms can fend for themselves just fine."

"But we have no idea how strong the demons are," Henchberry said. "We could lose tons of citizens because of this ridiculous idea."

The members started arguing and bickering. Back and forth, nonstop. Well, all except Bruno. He stood back and just watched. Then he gave me a look that seemed to say, *Do something.*

"Okay, okay," I said, frustrated. "We will think about this more tomorrow."

"Tomorrow?!" they shouted at me in unison.

"Fine, we'll vote on it now, okay?" I said. This meeting was getting on my nerves. "All in favor?" I said, raising my hand.

Maria, Chip, and Violet also agreed. Meaning the new law would be put in place. Everyone got out of their seats and shuffled out the door. Half of the members left hating me that day.

Half of Strelit seemed to hate me. Only half of the citizens' complaints got resolved. Only half of their suggestions were put in place. Every time I walked on the street, half of the creatures scowled at me or turned away. I was failing as a leader.

"Hey," Maria said. "This is good news. You should be happy." I ignored her words and continued out the door.

All I could think about was how this world was being torn in half, and it was all my fault.

Henchberry followed me toward my room. "Hey," he called out. "I don't like this idea one bit. So don't expect my help for any of it." With that, he turned around and headed outside.

What was that about?

I got to my room and plopped onto my bed. I groaned into my pillow out of frustration.

Bubbles perked her head from her nap. "What happened?" she asked. "Is everything okay?" I nodded, not wanting to talk. "Well, I'm here for you," she said. "And you can always talk to me."

I didn't really want to talk about it, though. I had to fix myself first, and I didn't need or want anyone's help. I had this huge responsibility, and it was *my* responsibility. I just needed to focus on being a better leader.

As I stressed over this, I slowly drifted into a deep sleep.

*   *   *

I gasped awake at midnight, panting. My shirt was drenched in sweat, and my face felt hot. I frantically looked around in fear. When I realized it was just Bubbles in the room, I relaxed.

I had a nightmare where all the citizens of Strelit had surrounded me and were yelling at me. They were all angry. And one face stood out in the crowd: Bruno's. He watched with the same look he'd had in the council meeting, but this time I sensed it was a look of anger. Had he been angry at me in the council meeting as well?

Out of all the people in Strelit, Bruno was the one I most wanted to impress. With each new law and regulation, I anxiously awaited his response, hoping he'd be satisfied.

Worried that he was angry with my recent work, I slipped out of bed. I tiptoed across the floor to the office to fill out some papers for the new law and get some other stuff done.

With the nightmarish image of Bruno's face haunting me, I got to work. I filled out the papers for the new law. Then I went to grab a glass of water.

But as I opened the door to leave, Bruno's face came back to me. That face sent shudders down my spine and quickened my breath. I didn't want to upset him.

I shut the door and went back to work instead. I felt a tremendous amount of pressure as I continued. I raced around the office, grabbing papers and files. My handwriting became vicious, and several pens broke in my hands as I wrote. I must have looked like a madman.

My breath began to shorten, and my legs became weak. But I needed to finish more work. I rushed to grab citizens' requests and read them in a hurry. I signed them and then crammed them in the OKAY box to be put into action. I ran to grab more and repeated the process. My eyelids drooped every so often, but I needed to keep going. I couldn't let Bruno down. I couldn't let *myself* down. I couldn't let Rebecca down.

And then, on my fifth trip to get more requests, I collapsed on the ground. *THUD.*

CHAPTER TWENTY-ONE

*D*RIP-DRIP-DRIP. I awoke to an IV dripping. A needle poked through a vein in my arm, and bright industrial lights hung from the ceiling. I was back at the hospital.

I sat up, and suddenly I felt a pulse in my head, and groaned in pain. Maria was in a chair, with Bubbles in the next one. No one else was there.

Maria set down her book and rushed over to my bedside. "How are you feeling?" she asked. Bubbles hopped onto the bed.

"I feel fine," I said. "What happened?" The last thing I remembered was my face hitting the ground.

"I think you passed out or something," Maria said. "But for a really long time."

Just then, the same unicorn doctor who'd treated me last time came in.

"Ah, you're awake," she said. "Do you feel okay?" I nodded. "That's wonderful news. Thankfully, Maria rushed you here as soon as she saw you. You could have been much in much worse condition."

Maria had found me?

"Where is everyone else?" I asked.

"Were you expecting company?" the doctor asked, surprised. I'd just thought that there would be more people, like last time. Maybe nobody cared that this happened to me?

"I brought you here as soon as I found you," Maria said. "I didn't want to wait any longer."

"How did you find me, though?"

"I woke up early to go do some work," she said, shocking me. She was actually dedicated and being responsible. "And when I left my room, I saw your door open. And so, I assumed you were working. When I got there, you had already passed out."

I swung my legs over the edge of the bed and stood up. I needed to get going with my day.

"Oh, no, no, no," the doctor said. "You need to stay here until your IV bag finishes." The IV bag was still full.

"But I have so much work to do," I complained.

The doctor shook her head. "You must recover so this doesn't happen again."

"What do I need to recover from?"

"You're mentally drained. You collapsed because of stress and fatigue. You had put your mind through so much tax and strain that it couldn't handle anymore."

I felt fine, though. But I didn't want to argue with the doctor. I looked at the IV bag again. The liquid was at the same level. I was going to be here for a long time.

The doctor left, and I stared at the ceiling. I counted how many panels there were. Then I counted how many panels there were, diagonally. And then on the other diagonal. I was getting bored, fast. Maria and Bubbles were still there, though.

"Aren't you going to leave?" I asked Maria.

"No way. I'm staying here the entire time. I'm not leaving your side."

"Oh," I answered. "Okay." I resumed finding more ways I could count the panels.

* * *

The bag finally finished dripping, after what seemed like forever. Maria was still reading her book when I was done.

The doctor came into the room. "You are done!" she exclaimed, removing the needle from my arm. "Just don't overwork yourself again." I nodded, only half listening.

What I wanted to do was start on the new law that we had voted on yesterday. But deep down, I wanted to start the new law so badly in order to prove to Henchberry and the others that I had good ideas. My focus for everything I did right now was proving Henchberry and the board members wrong.

I needed to show them that I was right.

"Thank you," I said to the doctor.

"You shouldn't be thanking me," she said. "Maria stood by your side the whole day."

Well, no one asked her to stay. I didn't need her to watch over me. I was fine.

Maria and I left the room and walked down the white-walled hallway. Once we got outside, we flew past the dry grass that had changed with the seasons. The weather was now becoming colder, matching my personality.

"Where are we going?" Maria asked.

"Um," I started. "I guess we should go to the closest kingdom and start there?" I didn't really know what to do first either. Maybe take measurements for the dividers?

"Okay," she said, beaming. "I'll go get the rest of the members of the Council. Should we meet you in Lucean?"

I mumbled okay and flew down. Maria didn't need to call the Council.

I could've done it myself.

Lucean was the light kingdom, and it was also the kingdom closest to the Palace. Strelit was formed with a forest surrounding it. Enclosed in the forest, the Palace was to the north, and then Crystel was to the east, with Lucean, Pharaoh, and Fiery following after, making a semicircle below the Palace. To the west of the Palace was the Academy. Creatures other than dragons, like the blubba gubbas and unicorns, lived in places near the Academy, or in houses behind the kingdoms.

The land in Strelit was mostly rolling hills and greenery. Inside of the thick forest to the east was the demon kingdom.

Right now, the kingdoms blended into each other with no separation, which was the issue we were trying to resolve. For instance, in Pharaoh, the land would go from dirt and mud, to grass, and then to hot rocks and ash. Nothing divided or showed where each kingdom stopped and started. And there wasn't anything to stop the demons from going from kingdom to kingdom and destroying everything.

I got to the entrance to Lucean. The floor reflected the sunlight so that everything was shining. All of the materials were either reflective or had some sort of shine to it. A lot of the buildings were tall and pointy so that they helped reflect light to practically everything in this kingdom. The rest of the Council was already there. They all greeted me—well, except Henchberry.

"Heh," he scoffed. "He's always late. Never can show up on time."

Well, Henchberry was the one who was always late for our meetings and got on my nerves. But he had come, even when he'd promised not to help. So, I guessed that was a good sign.

"Ready?" Maria said. I nodded, and we all flew to the edge of Lucean where it met Crystel. I carried Bubbles in my arms as we went.

Dozens of citizens from both kingdoms were gathered around. How had they known we would be there? I hadn't told anyone else.

"Henchberry," one of the ice dragons said. "So you were right. He really is doing this crazy idea," the dragon scoffed.

"Yeah," Henchberry answered. "I thought he would have come to have some sort of sense by now." All the ice dragons laughed.

Their laughs and remarks made me mad, and my face flushed with heat. All of them seemed to love Henchberry for no reason at all.

"Okay, so how is this going to work?" one of the light dragons asked.

Honestly, I didn't even know. Well, that was what I *wanted* to say. But I couldn't. As the leader, I had to pretend everything was okay.

"Um, well, I think the Council will discuss more about what actions need to be done next, but we will have protection up soon," I answered. The light dragons seemed to be okay with this idea, whereas the ice dragons absolutely hated it.

The light dragons shuffled away and started doing other stuff. But the ice dragons stayed and glowered at me.

"So much for a leader. He doesn't even know what he's doing!" an ice dragon said, and the rest agreed in unison.

"Okay," I said to the rest of the Council, trying to ignore what the ice dragons were saying, "So, we need to build a blockade so that the demons can't get through, but we can't just make a wall because they could just fly over." The ice dragons snickered. "So, we would need to deter them some other way. Any suggestions?"

We all thought about it for a second.

"Well, they are weak to water, right?" Maria asked.

"Okay, and?" I asked, not getting her point.

"Well, if we can somehow make a structure out of water, then we could at least slow them down and make them weaker."

That wasn't a bad idea, actually. And the structure wouldn't cost too much because it's just water.

"That would work," I said. "What if we did, like, a huge sprinkler system? That is, maybe, motion-sensored?" Violet, Chip, and Henchberry all looked confused.

"A *sprinkler*?" Henchberry asked. "What in the world is a *sprinkler*?" He laughed with the rest of the ice dragons.

Bruno stepped up to me. "Leon, we don't have sprinklers here in Strelit. Those only exist in Midgard." He stepped back and smiled.

My fists balled up in anger. Henchberry was still cackling with his minions. I jumped up in excitement. "Well, we could make one."

They all hushed. I finally had their attention.

"All you need is tubing, a water source, and then something to disperse the water." I started to pace around, talking faster. Everyone followed me and held on to my every word. "We can use a water source in Crystel, and I don't know if there is a motion detector here, but we could—"

"Or, what if we did a waterfall?" Maria interrupted. Everyone turned their attention to her.

"That could work, Maria," Bruno said. "We could make it so the water is recycled back to keep the waterfall going. That's smart."

Well, hold on. I had an idea first. Why wouldn't they listen? Why did Maria have to shut me out like that? My plan would've worked!

"She should be the leader," Henchberry said. "She comes up with great ideas!"

Everyone looked at one another with a *Why not?* expression, as if they were contemplating replacing me.

But *I* was the one who had the idea first! I should've been getting the praise! I had finally been making progress with the ice dragons and Henchberry, and all of a sudden, Maria had to cut in!

"What do you think?" Maria asked me, not seeming to notice my anger.

"Um, yeah, I think it'll work." I was still mad that she cut me off and stole my chance at being liked. "But wouldn't we need to build something to stop the demons from flying over that? If we go back to the sprinkler—"

"Oh!" Maria shouted again. "What if we did, like, ice cubes melting. So then, the water vapor stops them."

There she went again! I literally had a perfect idea.

"Hah!" Henchberry laughed. "She's a genius! Why isn't she the leader already?"

Maria smiled while I glowered.

"Okay," Bruno said. "Then it's settled. We will start it as soon as we finish our plans. Good meeting, everyone."

We all flew back to the entrance of Lucean and then parted ways. The sun was setting, so everyone else went home. I picked up Bubbles, and Maria and I both flew to the Palace.

"Good thing we figured that out," Maria said. "Right?" I just ignored her. "I'm going to go visit Kienan now. You wanna come?"

"Who's Kienan?" I asked, glaring at her.

"The kid who we helped with the ball, you don't remember? Right after we met with Victoria. I'm just going to go play with him."

"You don't have to make me look bad, okay?!" I shouted at her.

Maria's eyes went wide, and she stumbled as she was flying. "I wasn't trying to make you look bad," she said, her voice trembling a bit. "I was just offering if you wanted to come!"

"Yeah, right," I said, rolling my eyes. "It's like you want me to do bad as a leader. You make it look like I don't know anyone here, and then you steal my ideas."

Maria gasped in shock. "Why would I want that?!" she shouted back. "And I didn't steal your idea."

"You tell me. I was in the middle of talking about my plan when you decided to cut me off because you want to make everyone think I can't do anything."

"Leon, how could you say something like that? I'm trying to help you as a leader. I just had a thought for a plan, that's all."

"Well, I don't need your help," I snapped. "I can do this on my own. *I'm* the leader, not you."

Maria was speechless. Angry, I flew ahead of her.

I got to the Palace and slammed my door after Bubbles got in.

"You should apologize to her," Bubbles said. "She's probably really hurt."

"Well, she should be!" I shouted. "She humiliated me in front of everybody!" Why would Maria do something like that?

"She said she didn't do it on purpose, though."

"Do you really believe that? It's Maria, of course she wants me to look bad. It's who she is!"

I got in bed and tried to fall asleep. I was so angry about everything that had happened today. Half of Strelit hated my guts, and the other half barely tolerated me. Nobody was on my side. And now with Maria.

My world was crumbling!

CHAPTER TWENTY-TWO

I woke up the next morning. I squinted as the sun hit my eyes, and I got out of bed.

The pain of yesterday still struck me, and I dreaded seeing everyone again. Especially Maria. Would she yell at me? Would she make a scene? What would she say?

I opened my door and creaked down the stairs. Maria would already be down there because we had to leave for the Academy. I stood at the bottom of the stairs and saw Maria at the front of the Palace, facing the door.

My heart quickened. The last thing I needed was Maria to explode on me. She was going to if she saw me, though.

I gingerly walked to the lobby. I hid behind pillars and stayed out of

Maria's line of sight. I just hoped to avoid her for as long as I could.

And then she turned around. I dove for the nearest pillar and hid behind it. Had she seen me? What was she going to say?

"Good morning, Leon," Maria said from across the lobby. I peeked around the pillar. She was oddly cheerful, considering what had happened yesterday.

I shuffled my feet toward her. "Hello," I mumbled. I was still scared. Was this some sort of mind game? Was her calm manner supposed to make me vulnerable so she could then get angry at me?

"Are you ready for today?" she asked. "I'm so excited!"

I was shocked. She was so … nice, considering what happened yesterday.

"Yeah?" I stammered. "I'm excited." Today we were going to practice a Capture the Horn game. I was a little worried because it was a dangerous game. I didn't want to get hurt. But as the leader of Strelit, I had to participate.

Maria and I headed out toward the Academy. I tried to avoid talking to Maria, for fear of her lashing out at me. But Maria kept talking and talking like usual. She went off on all the strategies she'd read about, and how this tactic was better than that one, and how she hoped she got to hide the horn, and this and that.

And then, I just had to ask. "Aren't you upset from yesterday?"

She stopped rambling. "No," she said without doubt or hesitation. "We just had a discussion. You told me your thoughts, and that was it."

I guessed nothing had happened. So, I had gotten worked up over nothing?

We went directly to the edge of the campus, where it met the forest. Coach Carl was already there, as well as a lot of the other students. When we landed, the rest of the team snickered and whispered.

What were they saying about me?

"Okay!" Carl barked. "Today is a big day. This is where we take all those skills we have been practicing and put them to good use. The Wohna Games have already started, and the finals are coming up. And remember, Capture the Horn is the tiebreaker. If we win, then we win the Wohna Games. Now, let's do this!"

I gulped as I realized the pressure we were under.

We lined up per usual, and Coach Carl scrutinized us like always. What did he think about every single time he did this?

"Okay!" he shouted again. "Sam and Heather are the team captains for our two mock teams, and they'll pick their team members!" They both stepped in front of the line and turned around to start choosing their teams.

"Jovie, Maria, Lukas, Vett …" They called out names, and their teams started filling out. And then, it was just me and another kid whose name I forgot.

But the other kid was called.

CHAPTER TWENTY-TWO

And then it was just me.

Sam had the last pick, but he didn't want to pick me. He had a sour face, and he twisted and turned.

"Fffffffine," he said. "I pick Leon." He grumbled as I walked to my assigned group. "You better not mess us up, got it?"

Did he hate me now too? What was happening? And it seemed like everyone on my team hated me. Well, except Maria, who was the only one smiling. The rest of them glowered at me.

"Okay!" Carl shouted again. "Now, the team captains will choose their player to hide the horn. Choose!"

Sam immediately chose Maria, who then pumped her fist in the air.

"Any idea of where you're going to hide it yet?" Sam asked her. He had some sort of awe in his eyes, like *she* was the leader.

"Underneath the little waterfall that flows into the Lake of Luck," she whispered, and everyone *oohed*.

What was the Lake of Luck?

"That's a great spot," Sam whispered.

Maria smiled, blushing a bit. "Come on, let's talk about our strategy." Everyone huddled up, but I was left out of the circle.

They left me out of the team. They despised me! Maria gave me a pitying smile, but didn't do anything about it. She didn't want to help me!

I was able to pick up some bits of information, even from the outside.

Sam said that Maria would be the attacker, Heather would defend alongside him, and other people would scatter around and take different roles.

Then, another dragon asked, "What about him?" She nudged her head over to me.

Sam rolled his eyes. He broke the circle and stepped up to my face. "You better not mess anything up!" he yelled. "Just try to get the horn, and as soon as you do, you give it to Maria. That's ALL you do! Okay?"

Don't tell me what to do. I wanted to tell him that, but I kept my mouth quiet. But worst of all, Maria just stood there! She didn't even say anything! So much for a friend.

"Ready?" Coach Carl asked both teams. We all nodded. "So now, the team member who is hiding the horn has five minutes to place it and come back. Take your positions!"

At the entrance of the forest, Maria got into a running start position and held it.

"GO!"

Heather, who would hide the other team's horn, and Maria took off, and flew into the forest. Everyone whooped, cheered, and hollered.

And then we waited.

The silence was overbearing. This was the most dangerous part of the game because no one would know if something happened to them. Therefore, we all sat there, our bodies still and tense.

Three minutes had gone by when we finally heard rustling in the woods on our side. Maria emerged, and our team cheered. Maria was greeted with smiles and praises from all around.

But Heather was still not here. Another minute went by. Nothing.

"Forty-five seconds!" Carl yelled.

She was still not here. Was she okay? The last thing I needed was somebody to get hurt. It would all be blamed on me.

Everyone held their breath as we waited for any sign of life. But still nothing.

"Someone should go get her," Maria said. She went to go fly in, but Carl held her back from doing so.

"She's smart," he said. "She would yell for help if she needed it."

What if she couldn't yell for help? What if she was trapped? Or hurt?

And then we heard the rustling of trees. Was it Heather? Or just some animal? The rustling grew louder, and finally, she emerged. We all exhaled and congratulated her. She was safe.

"What happened?" Carl asked.

"My foot got stuck." She was panting. "I couldn't get it out." She was a light dragon, and because the sun was shining brightly today, she healed quickly.

And then the game started.

"Everyone ready?" Carl asked. We all nodded. "Okay, everyone, go into the forest to where your horn is hidden. I will announce the start of the game with the sound of the horn!"

Our team followed Maria into the forest, and the other team followed Heather.

Soon, we lost sight of the other team as they headed off in a different direction. We reached our horn quickly, which made me a little bit worried. Shouldn't Maria have hidden it a little farther into the forest?

We reached the Lake of Luck. Wow! It was gorgeous! A mesmerizing waterfall rushed into the crystal-clear body of water that sparkled like a diamond. The lake was serene and still. I went to touch the water. It was cool and icy.

"What are you doing?!" Sam said. Everyone gasped and looked shocked as I removed my hand from the water. "Don't go near that water!"

"Why?" I asked. "What's wrong with the water?" Some people on my team snickered, and others gasped again.

"Do you seriously not know?" Sam asked. "How can you be the leader of Strelit and not know about the Lake of Luck? Do you live underneath a rock or something?"

They all snickered again. Couldn't they just tell me?

"There's a water grim at the bottom of this lake," Sam continued. I was still perplexed. "Don't tell me you don't know what a water grim is."

I just stared at him. I had no idea what it was.

"A water grim is this long creature that dwells at the bottom of a lake or body of water," Sam explained. "They have arms and legs three times as long as yours, and they're skinny. Like, only bones. They look like an ancient witch, except they're green. They have green hair that looks like algae too."

"So, what's so dangerous about them?" I had come across many creatures in my time at Strelit. Some fat, others skinny. Some purple, others flaming red.

"They play the violin," Sam said.

I snorted, trying to stifle a laugh. *That's* what made them so scary? A violin?

"The music that comes off of it is hypnotizing, though. And the water grim will lure you down to the bottom, where it will take you hostage and bury you underneath the ground. Alive."

I gulped. Well, that escalated quickly.

"So, where did you put the horn?" I asked Maria. I still hadn't seen it yet. All I hoped was that it wasn't in the lake.

"In the crevice of one of the rocks at the waterfall," she said. We all gasped, and our jaws hit the floor.

"How did you get it there?" Sam said. He seemed to be even more in awe of Maria now.

"I teleported and came back," she said. Everyone started murmuring to each other.

"You can teleport?" Sam asked in amazement. "No one can do that. Well, at least no one for a long time. We are for sure going to win this. They'll never be able to get it. Did you see the water grim at all?" She shook her head. "Wow, that's legendary."

Maria blushed a bit. I guessed she liked Sam, and he liked her. They were always hanging out and laughing.

"Isn't that dangerous?" I asked her, out of jealousy. I wanted people to hesitate and question why she would put another person's life at risk.

"Well, the point is for them *not* to find it," a blubba gubba on our team said. "Do you not know anything?" The team sneered and laughed.

I felt like I was back at home, where I was hated on and bullied constantly.

But once again, Maria did nothing. I was angry at her; my hands balled and I was breathing hard. I tried to keep my anger to myself, but it wasn't easy. She wasn't helping at all! I thought she was on my side.

I went to the base of the waterfall to see where she'd hidden the horn. I was searching for it when I saw a symbol on the rock. I nearly stumbled back.

The symbol looked like Rebecca's signature.

Could it possibly be hers? I'd hardly considered her being here, like I had forgotten about her. But the symbol looked exactly like her signature: two *R*'s and a loop. Hope started rising in me. It could mean my sister was here.

All of a sudden, the horn sounded. We were all shocked for a second, and then ran into the forest, whooping and hollering. Well, I wasn't whooping. But everyone else was.

I took a deep breath. I needed to show that I was able to fight like them, even if I had Rebecca on my mind.

I had one objective for this game:

Show them that I could capture the horn.

CHAPTER TWENTY-THREE

I ran in with the crowd and hollered. I tried to match their energy, if not show more. I needed to show that I was one of them and that I was their ally and teammate. Both in the game and in life. But faking my dedication was hard. I couldn't stop thinking about the symbol I had seen.

Since this was a mini version of Capture the Horn, the coach had marked off a certain section of the forest for us to play in, to reduce the risk of injuries or someone getting lost.

Some members lingered behind to protect the horn, and slowly, our crowd of aggressors dwindled to four of us, including Maria and Sam.

But then my instincts took over: I froze as soon as I saw violence. People were fighting and pushing each other around.

I ran back and hid behind a tree. I didn't want to get hurt. I was better as a defender.

Maria kept moving forward and clashed with the other team. She teleported and shot fire around the opponents, attacked them, and ran forward. She did this like clockwork. How was she so good?

And here I was, standing around like a chicken. I jogged around nervously, never leaving a ten-foot radius. *Should I go in? I should stay back.* But Sam had told me to go in and try to get the horn and give it to Maria. Yeah, but I was the leader, not him. Who cared what he thought. But I needed his support so the rest of the team didn't hate me. I gulped so loud, I thought everyone could hear me.

I needed to stop overthinking everything. I wasn't going to abandon my oath to myself. I would bring the horn back and win the game.

I joined the fighting.

It was madness. Fights were happening everywhere as different creatures got tossed around. I weaved my way through and got pretty far without a fight.

And then I was attacked.

A blubba gubba came down from a tree with a war cry. He slashed down with his arm that he had turned into an ax, barely missing my shoulder. I fell to the side and stumbled on a tree root.

The only reason everyone fought with axes and weapons was that magical creatures have speed healing. An ax to the shoulder would heal as quickly as a cut with a knife. But it was still a cut. And it would still hurt, and I still didn't want to get hit.

The blubba gubba hovered over me and raised his ax-arm over his head. I blasted him with water, sending him back but sending myself the opposite way.

I crashed into a huge rock and slumped down. I felt woozy, like I had just been tumbled in a washing machine. I held myself steady, leaning against the boulder. And then the rock rolled out from under me.

This ten-foot-wide, gigantic rock moved like it was sliding on ice. It rolled and rolled until it banged into a tree. But what was left in the indent the boulder had made in the ground was a shiny object. I shielded my eyes and looked at it.

It was the horn! I had found it!

Its rainbow colors shimmered and glowed like a jewel. I quickly grabbed it and checked my surroundings. No one had seen. Now I just needed to run back to the Lake of Luck and we would win. I was so close.

I blasted off the ground with water and soared high up in the air. My face was hot with excitement. Everyone would look up to me and thank and praise me. And I would take the spotlight off Maria.

I passed most of the battles and fights, concealing the shine of the horn in my pants pocket. I looked behind me and laughed. They wouldn't even know what hit them once I sounded the horn, ending the game. Little did they know that they were all going to love me in about ten seconds.

My mind started wandering back to Rebecca. Why would she leave that sign? Was it even hers? Maybe she was calling for help.

And then, out of nowhere. I got blasted out of the sky.

I hit the ground with a thud. All the air in my lungs was gone, and I gasped for air. The horn had come out of my pocket and rolled about ten feet away from me. I went to grab it, my hand shaking

A fire dragon landed next to the horn and kicked it out of my reach. An earth dragon stood above me and was about to blast me with more wind when Maria teleported next to me.

She was finally going to help me. But she didn't. She picked up the horn and teleported away, without looking at me again.

What was she doing? How could she just do that?

But I didn't have time to think about that. The earth dragon blasted me with air, and I soared into the trunk of a tree. The tree groaned as I collapsed to the forest floor. I slumped down by the tree, and my head fell limply.

And then the horn sounded. The game had ended.

I croaked as I got up. I was in so much pain. I hobbled back to my team base, whimpering with every step because every ounce of my body stung and hurt.

"You did it!" they shouted to Maria. Maria held the horn high, proud like she was the one who found it. She'd stolen it from me.

"Where did you find it?" Sam asked. He beamed at Maria.

"On the ground," she said. "Leon had dropped it, and I picked it up before the other team got it."

All of a sudden, everyone glared at me.

"You had the horn?" Sam said. He snorted, and his face was angry. "You were just supposed to give it to Maria. Did you do that?" I shook my head. "You would've lost us the game if it wasn't for Maria, who saved the day. You shouldn't even be on our team."

Everyone else agreed and berated me even more.

I was like a dog who had just chewed up the furniture. I had just gotten severely hurt and might need medical attention. But instead, they were getting angry at me for dropping the ridiculous horn!

"It's just a game," I said. "It didn't really matter if we won or not. This is just a practice game." They all just looked at me with even more frustration and anger.

"*Just* a game?!" Sam shouted. "Do you even know what Capture the Horn means to Strelit?"

Was I missing something? It was just a game that was part of the Wohna Games.

"Of course you don't," he continued. "You're not part of Strelit. You're just a human. Capture the Horn is the finale of the Wohna Games, and if we lose them, we lose Yggdrasil. Do you know what that would mean, Leon? It would mean that crops wouldn't grow like they do now. Not just that, but we lose our strength as a world, and lose our honor to the other worlds. That tree Yggdrasil is what gives us our power."

I didn't know that. How could I not know that? Did Maria know?

Her face read that she already knew.

Why hadn't she told me? I was furious at her. She so badly wanted me to fail. Maybe if she'd told me, I wouldn't have gotten hurt. This was all her fault! Now it seemed like she was trying to hurt me!

"I'm so sorry." That was all I could manage to say. The rest of me wanted to blame Maria.

We all flew back to Coach Carl. Once we were all out of the forest, he clapped and congratulated each one of us, including me. That was the highlight of my day. At least someone still seemed to enjoy me being here.

We had a small talk about what we thought of the game and what we could've done better. Sam and my team just blamed me during the whole talk—how poorly I'd played, and how I shouldn't play during the Wohna Games. But what they also did was praise Maria for her *incredible* skills and talent for the game.

I should've been more aware and not dropped the horn. But Maria could've helped me. And she should've helped me. I could've been back in the hospital! Did she want me to die?!

Carl dispersed us, and we all flew back to our homes. But before I was able to leave, Carl said he wanted to talk about me.

"Look," he said. "You've got to do better, okay? You've got to pull your weight, got it? You're the leader here. You should be more active than what you're doing now."

"Okay," I mumbled. He didn't like me either. That was just great.

"Good game today," Maria said. "I can't believe I scored!"

"Yeah, me neither," I grumbled sarcastically.

"What do you mean by that?" She sounded scared. Did she not know what she had done wrong?

"You literally just let me get humiliated again," I shouted. "In front of everybody! Like, do you not want me to do well as a leader?" I wanted to erupt like a volcano. How could she betray me? After all we had been through together?

"What do you mean?" she yelled back. "You keep saying all these ridiculous things that aren't true!"

"Oh yeah," I said. "Everyone was making fun of me and saying I shouldn't play. And what did you do? You sat there silent. Silent! You didn't even say one word! And then you just snatched the horn while I was being attacked. Why didn't you help?!"

"Because you told me not to!" she yelled back. She was also erupting. The forest creatures passing by were probably all looking at us.

"When would I ever say that?" I snapped back.

"You said, 'I don't need your help, I'm the leader, not you,'" Maria mimicked my voice and made it higher-pitched and more annoying. "And now you get mad at me for doing what you said!"

"Well, yeah, I said that. But because you were literally shutting me out and not letting me talk. But you need to speak up for me!"

"Oh, I'm sorry," she said sarcastically. "I wasn't able to read your mind and know when you wanted my help and when you didn't."

"It's not that hard." I was frustrated. "You just let me get pummeled and sent into the trunk of a tree. But that's not as important as you getting the horn and winning the game. No, that's what is key. Forget about me and if I need to go to the hospital."

"Leon, you can't say that you don't want my help and then get mad when I don't give it. Either you want my help or you don't. I'm not a magician and can't read your thoughts."

"Well, you didn't have to let me get smashed and crumpled like a piece of paper! It's like you don't want me a part of the team either!"

We got to the Palace, and Maria and I continued to yell back and forth.

"Well, *you* can't tell me to stay out of your business and then blame me for doing exactly as you said. This is on you, not me. Make up your mind!"

Water began to form on my hands. Balls of water swirled on my palms, charged with energy. My emotions were becoming too much for me to handle, I needed to calm down somehow.

The staff of the Palace were looking at us, motionless, their mouths open. They'd all stopped what they were doing to hold on to every word of the commotion.

"How is it on me?" I asked. "You're the one who should've helped me instead of getting me humiliated. You probably wanted me to die by the water grim as well. That's probably why you put the horn in the Lake of Luck."

"Don't say that, Leon!" she yelled. "You know that's not true!"

I shrugged. It sure seemed like she wanted me dead.

We got to my room, and I opened the door. "You need to fix yourself first," I said. "Unless you're trying to make me look bad and fail. Cuz then you're doing a great job!" I went inside.

"That's not what I'm trying to do. Leon, just lis—"

I slammed the door in her face, cutting her off.

Bubbles was startled. Her ears were up and alert, and her hair stood like needles. "What happened?" she asked. "Take a deep breath. You need to stay calm."

"Maria did it again!" I yelled. I threw my pillow against the wall, wanting it to burst into a million feathers.

"Well, what did she do exactly?"

"She humiliated me!" I shouted. "She made me look bad in front of everyone and made them hate me and not want me on their team!"

"No," Bubbles said. "That's what you thought she did. What did she really do?"

I thought about what she said. "Well, that's what she did. And I knew she meant it because she was—"

"No!" Bubbles was getting stern. "What did she do that made you think she did that?"

I pondered her words. Well, Maria humiliated and brought me down. And she did that because she didn't help.

"She refused to help me," I said. "She hardly spoke up for me, and she let me get hurt. She was evil."

"Well, didn't you ask her not to help you?"

Was Bubble leaving my side too? Did no one want to support me?

But did Bubbles have a point? I did ask Maria not to help. No, no! *I* was the one who was being hurt here. I was the one who got betrayed by every single person here!

"That's not the point," I huffed. "She didn't help me because she doesn't want me to do well. That's what it is. I have to go."

I grabbed some stuff and stormed out the room. I needed to go see if the sign was from Rebecca.

I flew over to the Lake of Luck. The water swirled as the water grim moved underneath the surface.

I searched the rocks for the symbol. It was here somewhere. Where was it? I looked all over the rocks, like a madman, until I finally found it.

The symbol was caked with layers and layers of mud and dirt. This writing had to be hers. I scratched at the layers, the dirt getting under my fingernails and all over my hands. I splashed some water on the stone, and that cleaned it much faster.

My breath was quickening, and my forehead was sweating. What if it wasn't even hers? Should I bring this to Bruno?

I finally removed all the dirt and grime, but it was still unclear what the symbol was. I could make out a capital *R*, and a star—or at least what looked like one. Was my mind just playing tricks on me? Was I trying to force myself to see Rebecca's signature? It definitely could be hers, though.

I heard a rustling in the bushes behind me, but I was too concerned about the signature to care what it was.

I couldn't remember anything from Strelit that looked like the symbol. But why would her signature be here?

Blood rushed to my face. It had to be hers, it just had to be. All of a sudden, something spoke behind me.

"What are you doing out this late at night?" the voice asked.

I yelped and shot fire out of my hands at the thing.

Why did fire come out? My special power was water.

"Whoa, whoa, whoa!" Maria flew in the air and dodged my flames. "What are you doing? It's me!"

"What are *you* doing?" I asked. "You can't just creep up on me like that!" I went back to the rock.

"I saw you leaving, and I followed you here. What are you looking at? And how did you shoot fire?"

"There's a sign here," I said. "And it could be my sister's signature."

"The one who disappeared?" she asked as she knelt down to look.

"Yes, and this could mean that she is here in Strelit! But I don't know if it is hers. I mean, it looks like it."

"Um … Leon," she said. "That's not your sister's signature. I'm sorry to tell you this."

"What do you mean? It has to be hers. Look. There's an *R* and a star. That was her signature."

"That's not an *R*," she answered. "It's a *K*. It's a spell to keep the water grim from breaking the surface. I'm sorry to tell you this, Leon. I know it must be hard."

"Well, why didn't you tell me that before?!" I shouted. "You let me do all this when you knew it all along!"

"I didn't even know you were searching for this. There you go again, blaming your mistakes on me. I'm sorry about your sister. I really am. But this is not my fault."

"Yeah," I scoffed, "right. Just leave me alone."

I flew away from the lake and left Maria there alone. Tears streamed down my face, and my body shook with every breath.

My hands had balls of fire dancing on them. What was happening to me?

I felt broken after realizing the trail to my sister was useless.

She was gone. Why couldn't my sister just be here?

CHAPTER TWENTY–FOUR

The next day rolled in. And same as yesterday, the sun shone directly in my eyes.

I yawned and got out of bed. Bubbles, who had just woken up as well, was ready at the door.

I was tired. I didn't sleep at all last night. Mainly because I had been too anxious. My mind kept turning and turning, over and over. I kept getting worked up over what had happened with Maria and whether I would be able to gain her support back.

I also fretted over Sam and my other teammates and whether they would try to get me kicked off the team. The stress felt as though I was carrying a huge boulder on my shoulders.

And then these new fire powers. How was I able to shoot fire? I have so much trauma from the fire from the car crash that it should be nearly impossible for me to do that. I didn't really know what to think of it yet.

There was a lot going on.

I opened my door and walked down the hallway. For some reason, the hallway seemed endless, like I was a zombie shuffling my feet, barely getting by. I had walked down this hall so many times, it had lost its shine. As a matter of fact, being a leader had lost its shine. I was just barely getting by every day and doing the absolute minimum. And being a leader had become taxing and tiresome.

Every day, I dreaded reading the citizens' suggestions. I didn't want dragons and other creatures to berate me every day because I had made a decision they didn't like. I just wanted every day to end.

I went to breakfast and sat down. The waitress glowered at me.

"What do you want?" she grumbled.

"Can I get a soup?"

She nodded. "I've asked for a fence around my home for two months now. Two months! And I have been denied every time. Why can't I get a fence?! This is lunacy!"

I sighed. Now I remembered this lady. She gave me a headache.

"I can't approve the fence because your kingdom doesn't allow fences. You live in Fiery, and so the fence would get burned down. It would be a waste of money." I had to keep a calm face and force a fake smile, even though I wanted to scream and tell her that it wasn't going to happen.

"Hmph." She walked away, her eyes locked onto mine.

I groaned and rested my head on the table. Why was being a leader so hard? Why couldn't it just be a breeze? Or a walk in the park? Why did it have to be a battle?

Surprisingly, Maria wasn't at the cafeteria yet. Usually, she would already be at breakfast and waiting for me to come. But today she was nowhere to be found. I finished my soup and got up. There was no point in waiting for her.

When I returned to the main lobby, I saw Maria heading out the door. Where was she going?

She had on a black jacket, with the hood over her head. Her back was hunched over, and she seemed to be in a hurry. She checked her surroundings, her head frantically moving side to side. And then she looked back.

Her eyes met mine. Her jade-green eyes were filled with tears, and they streamed down her face. Her shoulders shuddered, and her lower lip quivered on every breath. She turned away and ran.

Was she okay?

I ran after her. "Wait, where are you going?"

But she had teleported already.

Mother Carla was there, though. She stood in the doorway, leaning on the door, and she was … smiling? No, she couldn't be. But she seemed happy? How could she be happy after seeing Maria like that?

"Oh, good morning, Leon," she said in her sweet tone. "Maria is a bit down in the dumps today. Do you know why?"

A bit down? She had been crying. And Maria wasn't one to cry. Mother Carla's voice seemed almost teasing. Like she was trying to blame Maria's sadness on me. But maybe I was imagining this. I was, after all, very tired.

"Yeah, we had an argument yesterday," I grumbled.

"Oh no!" she said. "No wonder why she asked to stay with me tonight. She was just a mess. Whatever happened must have really hurt her."

I was getting frustrated. This fight was not my fault. It was Maria's. She was the one who betrayed *me*. I should be the one crying. What did she have to sob for? And now she was leaving? And telling people? Pretty soon, she would tell all of Strelit that I was mean to her. That would be a disaster! I had to go speak with her right now.

"Where is she?" I asked.

"Why, she is at my home. I can take you there if you'd like?"

I nodded, and we both flew to Vanir Village.

On our way, we went through the more dangerous part of the forest. We had to cross treacherous lakes with currents that could have swept me off my feet.

"Oopsy!" Mother Carla said nonchalantly after I almost slipped off a rock.

"Oh no. Ha-ha!" She laughed after she accidentally knocked down a tree branch the size of me.

There was one danger after another. Thank goodness Mother Carla was here, or I would probably be dead already.

Finally, after almost dying five times, we reached Vanir Village. I felt like kissing the WELCOME sign after coming out of the forest alive.

"Quite the rush, wasn't it?!" Mother Carla exclaimed.

Quite the rush? That was more than just a rush. I could've died!

Anyway, we arrived at the village and walked down the beautiful path, with citizens here and there. Most of them said good-morning and welcomed me into the village, but all of them looked oddly at Mother Carla. Some had looks of disgust. Many pointed to her and whispered to one another, "There's the witch. Look, look." Some children ran away to hide, and some mothers shielded their kids' eyes.

I didn't realize it the last time we came here, but everyone seemed to despise Mother Carla. Why was that?

"Why ... um, doesn't anyone seem to, um, respect you here?" I asked Mother Carla, trying not to provoke her.

"Oh, I don't know. I guess I haven't been the most liked person here. I think it's because they believe I'm some sort of mean person whose powers aren't used for good. I try not to pay attention to it, though. People will say whatever they want to, I try not to let it bother me."

"So then why did Susan like you so much?" I asked. Susan was the one who had taken us to Mother Carla, and she had nothing but nice things to say about her.

Mother Carla seemed shocked, and stammered, "Oh, I don't know. Maybe there's always at least one person who likes you."

I shrugged. Maybe, but why was she acting odd about it?

We passed the fountain and headed to the dirt path that led to Mother Carla's home. As I stepped foot in her yard, I could hear someone crying.

Was it Maria? She was acting like a huge baby. She was the one who'd hurt me! I couldn't believe she'd turned this whole situation into a big fiasco. She was making me look bad again!

I opened the door to the house. Everything seemed to be exactly the same. Were those our cups from last time? But the flowers had wilted, and the fruit in a bowl had gone moldy. It was like nobody had been in the house for a while.

Maria was crying on the couch. Her face was buried in her hands, and she was shaking uncontrollably. She reminded me of a tree in a harsh wind, terribly uncontrolled and a mess.

"Hey, Maria." My voice came out as a whisper, and I thought she wouldn't hear it. But she raised her head from her hands and stared at me.

"What do you want?" she asked. She had a blanket wrapped around her legs, and a box of tissues next to her. A mountain of used tissues was on the floor already.

"Um … I came here to apologize," I said. Had I really come here to apologize? I made my way to the living room where she was.

"For what?" she snapped. She blew her nose into yet another tissue.

"For …" I couldn't think about what I had to apologize for. I didn't *have* anything to apologize for. "Um … you know. Like—"

"Just go. Leave."

"No," I said, stomping my foot. "I will not. You owe me an apology."

"Excuse me?" Maria scoffed. She stood up from the couch, tissues falling off her lap. "I owe *you* an apology?" I nodded. "For what?"

"For making me look bad in front of all of Strelit," I answered. "You might get me kicked off the team, Maria!"

"That was your own fault!" she yelled back. "You dropped the horn. Not me."

"This isn't about the horn!" I shouted. How did she still not get it?

"Then what is it about?!" she shouted over me. She walked from the couch up to me.

"It's about you being just so mean and not helping me, and trying to make me fail. You don't do anything right."

"Oh, is that so?" she said. I nodded. "So when you told me to not help you, I did just that. So you can't say that it's my fault."

"Yes, I can!" I shouted. "You set me up to fail. And that's what you've done since we got here!"

"Are you being serious right now?!" she screamed and walked back a few steps. Her hair was all over her face, and her shoulders heaved up and down.

"I have done nothing but stay by your side," she continued. "I help you try to come up with solutions, give positive feedback on what you do, stay next to your hospital bed, say encouraging words when you get down, try to do as many tasks as I can on my own so you don't have to deal with them. I probably do more work than you do. I even read books now, for crying out loud!"

"You've only made things worse!" I said. I threw my hands up in the air in frustration and groaned. "So why try? You just want to take over Strelit and have me thrown off and dishonored! That's probably why you've been supposedly doing more, to try to outshine me!"

"You have it all wrong!" Maria said, in between tears. "The only reason I came here was because of you. Sure, I-I used to be mean and selfish, b-but I've changed, and you don't see it!"

"Maria, don't you get it? You will never change! You were a spoiled brat when you came here, and you'll be a spoiled brat when you leave. Nobody wants you here! Nobody wants you in their family, including me! So just go back to living your rich life with your rich parents and your maid and chef. Because that's where you belong!"

When those words came out of my mouth, she gasped. And then she started sobbing.

I hadn't meant to say that.

"Just leave!" she shouted.

"Maria, I didn't …"

"LEAVE!" she screamed in my face and pointed at the door.

I ran out the door and flew away. I started crying, the tears flying off my face. How could I have said that? Why did I say it? What had I done?

CHAPTER TWENTY-FIVE

I ran up the stairs of the Palace, crying into the palms of my hands. I ran to the end of the hallway and went up the ladder into the attic.

I shut the door and slid to the floor. I was shaking with every breath, and my nose was running. I had lost the only friend I had. How could I have been so blind? So naïve?

Now I saw all the things Maria had done for me. Staying with me at the hospital, helping with work in Strelit, always trying to lift my spirits. She would never try to hurt me. But I had taken her for granted and not appreciated all her hard work. She really had changed. But now it was too late. She was never going to speak to me again.

I wanted to go home. Back to Hawaii. Where I didn't have to worry about leading a kingdom into battle or making everyone happy. And everyone seemed to hate me here. I would be doing everyone a favor by leaving. But how could I leave? I guessed I could just fly until I got home. Maybe the portal was still open.

I wiped tears from my eyes and cheeks. I wasn't meant to be the leader. Henchberry was right. It was an accident. Now I'd failed every citizen of Strelit and made them all hate me. I just wanted this nightmare to end.

* * *

I stayed in the attic for the whole day, crying. The tears stained my clothes and drenched my hands. I felt like I was going to cry forever. The sun set, and I stayed in the same position as when I'd entered. The guilt gnawed away at my stomach, like a parasite. It was consuming me. I hugged my knees to my chest and held my head low. I had failed everybody who had believed in me, and I had lost all my supporters. Maria was right—this was my family, but I had lost my family.

I couldn't do anything but mope. I tried eating some of the food that was stored there, but I couldn't. I tried reading an old book I found, but I couldn't do that either. My mind kept going to Maria and how she was doing, and how sad she must've been.

Over the next couple days, I became frightfully skinny, and strands of my hair fell out. When I wasn't crying, I was sleeping.

One day, I was sitting next to the window overlooking the forest when a feather fell on my shoulder. It was bone-white, almost translucent.

I had seen a feather like this before. With my sister, Rebecca, back in Boston. We'd been at the park.

The sun was high in the sky, and the park was bustling with kids of all ages running, screaming, and playing. But I was in the parking lot, not wanting to go up to any of the kids. I just wanted to stay with Rebecca, but she had to leave to take a test.

I sobbed as Rebecca held me. She tried to soothe me, saying, "I won't be gone for long" and "You'll be fine."

"I don't wanna go," I said in between breaths. "Can't I just stay with you?" She rubbed my head, and was trying to calm me down when a bone-white feather, so transparent it seemed invisible, fell on my head.

"Oh, what's this?" Rebecca said curiously as she picked it up. "It's a feather. That's a good-luck sign."

I looked up, my eyes bloodshot and red. "It is?"

"Yeah," she answered. "As long as you have this feather, I will always be right by your side, no matter where you are."

With that, I gave her a big hug and went into the park,

the feather clutched in my hand.

I now clutched a bone-white feather in my hand. No matter what had happened during the car crash, whether Rebecca was alive or not, she would always be with me. I had been so consumed by proving that she was here, but finding her had driven me crazy. I had forgotten all of the good memories I had of her. I needed to hold on to those. I had to know she would always be with me, in person or not.

I was about to open the trapdoor to head down when I heard a faint voice below. At first, I thought it was my imagination. But then I heard it again.

"Hello?" I sniffled, and my voice shook.

"Open the door," someone said. "I've been waiting out here forever. My legs are getting sore."

Bubbles? I unlatched the trapdoor and looked down. Bubbles was there, staring up at me.

"Well, aren't ya gonna come get me?" she said.

I climbed down the ladder and brought her up with me. She looked unhealthily thin, and her eyes drooped and didn't have that usual sparkle.

Her condition must have been poor because of our connection, and because we had been separated. Guilt sank in my stomach as I realized what I had done to her.

"What are you doing here?" I asked. I had been alone the whole time and didn't expect anyone to come to me after what I had done.

"Well, what are *you* doing?" she said. "You have the Wohna Games coming up. This is the big one. The one that gives all the points! The whole team is waiting for you!"

I had completely forgotten about them. "Well, they'll do better without me," I grumbled. "I'm no use. I'll make the team worse. And besides, they don't even want me there. They'd rather me stay away from them."

"I'm not gonna lie," Bubbles started, "some people like you not being there. But there are so many creatures who want you to come back."

Really? But I couldn't think of one person who liked me as a leader.

"You're just saying that, Bubbles."

I pulled out a book on spells and started reading it. Bubbles slammed her paw down onto the book, startling me.

"Leon. Don't you see it?" Bubbles shouted. "Your team needs you, whether you like it or not. If you don't go, Strelit will lose, and we'll lose Yggdrasil. The leader has to play. And they want you to play. So, you better get up out of this place, and get on out there. The world isn't against you, so stop acting like it is. Yeah, you're going to have some people who don't like you. You're gonna have some that hate you. You're probably going to even have some who wish you were dead. But you still have to go out and do what you are supposed to do, because of the people who love you and are counting on you. If not, I guess you can call this dingy little attic home. We can furnish it up. We can put up a sign: LEON'S PITY PARTY. That has a nice ring to it. Or another sign that says, SHHH … PITYING IN PROGRESS."

Did the team really want me there? Bubbles had a point. I couldn't let the team down. No matter how badly they hated me or how badly I wanted to stay away. And I needed to keep my head high, it was what Rebecca would've wanted. But Maria was on the team. It was too late to apologize to her. The damage had already been done. What would happen if she saw me?

"Maria's going to hate me," I said.

"She wants you to come back the most," Bubbles said. My eyes widened. "She is hurt, but she wants to win the Wohna Games. And she wants Leon back. We all do. Many of us believe in you, Leon, and we all want you to come back and fulfill your destiny. But as a new person. No one wants to see sad, zombie Leon."

I couldn't believe Maria wanted me to come back. After what had happened, I thought she would never want to see me again. And the truth was, I wanted to come back. I wanted to come lead Strelit and be the person I had always dreamed of being. This was my chance to help everyone, and to be part of a family. But I didn't know how the citizens would react. Would they reject me for leaving them? I guessed there was only one way to find out.

I looked at the feather in my hand. "Okay, let's go."

I opened the trapdoor and went down the ladder.

*　*　*

I walked down the hallway, this time with a different attitude. I wasn't a zombie walking through the Palace. I was hopeful. But I wasn't confident yet.

Was Bubbles right? Did the citizens want me to come back? Or was I just going to feel resentment from all directions again? I guessed there was nothing I could do now. I could only change how I acted. And I wanted to be better.

Bubbles led me out of the Palace. Some people smiled and greeted me. This reaction was so far better than before. However, a good amount of people still had angry looks or turned away from me. I guessed they needed to be convinced that I would be there for them, and I couldn't blame them for that. I would need convincing too if I were in their position.

Bubbles hopped into my backpack, and I flew down to the Academy. I felt a little nervous. What would they say? Would Sam say something? Was Maria already there? I just needed to apologize, though. I knew what I had done wrong and what I needed to do better, and now I wanted to be a better leader. I just needed to show everyone else that as well.

My team came into view. They were pacing around nervously. They must have thought I wasn't going to show up. One team member looked up, and he must have said something because everyone else looked into the sky at me.

I landed on the grass next to them, and they all looked at me. They didn't seem as angry as I'd thought they would be. But they still weren't happy.

"Where have you been?" Sam questioned me sternly.

"I, um … I took a little break. And I realized that I have made wrong choices in the past. And I am really sorry about those that I made. And now I want to come back and help lead Strelit."

They all just stared at me. None of them smiled, or relaxed. Why were they still mad at me? Were they ever going to forgive me?

"Fine," said Sam. "But only because we need you if we want to play. And we need to win. You got that?"

I nodded. As much as I didn't like Sam talking to me like that, I needed them to all trust me.

Carl ordered us to all line up. While he looked us up and down, I whispered to Maria.

"I'm sorry, Maria," I said. "I realized what I have done wr—"

"Can we talk about this later?" She cut me off. "We need to focus on this game." She turned her head back to Carl.

"Uh … sure." I was startled. I couldn't tell if she was still mad at me, or if she really did just want to focus on the game. But regardless of what her reason was, I felt uneasy.

What if she didn't forgive me? That would ruin everything! Or what if we lost this game and nobody forgave me? That would be even worse! Before I could worry any further, Carl spoke.

"Now! Listen up," Carl commanded. "This is the make-or-break moment. We either go into this game, win it, and keep Yggdrasil, or lose it and lose everything. And not to mention, we have a war coming up, so we need to keep the tree in order to have more strength in the war. I think we all know what we want. Now let's go make it happen!"

Our teammates hollered and whooped in agreement. I followed in their cheers as Carl started walking toward the arena near the Academy.

I tried joining the competitive atmosphere as much as I could. I hollered and cheered and shouted, which was not my personality at all. But I wanted to be a part of them and help Strelit. So, if this was the way, then I had to do it.

We shortly arrived at the arena. It loomed over us, casting us in its shadow. The arena reminded me of a renovated version of the Colosseum, even though I had never been there. The huge arena was made out of faded bricks that towered up. High arches separated each section of the seating, and on the highest level, the leaders of each kingdom watched from little towers.

I gulped as we got closer. So many legends had died during the Wohna Games. And those legends were talented and skilled fighters who had trained all their lives. I wasn't even an okay fighter! But I wanted Strelit to keep Yggdrasil, so I took a deep breath and kept walking.

As we made our way into the arena, the bustling crowd could be heard. The shouts, cries, and hollers drowned out any conversation as soon as we got inside.

All kinds of creatures swarmed every single inch of the arena. And many were creatures I hadn't known even existed. Some flew, others crawled or slithered. Some were ten feet tall, and other creatures were inches tall. There was no room at all to turn around, so my teammates and I crammed into each other and shuffled alongside one another.

When we got to our team bunker underneath the arena, we could finally breathe. Each bunker was divided by each world and separated by a one-foot-thick concrete wall. In the bunkers, the shouts of the crowd were muffled and reduced to barely a whisper.

"Okay, now, listen up!" Carl barked. "We have been training for this moment. All that hard work and dedication has led up to this. And we are not going to let all of that go to waste. Maria and Sam, you two will play offense. Julia and Mekus, you will stand in the middle. If Maria or Sam need help, you go and help them. And Heather and Leon, you will play defense and protect the horn. And Maria, you will hide the horn again, you got that?" We all nodded. "Perfect, now let's go win!"

We shouted and clapped one last time before getting ready. In each bunker, they had all sorts of armor, weapons, and gear used in the games. Everyone on our team was familiar with each item in the bunker, and we each had our specialties.

Each team member was allowed two items. Maria grabbed a chestplate and a fire sword. Heather picked a helmet and a freeze orb, which froze anyone who got hit. (The reason she picked that was we were both ice types and wouldn't be affected by it.) I grabbed a chestplate as well, and also midnight boots, which made me invisible if I stayed still for long enough.

The rest of the team grabbed their gear, and we prepared to enter the forest. First, our team would go to the arena and face the other team. One of the Wohna Games rules is we wouldn't know who our opponent was until we faced them in the arena.

All of a sudden, a loud boom echoed from above, and a voice said, "WE WILL NOW BEGIN THE FINAL FIGHT! THIS ROUND IS CAPTURE THE HORN! OUR FIRST TEAM IS STRELIT!"

The wall of the bunker slid up, and we walked up a set of stairs into the arena. Everybody's eyes were glued onto my team, but it felt like they were watching me. I wanted to crawl back into the room and wait for this to be over. But I wanted more for Strelit to keep Yggdrasil, so I wiped the sweat of my palms on my pants and marched forward.

"AND OUR NEXT TEAM IS JOTUNHEIM."

The wall slid open on the other side, and six giants had to literally crouch under the wall just to get into the arena. They towered above us like a human does to an ant. The crowd erupted when they stepped in. The giants all waved and smiled at the crowd.

"FIRST TEAM TO CAPTURE THE HORN OF THE OPPOSING

CHAPTER TWENTY-FIVE

TEAM WINS THE WOHNA GAMES. PROCEED TO YOUR BUNKERS!"

The crowd cheered as the teams returned to their bunkers. The wall slid back down, and the opposing wall opened up, with a new set of stairs. We went up this set, exited the arena, and faced the edge of the forest. The other team pounded around the arena and met us in the forest.

There were three referees here: a dwarf, a Vanir God, and a unicorn. The Vanir God stepped forward and spoke. But the Vanir God looked a little odd. Its feet didn't have fur, and its back was more curved.

"Each team has five minutes to hide the horn. The five minutes starts now!"

Maria zoomed into the forest, and a giant clambered into it. Maria was going to hide the horn in the same place as last time, behind the waterfall of the Lake of Luck.

Maria came back within two minutes, and the giant followed soon after. Once they were back, the Vanir God spoke again.

"Now each team will go to their horn and wait for the start of the game. Proceed!"

Maria led us to the horn, and the giants went the other way. We tried to see which direction the giants were headed, but we soon lost them.

The referees flew in circles, staying near the trees as each team headed to their bases. But the Vanir God kept moving closer to us. Was it following us? Was it going to give our hiding spot away? But they couldn't do that. All the referees had to promise under an oath not to tamper with the outcome of any of the games. Maybe he was just overseeing more of the forest.

We got to the Lake of Luck and prepared for the game.

"Let's go win this," I said to my team, and for the first time, they seemed to respond with positive reinforcements. They agreed and became energetic.

A smile stretched across my face. I might actually be gaining a little ground. But now I had to focus so we could make this win ours.

The horn sounded from a distance, and Maria, Sam, Julia, and Mekus all ran forward. Heather and I stayed back, waiting anxiously for anyone to come.

While we waited, the Vanir God showed up. It was walking slowly around the trees. It acted like it didn't pay attention to us, but it kept eyeing Heather and me. It moved closer.

"I think that Vanir God is following us," I whispered to Heather. She eyed him closely.

"Something's up with him," Heather whispered back. "Let's hope it's nothing."

She turned her head back to the game. I looked at the referee, worried, and then focused on the game.

I could hear movement in the trees every once in a while, but those were just birds and little critters. They must still be trying to find their horn. I stayed active and vigilantly looked around.

And then I gasped.

The Vanir God was charging at us and, at the same time, removing its fur. But it wasn't fur. It was just a covering. The referee wasn't really a Vanir God.

It was a demon! And he was coming right at us!

"Heather, watch out!" I shouted.

Heather saw the demon just in time and dodged his attack. The demon flew past us, but then charged after us again. I blasted him with water, thinking it would hurt him.

Nothing happened to him.

Why hadn't it worked? The demon was wearing some sort of armor that reflected any damage. The demon slashed its talons at me, but I dodged it. I needed to protect Heather: there was no way she could protect herself because her powers didn't work against him. I shielded her with my body and blasted the demon with air.

The demon was hurled back into a tree. He got back up slowly. He looked stunned and badly injured. But still, he hit me with a blast of fire, and I was knocked back into the dirt. And then the demon hit Heather.

She was sent far back, over the lake and onto the other side. She barely missed falling into the lake, but she couldn't get up. She was unconscious. She had been struggling a lot after being hit by the fire. I tried to get to her, but I was too late.

The demon flew to her and blasted her into the Lake of Luck.

I gasped. The water grim would get her. She was going to die. But the demon was injured. And if I let him get away, who knew what he would do next. But I couldn't let Heather die. Not if I could help it.

The demon gave me a wicked smile. He knew what he had done.

I dove into the water after her.

The surface might have been clear, but as I got deeper, the water became murky. It had a greenish tint, and it was so cloudy, I could hardly see four feet in front of me. I casted light in the palm of my hand and continued going deeper. Heather was unconscious, so she must be sinking to the bottom. I couldn't let the water grim get to her.

As I searched, I heard a violin playing. My eyes became fixed and motionless, and my breathing seemed to slow. I was being hypnotized. I couldn't let that happen. I needed to find her.

"Two preysss in one day," a voice slithered faintly. "What a pleasssant surprissse."

A green blur zoomed in front of my face and zoomed behind me again. My heart quickened, and my breath shortened. It was the water grim.

I swam away as fast as I could, all the way to the bottom. That was probably where he was keeping Heather.

I got to the bottom and searched the entire area, feeling around for anything. And then I came across an object. I bumped into it and stopped. It was a clear half dome that seemed to be a sturdy bubble. Inside was Heather. But how could I get to her?

I started banging on the bubble, trying to break it. But the transparent, rubberlike shell of the bubble would just cave in and pop back out. It was indestructible. There was no way I could break it.

But what if I could puncture it?

I made an icicle in my hand and stabbed at the bubble. A tiny fracture appeared on the outside. It was working. I kept stabbing over and over, expanding the crack. But then I heard the violin again. My breath lingered in my throat, and my blinking seemed to slow down. I had to keep going, though.

I stabbed and stabbed and stabbed, over and over, trying to drown out the violin, but the sound grew stronger.

I was so close to breaking the bubble.

I saw the green blur again.

"I wouldn'ttt do thattt iffff I were youuu."

My pace quickened. The violin quickened. My stabs quickened. Was I going to make it?

The green blur came closer and closer. Now I could make out the shape.

The water grim was long and had yellow eyes that narrowed angrily. His body was shaped like a serpent, and it slithered like one as well. Two long arms held a violin and a bow. Its body had yellow streaks, and yellow lightning seemed to form around it.

As he came closer, about to hit me with his bow, the bubble burst. A gush of water sucked into the air pocket, taking me with it. Thankfully, this let me dodge the bow, and now Heather was free. But she was still hypnotized.

I snatched her body and started kicking up to the surface. But the violin was playing, stronger this time as well.

My eyelids became droopy, and my arms suddenly felt twenty pounds heavier. I let go of Heather, and blasted her with air, creating a jet of bubbles that surged her upwards. She broke the surface and landed on the ground, away from the water grim.

But I was still in the lake and was getting hypnotized. And I didn't know why, but I thought of Rebecca in that moment.

"There is always a solution," she once told me, when I was struggling with my homework. "Whatever you are doing, there is always a way to solve the problem. All you have to do is find it."

I turned toward the water grim and tried to examine everything, all while my eyelids drooped. The water grim was playing the violin furiously. But he also had his eyes closed. So if I took out his violin, he wouldn't even see me coming.

This realization gave me a surge of energy I didn't know I had. My veins pulsed and my power surged through my body. I held my hand out in front of me and charged with all my power and energy, blasting dirt directly at his violin.

He didn't see it coming, and I knocked the violin right out of his hand. With no more music, I was able to surge to the top of the lake; I could see the light. The water became clearer.

But then two slimy green hands covered my face and dragged me down. I tried to fight it, but his whole body was strangling me. I couldn't move.

But I could still use my powers.

I closed my eyes and used all my remaining energy to blast air around me. My clothes fluttered with the windstorm around me. And then a violent, hurricane-like cyclone of wind blasted him away from me as I rode the wind to the top of the water.

I broke the surface and tumbled onto the dirt. Maria, Sam, and Heather all rushed to my side. I threw up water onto the ground multiple times, shaking. My eyes were wide, and I felt like I was going to pass out.

"Oh my gosh, are you okay?!" Maria said to me. I flopped onto my back and took short, ragged breaths as Maria knelt by my side.

"D-d-did we win?" I asked.

My teammates laughed, and Maria hugged me.

"Yes, we won," she said. "We won the Wohna Games."

CHAPTER TWENTY-SIX

"What happened to you two? You were both gone. How did you end up in the lake? How did you come out alive?"

I slowly stood up with the help of Maria. My whole body was wet, but I wasn't cold. I blew wind around me to dry myself off. As we walked back, I told my team the story.

"Wait, so a demon attacked you!" Sam exclaimed. I nodded. "And he was dressed as the referee!" I nodded again. "And then he pushed Heather into the lake!"

"Yes, and then I saved Heather," I finished.

"You saved my life!" Heather exclaimed. "I would've died! How can I ever thank you enough?!"

I gave her a warm smile. I had gained the team's trust. I was back to being loved by them.

When we got back to the arena, the crowd awaited the winner and the loser in tense anticipation. Both teams walked to the arena. Carl led our team in. He tried to conceal his excitement so the crowd wouldn't know, but he hardly could. We all tried to hide our excitement. We had won the Wohna Games and kept Yggdrasil.

"AND THE WINNER OF CAPTURE THE HORN IS ..." The announcer paused. "STRELIT!" The crowd erupted in cheers and shouts.

Someone in the crowd shouted, "YOU'RE THE BEST, LEON!" and countless other creatures shouted and cheered in agreement. It was the most praise and welcome I had felt in my entire life. I guessed they did want me to come back.

*　*　*

We exited the arena and had a small celebration outside. Bruno, Violet, Chip, and even Henchberry came alongside our team and Carl.

"We did it!" Carl shouted. "We're going to keep Yggdrasil!" He jumped and pumped his fists in the air.

"Thanks to Leon," Sam said. "We would've lost Heather."

I was shocked. Sam was complimenting me?

"You guys were amazing out there," Chip said. "Now we can still say that Yggdrasil is a part of Strelit." We all cheered and then parted ways.

Maria and I met up with Bubbles. This was my chance to apologize.

"I'm sorry for the way I acted. I know what I did wrong. I've realized that you have been by my side all this time, and I didn't appreciate it and chose to ignore it. But I do appreciate all that you have done. And I see that you have changed. When we were with the little dragon, Kienan, you helped him with his toy, and then went to visit him afterwards. I see that you wanted to be here and help this kingdom. And now, I want to as well. So can we do that toge—"

Maria interrupted and hugged me. She flung her arms around me tightly.

"Yes, of course," she said. Her voice broke a little. Was she crying?

I hugged her as well. A tear rolled down my face. Was I crying? I felt emotional. I was a different person with a different purpose. And I had my new family to support me. And Rebecca would always be with me.

"I am right by your side. No matter how far away you are." Rebecca had said that to me all the time. Now, I truly believed it.

"You guys are beautiful," Bubbles said, sniffling. We laughed, and I went to pick up Bubbles.

"Now, let's get out of here," Maria said.

"Wait, but first I have to get my stuff from the secret room underneath the Palace," Bubbles said. "I stayed there because I couldn't bear to stay in your room without you."

Maria, Bubbles, and I talked and laughed the whole way to Strelit. Experiencing this closeness and family-like relationship, and living in this moment, made me realize this was what I had been missing ever since my parents and Rebecca had gone. I smiled to myself.

I was happy for the first time since then. And of course, today was only the beginning. There would be times we didn't get along, and there would be times we would fight. But it was a start. And I was willing to put in all the effort.

When we got to the Palace, we walked around the building, and Bubbles led us to the secret entrance we'd come to when Henchberry went down with the blubba gubbas. She knocked on the wall, and the door revealed itself.

We went down the cold stairs, our footsteps echoing along the concrete. Neither Maria nor I knew where we were going, but there were pawprints from when Bubbles was last here. We followed the prints until they led to a room where Bubbles's stuff was.

Once Bubbles had grabbed her stuff and was ready to go, we left for the exit.

We took a left turn, but then we didn't know where to go. We all looked to the floor, and our eyes widened and our mouths dropped.

The paw prints were gone. They had dried up. We had no way to get back.

"What are we going to do?" I said. I didn't want to be stuck here forever. I was only fourteen!

"I know where to go," Bubbles said. "I have been here many times before, and I know it like the back of my paw. We take a right."

We both followed her, praying that she could get us out.

We reached the next intersection. There were two ways we could turn: right or left.

"Left," Bubbles said without hesitation. "No … right.. Yeah, it was right."

We followed her. Our feet pounded against the cold floor, and Maria started shivering. We reached the end of the tunnel, but there was a different door than the one we had entered. We had taken a wrong turn.

Out of curiosity, Maria opened the door. Inside, it looked like a classroom. But the books appeared untouched for ages. The wooden chairs were moldy and had been chewed by the termites.

"Okay," Maria said, shutting the door quickly. "That wasn't the exit." We turned back to the intersection.

This time we took a left. We came to another intersection.

"It was right this time," Bubbles said. "Yeah, it was for sure right."

We trusted her and continued. But we reached yet another door different from the one that would lead us out, and this one was a classroom as well. It was just as scary and creepy. It gave me an eerie feeling, exactly how the last one had done.

"No, it was left. I'm sorry," Bubbles said as we walked back.

This process lasted forever. Bubbles second-guessed herself all the time, and we encountered all sorts of rooms. A lunchroom, a bathroom, an ancient gym. They all were old.

I started to get a hunch about where we were. By the time we had found our twelfth classroom, I asked, "Why does this look like a school?"

Bubbles got all nervous. "Oh … ha-ha. Um, no reason. Matter of fact, I don't think this is a school. It doesn't even look like a school. So many places have lunchrooms and classrooms and bathrooms, right? It's not like it's abandoned or anything."

Maria and I both looked at Bubbles, and as we expected, she cracked.

"Okay, fine! This place used to be a school. But it was shut down because staff members and students kept going missing. There, I said it!" Maria and I gasped.

"So," I started, "t-t-this place is a—"

"Abandoned! Yes, it's abandoned. And I don't want to be here just as bad as you guys. I don't wanna go missing!"

"Okay, um … Maria, you can teleport us out," I said, and looked at Maria.

She nodded and closed her eyes. But nothing. She tried again, and this time she started to fade a little, but still nothing.

"I can't," she said. "I think my powers are too drained from the fight, and it's too cold. They're not working."

"I can make a fire!" I exclaimed. "And then you can regenerate your powers."

I made the fire and placed some old papers from one of the classrooms to keep it going, and Maria huddled next to it to warm up. While she became stronger, I looked into some of the other rooms. And then I came across a room that was different from the others.

Inside, the chairs were pulled together around a desk. Papers were strewn on the table. The chairs had no dust, and footprints could be seen on the floor.

"Hey, guys," I shouted. "Look in here!"

Maria and Bubbles both came in and were equally as puzzled. Who would have been in this room, and what would they have used it for?

"Look at the footprint," Maria said.

We crouched down and examined it more closely. It was big and had four long claws. I had seen this foot before. It was a demon footprint.

"Why would the demons be here?" I said. Maria and Bubbles shrugged.

I became worried. Were the demons planning something? And did it have something to do with the Palace?

I studied the papers. Some of them were photos of me and Maria! They had followed us to our practice game of Capture the Horn. They knew that we had placed the horn at the Lake of Luck. That's why the demon knew where we would be!

The other pictures were of me around the Palace. They knew my room was on the second floor. That's how they knew where I was when they ambushed the Palace. They had been using this room as a hideout to plan everything! All along they had been hiding right below us!

"You guys, this is like their second base. The demons use this room to spy on us, I think, and to gather info on what we are doing," I said.

But Maria was still busy with the footprints. "What's wrong?" Bubbles asked.

"Come look at this," Maria said. I crouched down again and saw what she was pointing at. "This isn't a demon print. Look." She put her foot next to it, and it was about the same size. "It's almost like my foot. This is a different creature. And the shoe print has a certain tread pattern, like the creature who made this print was wearing some sort of shoe. I think this is a human since creatures don't wear shoes."

"Well, that can't be," I said. "Right?" No humans except Maria and I were allowed in Wohna. I looked at Bubbles for confirmation.

"I mean, no other humans have ever been in Wohna that I know of. But it's not impossible that they would be here. But somebody would have had to bring them in."

Was it a human? But why would the demons work alongside a human?

Weren't there other creatures that could help them?

"Well, all we know is that somehow a creature was wearing a shoe and helping the demons with their plans. We just don't know what that creature is."

The footprints seemed to lead to a corner of the room. As I searched, something on the floor caught my eye.

It was a circular pin. It had two *R*'s and a loop in a royal blue against a pink background.

I stumbled back and toppled a chair. My breath quickened. My hands and legs were shaking. My chest heaved up and down unsteadily.

"What's wrong?" Maria asked, alarmed. She picked up the chair, and then steadied me.

My hand clenched the pin so tight, my knuckles turned white. "My sister is here."

As soon as I said those words, we heard footsteps. They were coming from underneath us. I turned to the corner where I'd heard the noise and noticed that the floorboard over there was loose.

"We have to go," I said. "They're coming. Can you teleport us now, Maria?"

Maria nodded. We quietly ran out of the room. Still shaking, I took the pin and some of the papers with me. I blew out the fire, and then teleported away with Maria and Bubbles.

We landed on the green grass of the Palace. I fell to my knees because of my shaky legs. I held the pin in front of me, my hands trembling. What was going on?

CHAPTER TWENTY–SEVEN

The pin couldn't be Rebecca's. There was no way it was hers. And yet it had to be. My shaky hands traced the pin. The *R*s were exactly as I remembered. Every point and edge was just the same. And there was no way I would mistake her signature for something else.

Literal fires danced on my fingers, similar to what happened when I thought I saw the *R*s at the Lake of Luck.

"What do you mean your sister is here, Leon?" Maria asked. "Your sister disappeared."

"Look." My voice trembled and my eyes were wide. "Look at the initials. That's my sister's name. Rebecca Rodriguez. A-and the loop. This is what I thought was next to the Lake of Luck. I made this pin for her. I made two of them, and she always wore them on her shoes. Guys, this is my sister! She's here! A-and she's being captured by the demons! We need to go save her!"

I started to run away, but Maria grabbed my hand.

"Okay, slow down," Maria said. "I agree with you that this could mean that Rebecca is here, but we can't just go running into the woods to find her. We need to gather more info and evidence. And we are going to need a team if we want to bring her back. Let's gather the Council."

I agreed with Maria, although I was still anxious to find my sister. But if Rebecca was here, then we needed to be as prepared as we could be. The demons were dangerous creatures.

We ran to the Palace and met Simon. "Can you tell the rest of the Council to meet me now, here?" I asked him. He looked at me, concerned, and left.

Maria, Bubbles, and I hustled up the stairs, and waited in the office room. I held the pin in my hand the entire time, never letting it out of my grasp. My legs shook while we waited. I traced the initials over and over.

Rebecca was here, I knew she was here. I was so close to being able to see her, after eight years.

But what if she was hurt? The demons could have done something to her already.

No, I couldn't think like that. I had to hope that she was still alive.

Slowly, the Council arrived. Once they were all seated, I showed them the pin.

"My sister's name is Rebecca Rodriguez. She went missing eight years ago, and no one knew where she went. And this is hers, I made these pins for her. M-m-my sister is here in Wohna, and she has been taken hostage by the demons! So we need to come up with a plan to get her back."

The Council didn't show excitement. They were still and silent. What were they waiting for?

"It's okay if you miss your sister, Leon," Bruno said. "You don't have to hide your feelings away."

"Well, I do miss my sister. But now I can see her again! All we need to do is come up with a plan to find and bring her back." What was happening?

"Leon, it is impossible that your sister is here. I'm sorry to hurt your feelings. But no humans can carelessly wander into Wohna. They must be brought in by a creature. And you and Maria are the only humans to have ever stepped foot in Strelit."

How could they not believe me? It had to be her. Maybe the demons had captured her?

"But we saw footprints," I said, looking at Bubbles and Maria for reassurance. "They were for sure hers." Why were they skeptical about this?

Violet spoke. "There are many creatures that look like humans. And Leon, that could be anybody's initials. There are five billion creatures in

Wohna. It could be any one of those. And the creature being a human is an even slimmer possibility. I'm sorry to ruin your hopes, Leon." She quieted.

I stared at the pin and traced the initials again. Tears rolled down my cheeks. I knew Rebecca was here. I just knew it. But I kept thinking about what Violet had said. There was such a small chance that it was her. Was I just imagining this?

"And why would her initials be on the plans for the demons? Whoever this is might be working *with* them," Henchberry spoke in his usual negative tone.

"No, no way. Rebecca wouldn't do that," I said, becoming defensive and standing up for my sister.

"Then it's probably not her," he said.

"Leon, we are all so sorry for your loss," Bruno said. "And we all wish that she was here with you. But we believe that it is nearly impossible for your sister to be here. And for your safety and the safety of everyone else, we don't want to explore this further."

I looked at the pin again. Was I just being blinded by the fact that there were two *R*'s? Was I just getting my hopes up for nothing?

And Henchberry had a point. Why would her pin be with the demons? But I was so certain it was hers. And the certainty overpowered and pushed away any doubts. I knew she was here. I didn't know how, but I had to find her. But I couldn't let them know that I was going to look for her.

"You're right," I said. "I'm sorry for bringing you all here. I do miss her, and that was clouding my judgment." It was hard lying to them because I didn't want to betray them and go back on my word. They were my family. But somewhere deep down, I knew that my sister was here, and I needed to get her back.

The Council shuffled out the door, leaving Maria, Bubbles, and me in the room. Maria turned toward me and whispered.

"But what about your sister?" she said. "She's here! Don't you want to get her back?"

"I do, and I will. That was just a setup. I didn't want them to keep a close eye on me. I know she is here. Can you just please just not tell them what I'm up to?"

"Oh, I want to help you," Maria said. "And I want to work with you to find your sister."

I smiled. It felt nice to know someone had my back and was willing to give their time and support to help me find Rebecca.

"Thank you. That means a lot to me."

Maria patted me on the shoulder. "Now, come on," she said. "What do you think is the first step?"

"Well, I don't think we can just go back to the demon kingdom or that secret hideout we found," I said. "We wouldn't be prepared."

"Maybe there is some way we can find clues from the pin?" Maria asked. "Kind of like dusting it for prints, or traces of something?"

"Yeah, that would be good," I said. "I don't know where we would go to do that. And we can't ask Bruno."

"Well, good thing I'm here!" Bubbles announced. "You know, Schnawegians have a very good nose and taste buds. We can identify almost all of the elements Wohna has to offer. That is, if we have come in contact with them before."

"Really?!" I said. "If we could find something, that could help us." I was getting closer and closer to finding my sister after all this time. Was it becoming too good to be true, though?

"Okay, then," Bubbles said. "But we can't do it here. Someone might catch us. Let's go to your room."

We all exited the office and went to my room. We didn't pass by anyone on the way, but Bubbles kept acting like we were in a spy movie. She would peek around the corner, and then roll across the hall. She would make all these signals to us as well, which Maria and I didn't understand at all.

"It's okay, Bubbles," I said once we got to my room. "You didn't have to be all secretive. We were just going to my room."

"I know," Bubbles said. "But this is my first time being a detective! I had to do all the moves. It gets me in my groove." Maria and I laughed.

"Okay, Bubbles," I said. "What's next?"

"So," Bubbles started, "put the pin on the floor. And then, I perform my magic!"

I set the pin down and then stepped back. Bubbles closed her eyes, took a deep breath, and then gave it a tiny lick.

"Hmm," she said. "I taste … dirt." She licked it again. "And … rock. Like a … a volcanic rock. Obsidian, that's it."

Then she started to lick the entire pin, stroking her tongue across as if it were a paint brush. Up and down, and up and down, until she had licked the pin about five times over. And then she sniffed the entire pin as well. She pressed her nose against it and went across every millimeter. And then she paused abruptly.

"Okay," she said. "So far, I have detected dirt, obsidian, sweat, blood, ink, dust, cobwebs, and the scent of demons.

"Ok," I said. "At least we know there's a connection to the demons somehow." But that was kind of a dead end. What were we supposed to do now? Maybe the Council was right. This was a crazy idea. I just wanted Rebecca back so badly.

"But," Bubbles said, "there is something on this page that I think might help us. But I don't know what it is exactly. So we need to make a trip to the library."

We all nodded, and held on to Maria, who teleported us to the Tower of Magic. We went to the library and followed Bubbles inside.

She went to the aisle with the letter *S* and told me to pull out a book.

The title read, SCENTS FOR SCHNAWEGIANS. She opened the book and started flipping through the pages with her paw. Her eyes scanned each page for a second, then went to the next one.

"Come on, where is it?" Bubbles said. She flipped through the pages so fast, I thought they would rip out. "Aha! There it is."

Bubbles's paw pointed to a black orb with swirls of purple in it. The orb was called *The Orb of Impius*.

"I knew it!" Bubbles shouted. "This is what was on the pin. This explains it! It was such a faint smell. It must have been used a while ago."

"Explains what?" I asked.

"Okay, so," Bubbles started, "Orbs of Impius are illegal. And they're used to combine two kinds of creatures together, including humans. And they can only be used once. But they are so rare that only three have been seen in history. Two of them are in Asgard with the gods. And the third one was in Strelit a long, long time ago. But when the war between the demons and the dragons happened, the orb shattered, and rained down on so many people. This means that whoever was hit with a shard would've been fused with a different creature. This happened tons of years ago."

"Was that how we got our powers?" I asked her, getting carried away.

"Well, I think so," Bubbles answered. "The shard exploded far, and I heard some of them even reached Midgard. That's really the only way a person in Midgard could've gotten powers, and also been able to cross into Strelit."

Why hadn't Bruno told us about this? I shook the thought out of my head and focused on Rebecca.

"Ok, wait, so how does that relate to Rebecca?" I asked.

"Well, maybe they were able to steal a shard from the explosion, and use it to turn her into part demon and then get her into Wohna since pure humans can't enter on their own," Bubbles answered. "That would explain why the scent is so faint. It was used a long time ago.

"But how would they use it?" I asked. "Wouldn't they have to hit her with it?

"Yes," Bubbles said. "The shard would have to cut her in order for the DNA of a demon to enter and transform her."

"When did the demons do tha—" And then I remembered.

It was Sunday. Rebecca had taken me to get ice cream, and we were walking back to our home. It was a nice sunny day. The trees were swaying in the light breeze, and the birds were chirping in perfect harmony.

"Hey, Leon," she said. "Do I look any different to you?"

"No," I answered, licking my ice-cream cone. "Why?"

"I think that mean old person at the bakery put something in my lunch. I'm starting to see things, and I can

sense things I wasn't able to sense before. Like, I can almost feel some people's emotions. And I think my vision is better."

"You're just saying stuff," I answered, not really paying attention to what she said. "No one can see people's emotions."

"I'm not joking," she said, looking straight into my eyes. She looked scared, with her wide eyes and quivering lips. "Something is wrong with me. I don't feel right."

She pulled me to the side of the street where no one was. She rolled up her sleeve and showed me her arm. Part of her forearm was inflamed and looked scorched. And it seemed to glow.

"What's that?!" I shouted.

"Shhh," she whispered. "I don't know. It has just been growing and growing. I can't make it stop."

"Does it hurt?" I asked. She shook her head. "Maybe you should tell Mom and Dad. They can help."

"No," she said. "I can't tell them. They would just send me to the hospital. And it's not a burn. It's like a fire or something."

That's probably when the demons hit her with the shard. How could I forget that? She showed me her arm, and the skin had looked burned, but she said the wound was a fire, not a burn, similar to how the demons have the glowing veins on their skin.

I retold the story to Bubbles and Maria, and they nodded.

"I mean, it seems like the reason," Maria said. "But why would they need your sister here? I mean, that seems like a huge coincidence for you and Rebecca to both be brought to Wohna."

"Well, maybe they heard about the prophecy Mother Carla made a couple years ago saying that I was going to be the next leader. So then they took my sister. My sister could really be here!"

But then doubt poured into my mind. What if she didn't remember me? Did they wipe her memory? Was she a full demon? I didn't know anything about this Orb of Impius.

Well, there was only one way to find out.

"We need to go get Rebecca back," I said. "And I think the Council will help now."

CHAPTER TWENTY-EIGHT

We raced back to the Palace and gathered the Council one more time with our newfound information. They all came in, complaining and whining.

"What now?" Henchberry said to me. "Some of us are trying to sleep."

"My sister is really here," I said, and they all rolled their eyes and sighed. "No, we have proof. Bubbles sniffed a paper we found and discovered that the demons used an Orb of Impius."

When I said that, everyone's head turned as their curiosity piqued.

"And when my sister was back in Midgard, she showed me her arm once, and it had the same cracks of red as the demons. And when you add in the prophecy, all of it makes total sense."

Everyone muttered to each other, shocked. They seemed to believe me more now. They *had* to believe me. We had all the evidence to show that Rebecca was taken by the demons.

"Okay," Bruno said. "There is a higher chance that she is here, now that we know these facts. And we will help you see if she's here." A smile spread across my face. "But you shouldn't have gone behind our backs in the first place. Something could've happened. And we do need to come up with a plan first. We won't simply walk into their castle looking for her."

I nodded. "We can use the second base under the Palace if we need to. I marked it in case we needed to go back to it."

"No," Chip said. "We don't know where that leads to. There could be a whole army of them waiting on the other side."

I thought of other ways we could get Rebecca back. We could sneak into the castle, but there would be a high chance of getting caught and maybe killed. We could somehow create a distraction, but then every single demon would have to leave in order for us to get her.

Maria spoke up. "What if, when the demons attack us, some of us use that opportunity to go search for Rebecca? They won't suspect that at all."

Everyone looked at each other. That could work. It was our best option right now.

"How would we decide who goes?" Violet asked. "And how many people would go?"

"Well, we would want people who are good at sneaking in. And we wouldn't want them to be our best at fighting, because then we wouldn't have as good of a chance to win the battle here," Bruno said.

"We could go with Heather?" I said. "She's really good at hiding and being stealthy."

Everyone nodded, and we all thought of who else could go. But then we received news that completely changed our decision.

A dragon burst through the office. Papers scattered as he flung the doors open. He was panting when he came in.

"What's wrong?" I asked.

"The-the demons," the dragon, who was named Leto, said. "They're coming! They're on their way here. I was outside of the Palace when I heard someone's cry of agony when he was killed in the forest! He shouted before he died that the demons were coming!"

The news shocked all of us. We all looked at each other for a few moments, speechless. And then we regained our senses. What he said matched what was in the poem "The Sun Shines at Night": *the havoc will shower when the wind blows a cry from afar.* The death in the forest was heard all the way here.

"Okay," I said. "Okay. Let's go inform each kingdom's leader and tell them to bring all citizens to the Palace. It's the safest place for them." Leto nodded and was off.

"The rest of us, let's start executing Plan A." They nodded and were off as well.

We'd come up with Plan A when we first heard about the war. It started off with a bunch of traps and defense mechanisms in the forest to kill off as many demons as possible. And then the ice and fire creatures would battle them first. The earth and light creatures would be archers, medics, and really anything else they could do from afar because they were the weakest against demons.

Maria and I flew down to the Academy as fast as we could. I was still in shock. I mean, for almost the whole time we had been here, we'd known of the war, and that there would be one. But we'd never known when it would happen. It was always something in the future, not now. And now that the war was actually here, I felt like someone had poured a bucket of ice water on my head.

We reached the Academy and rushed inside, trying to find Carl. We told everyone who we saw on our way to go to the Palace. They rushed out in a frenzy, all flying like a flock of crazed birds.

We found Carl. He didn't know about the war yet, so he looked with shock at all the creatures who were flying.

"Carl! Carl!' I said. "The war is coming."

"Wait," he said. If he'd been shocked before, now he was really shocked. "The war is here. Like, it's happening?"

"Well, not right this second," Maria said. "But soon. And we need your help. Can you get the Elite Team ready? And tell everyone you see to go to the Palace."

"Okay," Carl said. "I can do that! Okay, I'm going!" He ran down the hall, all eight of his legs squiggling around.

"Let's go get weapons," I said to Maria. "Just teleport them to the Palace."

We both went into the training rooms. As I threw stuff into piles, Maria teleported it. Pretty soon, we had cleared almost everything. Then Maria teleported us back to the Palace.

When we got there, everything was almost prepared. All the citizens were in the safe of the Palace, and soldiers were around the building, guarding it. Unicorns were casting spells over the Palace to keep it safe and creating a magical border on the forest that would kill anyone who touched it.

The traps inside the forest had already been set up by the earth dragons. All sorts of trip wires, claws, spikes, cages, ditches, you name it. The fire dragons were setting up a medical center with bandages, burn treatments, and all kinds of potions and medical equipment. The ice dragons had also dug a moat separating the forest from us.

I was impressed. Our setup looked impenetrable. There was no way they would be able to win now. But I was still scared. I had no idea what the demons would bring to the fight. They could have a secret weapon that would kill us all.

But I couldn't think like that. I had to do everything in my power to win this battle.

Henchberry came up to me. "Leon, your room has been protected. You can stay there, it's safe."

"What do you mean?" I asked. Stay inside? I wanted to fight. I wanted to help Strelit. "I'm going to fight. I'm part of Strelit too."

For the first time, Henchberry smiled. He patted me on the shoulder and went away. Did I make him proud?

Victoria, who had taught us about our powers, and Julian, the leader of Crystel, came up to me. He carried a big package in his arms. He also had a smile, which I had never seen before.

"Hello," Victoria said. "Everything is prepared. We have the front lines, medics, archers, and everyone else all set."

"Thank you," I said.

"Maria, can I talk to you for a second," Victoria said. Maria nodded, and they went off, and I was left with Julian.

"Sir Leon," he said, "it is ready."

"What's ready?" I didn't remember talking to him about anything before. Did I forget something?

Julian opened the package. I gasped.

Inside was the ice armor that Crystel had been working on when we visited. It was finished. I picked it up. The ice glistened in the sun, showing each swirl and pattern carved to perfection in the ice. The edges were smooth, but as sharp as knives. The armor felt indestructible.

"For you, during the war," he told me. My mouth gaped open. This was for me? Wow. I slipped on the chestplate. Instantly, I felt stronger and healthier.

"Crafted out of sheer ice, and strengthened with the power of the Enchanter," he added.

"Thank you," I said. The Enchanter was the large book in Pharaoh that had healed Maria and could make virtually anything. "I'm honored." He nodded and went off.

I put on the ice boots as Victoria and Maria came up to me.

"Leon, I need to show you one more thing," Victoria said. I followed her to the base camp on the lawn of the Palace. Sitting right there, in all its glory, was the Enchanter.

"Wow," I exclaimed. "How did you move it down?"

"It took a while," Victoria said. "But I was able to do it with the help of some others. I think we can use this to strengthen our team. The Enchanter can heal our warriors and strengthen them if we're falling back."

"This is great," I said to Victoria. "Thank you." She nodded and went back to work on another thing.

I walked around, making sure everything was how it should be. I felt as though I couldn't be too prepared. Who knew what the demons were going to do.

I noticed Maria in the corner fiddling with her armor. "Hey," I said. "How are you doing?"

She suited up and grabbed a sword and shield. "I'm about to go fight to the death against a bunch of demons," she answered, looking down, shifting her feet in the grass. She was nervous and worried, something I had never seen in her before.

"Hey, it's okay," I said, comforting her. "I won't let anything happen to you, okay? We are both staying alive." She nodded, but I could tell she was still nervous.

Suddenly, she flung her arms around me, her breath shaking as she buried her face in my shoulder. "This could be it, Leon," she sobbed. "This could be my last day here!"

I patted her back and held her. I understood what she was going through. I was scared too. I might not see tomorrow. I might never see anyone ever again.

"It's okay, Maria," I said. "I understand. Just relax. We have trained so hard for this, and you're the strongest fighter here. We're going to win this."

Maria let go of me. "I'm not letting this team go into war without me. We're going to win this thing." She looked up, and her eyes danced with flames, literally. She was prepared.

Bruno came up to us. "The demons should be here any minute now. Everyone is in position."

"Thank you, Bruno," I said. He walked away, and I turned to Maria. "We've got this, okay?"

Maria thanked me, and we parted ways. I went over with the ice creatures, and Maria gathered with the fire ones.

Everything was taken care of. We had protection, warriors at the ready, you name it. Whatever the demons could throw at us, we had something to counter it.

Was Rebecca with the demons? She could be in danger as they attacked us. But there was no way I could go to her. I needed to be here with everyone to help win this.

Maybe there was still hope of seeing her later.

If we won the war.

Everyone was silent. The trees whispered in the wind, creating tension in the air. The archers stood ready on the roof of the Palace, their bows drawn and aimed toward the forest. We all looked around for any movement other than an innocent squirrel or critter.

And then we heard it.

Their army sounded like a stampede thundering in the forest. The demons' feet pounded on the dirt. Even though we couldn't see them, it sounded like they were right next to us. How many of them were there?

We heard groans and cries of pain. They were getting caught in the traps. It seemed like every one of them was getting hurt, that's how much noise was coming from the forest.

"Fire the first one!" I shouted to the earth dragons. They launched a freeze orb into the forest. A plume of icy blue smoke rose up. Shouts and screams cried out from the trees.

"Keep moving forward!" I heard a voice call from the forest, and then the demons kept moving forward. Their footsteps grew louder.

We all tensed up and dug our feet into the ground. And then we saw them.

They came as a horde. A black horde with red lines glowing and pulsing. They stampeded across the ground, all holding weapons and shields.

But they also had on the armor that the demon who attacked us at the Lake of Luck had been wearing. They were immune to ice powers. Our plan wasn't going to work.

How were we going to beat them now?

"Fire!" the lead archer said from the top of the Palace. A volley of ice arrows rained down and struck the demons. They fell back a few steps, but they just plucked out the arrows as if they were splinters.

"Fire, fire, fire!" Hundreds of ice arrows fired down at the demons, but each one harmlessly bounced off them.

And the more arrows we shot, the angrier they got.

I panicked. At this point, they were unstoppable. Their armor was too strong. Nothing would get through. And it seemed like the whole body was protected, leaving no openings.

But I noticed something.

Each time an ice arrow hit the armor, the armor would shine brightly, and the arrow's ice would evaporate.

Not melt, *evaporate*.

The armor was fueled by light. That's why ice wasn't doing any damage. Ice was weak against light. So we needed to beat them with light's weakness. *Earth.*

"All earth creatures, come up!" I yelled. "Ice creatures, step back!" Everyone looked around at each other, confused. "Just do it!"

The ice creatures ran back and traded places with the earth ones. I ran back with them, hoping I had made the right choice.

Maria ran up to me. "What are you doing?" she asked. "You're going to get them killed! They're weak against fire."

"Right, but not against light," I answered. She didn't seem to understand. "Their armor isn't made by fire, it's light. That's why the ice arrows aren't doing anything."

"Ohhh," she said. "Okay, well, the demons are about to break the border. Let's go win this." She left and went back over with the fire creatures.

The archers switched their arrows to earth, and now progress was being made.

The armor began to chip and crack with every arrow. By the time the demons broke the border the unicorns had set up, their armor was tattered and beat up all over.

The earth creatures attacked. Some threw rocks or chunks of mud at the demons, which split their chestplates in half. Others made vines grow around the demons' legs, cracking their boots, leaving the shattered remnants on the ground.

Some of the dragons went into a full-on battle with the demons. Their talons flew at each other, and swords slashed down.

But we were getting beaten. Dragons fell to the ground in agony.

"Ice creatures, move forward!" I yelled. We all launched ourselves into the battle and helped the earth dragons. The demons were still fire types, even if their armor wasn't, so they would be strong against the earth types.

Lucky for us, almost all of their armor was broken, so we took charge instantly.

Deadly icicles flew toward the demons, puncturing their skin and making them collapse.

I thrust my sword at a demon who was standing on top of a hurt dragon. He dodged the blow, and then he slashed his claws at me, just barely missing taking my whole nose off. I slashed my sword at his claw, leaving a deep gash.

He howled in pain and retreated back to the forest.

I helped the earth dragon up off the ground. She looked young, like she had just finished her training. She had a deep red burn on her back that looked raw.

"Go to the medic center," I said. "They'll help you." I protected her as we hurried to the tent. I dropped her off there and rushed back into the fight.

But by the time I came back, we had lost the lead.

The demons had pushed toward the Palace with another huge wave. They outnumbered us three to one, and they had more soldiers coming.

We needed more fighters.

"Fire types, move forward!" I yelled. The new fighters ran in, but our army still wasn't enough. There were too many of them.

A demon charged at me with a blazing hot sword. He swung it in the air maniacally, like he was just hoping to hit something.

I managed to dodge each of his swings. I blasted him with ice, and he collapsed on the ground. I was panting hard, but I couldn't stop to catch my breath.

Countless dragons and other creatures of Strelit were on the ground, either badly injured or dead. The medic center overflowed with dragons being healed and mended.

As I looked around, horrified, two demons charged at me, completely taking me by surprise. They crashed into me, and I tumbled back in the dirt.

My sword and shield scattered on the ground, and I felt bruised in multiple places.

One demon hacked at me, but I managed to roll out of his reach just in time. I got back up and threw an icicle directly into each of their chests.

They fell onto their backs as I scrambled to get my sword and shield so I could attack them, but then I heard a cry.

To my right, Maria had been struck badly by a demon. The demon struck her again with a club to her side, and she fell to the ground with a *THUD*.

She couldn't get back up.

She tried to scramble away from the demon, but she was too slow. The demon was gaining ground as he raised his club.

Without thinking, I dropped my weapons and flew toward her.

The world seemed to slow as I flew. The cries of the war were drowned out as I harnessed all my energy into flying to Maria. I was too far away to get a clear shot at the demon, so I kept a straight path toward her.

Maria saw me coming. Tears streamed down her face as the club came down. I wasn't going to make it in time.

I raced to her at breakneck speed, the air tearing at my skin. My hands burned from the pain, and I let out a cry. I pummeled into the demon and sent him crashing to the ground.

I panted and gasped for air with my hands on my knees. Maria was in tears as she struggled to catch her breath. I helped her out, groaning as I picked her up.

"How bad is the cut?" I asked, but I didn't need to. At her side, just below her ribcage, her armor had been cut off, and she had a bloody wound that looked like it reached the bone. I looked at the medic center. It was too full. She wasn't going to heal there.

"Here, drink this," I said. I grabbed a bottle I had kept with me in case someone needed it during the fight. The regeneration potion would almost instantly cure her.

She drank it down. The cuts and nicks on her face healed, and the wound on her side began to shrink.

"Thank you," Maria said. "For the potion, and for saving my life just there. I would've died if yo— Leon, look out!"

I didn't have time to turn around. I had been attacked.

A sword sliced right through my back. The enemy must have used a sword made of light because it cut through my armor, and me, like butter.

I was being burned alive. The pain was searing. Someone had literally taken a knife and dragged it down my back. My knees buckled underneath me, I collapsed to the floor, and all I saw was black.

* * *

I awoke in my room. I was lying on my stomach, and I could still feel the pain in my back. It throbbed as if the wound were alive.

My vision was blurry, and the room looked like it was spinning. I couldn't focus on any one object clearly. Everything seemed to mush itself into one blob.

Bubbles was curled up on the bed, sleeping. I tried to speak, but nothing came out.

"Bubbles," I managed to get out. Her ears shot up and her head perked up. She looked around, and then found the sound had come from me.

"Leon!" she shouted. "You're alive!" She jumped up and down on the bed. "Oh, what a relief!"

"You thought I died?" I tried to sit up but ended up collapsing back onto the bed with a grunt. My back flared up, and I groaned.

"Don't try to get up. You're not healed yet. But yes, we thought that you might've been dead. You were out cold. You were hardly breathing when Maria brought you in."

"Maria," I panicked. "Where's Maria? Is she okay?"

"She's doing well. She's here as well."

Maria came in the door. She looked much healthier than the last time I saw her. The caked dirt on her face and arms was gone. She had a slight limp. Her eyes seemed to be a little wet. Was she crying?

"Are you okay?" I asked her.

"I'm fine. Thanks to you. You saved me during the war. I would've died for sure."

"The war. What about the war? What happened?" My stomach turned into a knot. Did we win? What had happened?

"They just left," Bubbles said. "When we rushed you into the Palace. They retreated back as soon as you went in. They probably thought you died. We were so lucky they left. I don't think we could've been fighting much longer."

Something didn't seem right. Why would the demons just leave? I didn't like the sound of that. They must've been planning something else. But when would they strike again?

Outside my window, it was nighttime. The moon was high in the sky, and it gave off a slight glow that cast the forest and the grass in a faint white light.

From what I could see, the place where the battle took place was awful. The grass was burned to a crisp. Chipped weapons and broken armor lay scattered on the ground.

"How long was I out for?" I asked. It couldn't have been that long, right?

"Like, twelve hours," Maria answered. My eyes widened. How could it have been that long? "It's three in the morning. And that reminds me, the doctor told me to not keep you up. So, you need to go to bed. I will be right here the entire time."

Maria brought a sleeping bag and rolled it on the ground. She grabbed one of my pillows and laid her head down.

"I'm gonna go help people outside," Bubbles said. "But you guys are in the safest room in the entire Palace. The glass has been completely reinforced so it's unbreakable. Henchberry is positioned right outside your door. No one is allowed to come in. You guys are safe."

"Thank you, Bubbles," I said, "for helping us. It means a lot."

Bubbles smiled. "Glad to be here," she said. She walked out the door, and I heard her footsteps fade away.

"Thank you for being here with me, Maria," I said. "I wouldn't be alive right now if it wasn't for you."

"Well, you saved my life too," she said. "I guess we both saved each other today. You should try to get some sleep so your back can heal. Good night."

"Good night."

I tried to get as comfortable as I could, but I couldn't fall asleep. My mind just kept wandering. Maria couldn't sleep either. I kept hearing the sleeping bag rustle as she moved from side to side.

And then I heard a commotion outside my door.

"I don't care who you are," Henchberry said. "No one is allowed in. So get on out."

"No," the other person said. "I need to see him. He knows me, just let me see him. I need to get in there." I recognized the voice. It was Mother Carla.

Why did she want to get in so badly?

"No one needs to get in there," the professor said back. "And no one is going to get in. So leave." I heard Mother Carla groan in frustration.

"It's okay," I said. "You can let her in."

"No!" Henchberry shouted. "My job is to not let anyone in. And that's what's going to happen."

"Henchberry, just let her in. I know her."

Henchberry grumbled something under his breath, but he opened the door. Mother Carla came in. Her hooves made the usual *CLOMP-CLOMP-CLOMP* on the floor.

"Hi, Mother Carla," I said. "What are you doing here?" I turned my neck as much as I could without hurting my back. She looked the same as usual, with her spotted white fur nearly touching the floor.

"Hello, Leon. Hello, Maria," she said with her melodic voice. When she spoke, my eyes became droopier, and my body seemed to sink into the bed like it was a cloud. "I'm just here to check in on you guys."

She went over to Maria and raised one of her paws. She swished it above her head two times. Maria instantly looked incredibly tired. Mother Carla went over to me and did the same thing. Suddenly, I felt as if I could've fallen asleep for ten days.

"We're— we're doing well," Maria said, her voice slower and a little bit slurred. "Just trying to sleep." She blinked twice as if she was trying to stop herself from falling asleep.

"Good," Mother Carla said as she moved to the window. She raised her paw and knocked on it twice. The glass shimmered for a second and then went back to normal. "That's really good."

I had to blink to keep from drooping to sleep as well. Suddenly, I was so tired, I didn't know why. My vision would go black as I closed my eyes, and then I would open them after, like, five seconds. What was going on?

Mother Carla was still at the window. And then the window seemed to expand. Was I imagining it? It grew from a small window to five feet tall.

And then someone came through the window into the room. Two creatures, actually.

"Oh, hello," I said to them. I gave my best smile as my eyes drooped shut. When they opened again, the two creatures were standing next to me.

My eyes focused on the creatures the best they could, but my eyesight was blurry and fuzzy from being so tired. All I could make out were glowing red cracks.

And then I fell asleep.

CHAPTER TWENTY-NINE

My eyes slowly opened. The ground beneath me was moving. No, *I* was moving. I was being dragged along a black stone floor. Where was I?

My hands were chained to a cold metal rod above me. My feet were in shackles. I turned my head to my right, wincing as I did so. My back was in searing pain, as though someone had stuck a pole in my long wound, but I didn't have the strength to make any noise.

Maria was there. Her hands were attached to the rod as well, and her feet were chained too. She looked as groggy as I felt. She could barely lift her head, and her fingers dangled lifelessly.

Beyond her, I could see rows and rows of creatures in full armor, lined up with spears at the ready. My vision was blurry, but they looked like demons. Two demons flanked Maria, and me as well. They too carried spears with metal tips that gleamed even though there was no sun.

They marched steadily down the pathway, slamming their spears down with each step, but to me, everything sounded like it was happening underwater. The noises were drowned out to a deep and low beat.

We went up a spiral staircase in the middle of the room. As we went higher, it started to smell musty, like wet socks. The air became colder. All around us were rows and rows of empty jail cells. Cobwebs hung from every direction, and insects skittered away as the demons walked along.

We reached the end of the hallway. To the left, there was a jail cell with thick black bars, different from the skinny silver bars that all the other ones had. A pool of lava lined the edges of the floor. To the right, another jail cell had the same black bars, but this time, the pool along the edges was a sheet of ice.

The demons unchained Maria and me from the bar. My arms fell down, limp. They ached in every spot imaginable. Two demons grabbed me and threw me into the lava jail cell, and the other two put Maria in the ice cell.

They then chained our hands back up to rods on the ceiling. Now, we dangled from the top of our cells, with our toes barely touching the floor. My cell was warm, too warm. I started sweating and panting.

Maria opened her eyes and found mine. Her eyes seemed to have no soul, like there was nothing left inside her.

She looked frail, as if a single touch would send her shattering into a million pieces. Her hair was matted against her cheek. She had scrapes and bruises all over. She was shivering, and her teeth chattered.

Seeing her like this made my heart crumble. She'd always had this fire in her eyes that kept burning. But right now, she looked defeated.

Down the hallway, footsteps echoed. A figure took shape: it was a demon. But this one was different.

The first thing I noticed was the cracks in his skin. They weren't red like the other demons. They were golden, as if they were literally made of gold. His eyes matched that gold color as well. He was about two feet taller than normal demons, so he loomed over us as he walked toward us.

"Ahh," he said. His voice was deep and grand. It boomed throughout all of the cells, and even vibrated the black walls. "So I finally get to meet the famous Leon and Maria. What a pleasure."

"W-w-who are you?" Maria said. Her voice was barely a whisper. "Where are we?"

"Well, you should've figured it out by now," he said. "All the demons would kind of give it away. You're in the demon castle. And I am Demond Scarlatti, the leader of the demons."

My heart dropped to my stomach. What had happened? We had been abducted to the demon castle and thrown into their jail.

"How did we get here?" Maria asked. She seemed to be in pain, as she winced with every word she spoke.

"Do you remember anything of your little journey?" he asked. He seemed to taunt us with his voice. Like he was teasing us.

"We were with Mother Carla," I said. "And then, we were here."

Was Mother Carla okay? Did she get hurt?

It suddenly came to me. The red cracks of the creatures in my room. Mother Carla had led the demons in.

Mother Carla was a traitor! She was working with the demons!

"Mother Carla," I said. "She works with you. She's part of the demon team."

"Yes, yes!" Demond said. "It took a little convincing, but with the right temptation, we got her on our side."

I was at a loss for words. How could she do that to us? She was part of Strelit, but she had walked away and joined our enemy. She had backstabbed all of us!

"What are you going to do to us?" I asked.

"Well, I'm going to kill you," he said. "If you were a mere citizen, then I could spare your life. But since you are the leader, if I kill you, then …"

"Strelit would die," Maria finished.

"Ah, she's smart," Demond said. "That is why you cannot live."

"Wait, what do you mean, Strelit won't live?" I asked. This was something completely new to me.

"Because," Demond started. "When someone becomes a leader, they are infused with powers that only they have. They are stronger, faster, more powerful. But that power lets all of their kingdom become alive. If they are killed before their power is stored or moved to another creature, then the power dies and ..."

"The kingdom goes with it," I whispered. How did I not know that? I should've known that. Now I had put all of Strelit in terrible danger.

"Wow, both of you catch on pretty quickly," Demond said. "Very smart humans. Very smart. But I don't want Strelit to just die. You see, I want to rule Strelit. So, before I kill you, you will give me the powers of Strelit. And finally, after waiting for an eternity, I will rule Strelit."

"I would never give you control over Strelit," I said, trying to sound as menacing as possible.

"Oh, ha," Demond laughed. "You don't stand a chance against me. I'll have you handing over power in no time."

This creature was downright evil. How could he do something like that to Strelit? What trauma had he suffered?

It was as if he had read my mind. "When the demons lived in Strelit, we were treated like pigs. Midgard pigs, of course. The ones here are treated like gods. But back to the story. We weren't given any freedom. My home was as small as your cell. And there were five of us in that one single-story home. But since the beginning of time, the demons went along with it. We all lived in misery, but none of us dared to retaliate. But I did. And I was so close to taking over. And I would've won, if it wasn't for your ancestor." He pointed to Maria.

My eyes widened as much as they could. Who was her ancestor? Maria was shocked as well.

"Oh," Demond read our expressions. "You don't know? Well, have you ever wondered why Maria can open portals?"

I'd never thought about it before, but I had never met another person who could open portals. But I'd just thought the power was something unique and rare. Was there a meaning to it?

"Well, it's because you aren't a dragon. Nor are you a blubba gubba, Maria. You come from a huldra," Demond explained.

I had heard about a huldra before. Kimyo had called Maria that when we fought him in my room.

"A huldra is a creature that is extinct," Demond went on. "And I will tell you why. Before the war, huldras roamed Strelit just like demons and dragons did. But over time, huldras created so much destruction. And it got worse, until it was too much at the battle. One huldra named Trinity—your specific ancestor, Maria—blew up the Palace. Not this Palace, the old Palace. She blew it to smithereens. She was with Bruno, and she protected him. She killed some creatures that she wasn't able to protect, though, including some demons. And that's when Strelit realized that huldras were a ticking time bomb, and the next time, they could wipe out all of Strelit. So Trinity and the rest of the huldras killed themselves, never to be seen again. Which means you need to die too, Maria. I can't have you roaming around causing destruction to all of us."

I was speechless. I never knew this history. Why did I not know this? Why hadn't Bruno, or Chip, or anybody ever told me this?

Bruno and the rest of them had kept so many secrets from us. I began getting angry at Strelit. We were uncovering so much that we had never known.

I had to stay calm, though. Strelit wasn't the bad guy. The demons were, and why should we trust Demond anyway? He was our enemy and wanted to kill me and Maria.

But at the same time, his huldra story would explain everything about Maria's powers and why we had never seen them before.

But I had to set that aside for now and focus on how to save our lives.

Demond went on and on about his plans to take over, but I didn't listen to him because I'd started to hear something else. *Someone* else.

Leon, Leon. Are you there?

I looked side to side but didn't see anyone.

"What are you doing?" Demond asked sternly. His golden eyes stared at me.

"Nothing," I answered immediately. What was that noise?

Leon, come on. Give me something.

I then realized I was hearing the words in my head. And I recognized the voice.

Bubbles? I asked—well, more like I thought.

Oh my gosh, he hasn't killed you yet. Is Maria alive? she asked.

Yes, but—

She cut me off. *Woohoo, they're alive, everyone!*

Wait, what's going on? I asked, trying to keep a straight face so Demond didn't suspect anything. *Are you in my head? Is this the telepathic connection that can form between us?*

Yes! Yes, it is! Bubbles shouted. *We're connected, baby!*

Wait, who's with you? I asked her.

Some of my Schnawegian friends. I guess the demons didn't think we could do anything to stop them. Everyone else is being held hostage in the Palace.

What?! What happened? I asked. No one had told me how I ended up in the demon kingdom.

They stormed the castle.

I knew it! I knew they were planning something else.

I managed to sneak out and gather some of my friends, she said.

Wait, where are you guys? I asked.

We're in the wall. We dug through the side of the demon's castle and tunneled through until we got to you. We're right above you. And we came prepared. Now we're going to get you guys out of here. Just make sure he keeps talking. They can't move you from here, or else we might not be able to get you out.

It turned out I didn't even have to get him to talk: he just kept talking.

"—after the war, there was nothing here," Demond was saying. "I built this kingdom from the ground up. It is impenetrable."

I chuckled. Little did he know that Bubbles had just broken in.

He looked at me again, those golden eyes boring into me. "Is something funny?"

"No," I said. And then, something happened.

One black brick fell from the ceiling, just past my arm. More bricks fell down. One, two, three, four. I started losing track. They all started falling, creating a hole. The same thing happened in Maria's cell. She was shocked and confused. I would be confused too if bricks started dropping with no explanation.

"What's going on?" Demond asked, alarmed. "Open the cells," he ordered his minions. Two demons came to open mine, and two more for Maria's, but before they could do so, a yellow ball emitting yellow smoke dropped from my ceiling, and a second one from Maria's. They exploded, and yellow smoke filled the entire floor.

The demons were coughing and hacking. I felt fine, though. Maria was still confused, but she wasn't affected by whatever the smoke was.

"This won't be the end of me!" Demond wailed.

Before I could see what happened next, the chains on my arms broke loose, and sets of paws grabbed my arms and heaved me up.

I collapsed onto the floor above. Well, more like the *tunnel* above me. My arms ached like they were going to fall out of their sockets. But I was relieved to be free.

I turned around and saw Bubbles, who was caked with dirt and had a camo bandanna wrapped around her forehead. "You saved me," I said. "Thank you, thank you."

"Any time," she said. "I've got your back." I smiled.

Maria was also in the tunnel, smiling from ear to ear and hugging the ground. "We're safe," she said to Bubbles. "How can I ever thank you?"

"By moving out of the way so I can seal the hole in the ceiling," she said jokingly.

Maria and I both got up. I was still sore and groggy. Maria looked like she was too. At least two dozen Schnawegians were inside this little tunnel, all grabbing and replacing the black bricks that they had dug up into the holes that they'd made.

"Here, each of you, drink this," Bubbles said, and handed us each a regeneration potion.

I slurped it down, and instantly started feeling better. The fuzziness in my brain went away, and my vision became sharper. My aches went away and my cuts healed.

"What about the demons?" I asked. "They're still down there."

"Nah," Bubbles said as she placed bricks. "That yellow thing I threw down there. That was a nescius orb. They'll be sleeping for a long time."

"Bubbles, the demon told us about these creatures called *huldras*. Is the story true?" I asked.

She immediately tensed up. Her body became rigid, and she stammered, trying to find words. "I mean, I don't know what he told you," she said. "But yes, there were huldras before, and I don't know if he told you, but you, Maria, are part huldra. But this is not the time to talk about it. I'll make sure someone explains it to you after we get out safely, okay?"

I narrowed my eyes at Bubbles. What was so secret about this? And why did Maria of all people have this power?

Behind Bubbles, I noticed a pile of daggers that I had never seen before. They shimmered and seemed to phase in and out of existence whenever they were hit by slivers of sun that seeped into the tunnel.

"What are those?" I asked.

"Those are what cut your chains free. Pure Elvian Crystal. The only element that can break a power-dampening cuff, which is what you had on. They are the most powerful material."

Her two tiny paws raised the crystal dagger with ease. She slashed down at my feet and cut the shackles off. She did the same with Maria's.

"You each take two. They'll be useful," Bubbles said.

I grabbed two daggers. They were as light as a feather. I wielded them around quickly. They felt nice and glided smoothly through the air.

"All set," one of the Schnawegians said to Bubbles once they finished patching up the ceiling.

"Okay," Bubbles said. "Let's get out of here." She ran out of the tunnel, with her friends following her.

I was going out the tunnel when Maria grabbed my hand. "Leon, wait," she said. I turned around. "This could be your only chance to find your sister. She could be somewhere here."

She was right. Rebecca might be in here, and I was in the best position I would ever be to find her. But should I save the rest of the citizens of Strelit, or should I save my sister? I didn't want to be selfish by any means, but at the same time, Rebecca had been missing for eight years. This could be my only chance to get her back.

"Go," said one of the Schnawegians. "I have a plan to save the rest of the creatures. And it'll work."

"You sure, Nilo?" Bubbles asked the Schnawegian with the plan. He nodded. "Well, I'm coming with you two," Bubbles said to us. "There's no way I'm letting you guys creep around the demon kingdom by yourselves."

I thought about it. If this Schnawegian had a plan, then I could go. But what if the plan failed? Or what would the rest of the creatures think about me leaving them alone?

Hey, Bubbles said to me in my head. *Strelit will be fine. I know this Schnawegian. He's the only one I know that will come up with an undefeatable plan. Plus, all the creatures would understand. Let's go save Rebecca.*

With a renewed energy and spirit, I lifted my head. "Let's go find Rebecca."

CHAPTER THIRTY

"Let's do this!" Bubbles shouted. "Nilo, you have a plan?" He nodded. "Then go! You got people to save!"

With that, the crowd of Schnawegians left, going out of the tunnel and down a ladder that they had brought. We saw them run down to the forest, but in the opposite direction of the Palace. Where were they going? They disappeared into the forest.

Now it was just us three.

"So, where do we start?" I asked. "We need to have a plan if we want to stay alive."

"Well, I think we have to start on the first floor," Maria said. "We can't just keep skipping floors. We'll never find her like that. We need to start from the beginning."

"Okay," I said. "And how are we actually going to get to the first floor? We can't just walk through."

"I think we're going to have to sneak through the castle," Maria said. "And just hope we don't get caught."

"I guess so," I said. What other options did we have?

And with that, Maria, Bubbles, and I flew out of the hole the Schnawegians made and down to the forest.

We lurked in the forest, within view of the entrance. We hid behind bushes, just out of sight of the two guards at the front.

"So, what do we do now?" Maria asked. "They'll never leave. We won't be able to get in this way."

"I can help," a voice called from behind me.

I yelped and shot up. The guards jolted to attention and had their spears at the ready, but then resumed their normal state.

Henchberry was behind me. How did he get here?

"Henchberry." I relaxed. "You're alive. How did you get out of the Palace?"

"I was able to sneak away," he said. "And then I ran into some Schnawegians on the way, and they told me you were here."

"Well, we're glad that you're safe," I said. "But how do you think you can get us in?" It would be almost impossible.

"Just follow my lead," he answered.

* * *

We walked up to the demon castle entrance. We were in handcuffs, and our feet were chained. Bubbles was stuffed inside my pants pocket, but the top of her head and ears were hanging out, so I had to cover her with my shirt. Henchberry was in between Maria and me.

He held on to me with one hand and Maria with another. But he wasn't a blubba gubba anymore. He had shape-shifted into a demon, and it worked perfectly because his black skin looked just like a demon's. And we had painted gold lines on his skin with leaves and sap. Now he looked like Demond, except smaller. Hopefully, they wouldn't catch this small detail.

Henchberry would get us into the demon kingdom by disguising himself as Demond and pretending we were prisoners. And then he would be able to walk us through the entire kingdom with ease. That is, if everything went well. We just had to hope.

Henchberry marched up to the two black doors that led to the area where I'd first woken up. Henchberry flung open the doors and stepped in with ease. The guards didn't even bat an eye.

"To the basement," Henchberry said.

"What?" I whispered. I didn't even know they had a basement. How did Henchberry know?

We followed him down a set of stairs, and with each step, the air got colder and colder. My teeth clattered against each other. When we finally got to the basement, it was so cold, I could see my breath!

I had to keep my head low and limp, but from what I could see, the basement was another prison. How many jails did this place have?

But these cells were actually occupied. Cells lined the right and left walls. This prison was smaller, with only four cells on each side. All of them were occupied by creatures I had never seen before. But Rebecca wasn't in any of them.

Wait, Bubbles said to me in my head. *The pixies. We need the pixies. The pink ones.*

In the farthest cell to the right, which was surrounded by chicken wire, were a dozen creatures, each the size of my palm. They had beady yellow eyes and tiny wings. They buzzed around like oversize bees.

Yeah, those, she said. *They'll help us.*

How will they help us? I asked. *And how are we supposed to free them?*

All around the basement, demons walked around. There were at least twenty of them. And they each had on armor and were carrying a weapon. We couldn't just walk out with pixies. We'd be dead!

But Henchberry was Demond. Maybe he could get the demons to leave?

"They need to go," I mumbled under my breath, hoping Henchberry heard me, but he didn't. "They need to go," I said again, this time a little louder. The demons looked at me.

Henchberry must've heard me this time. He cleared his throat. "Demons," he said. "I need more pixies. Go catch me some more."

"Are you okay, sir?" one of the demons asked. "Your voice is … different."

"Did you question the leader?" Henchberry said, raising his voice. "Next time you do that, I'll have your head torn from your neck! Now go get me more pixies!"

All of the demons scrambled for their lives out of the exit. Pretty soon, they were gone.

"Bubbles said we should take the pixies," I told Maria and the Henchberry.

"Smart move," Henchberry grumbled. "Pixies bring bad luck to others and good luck to themselves."

"Well, how does that help us?" I asked.

"Because if you can get them to trust and like you, then good luck comes to you and bad luck to whoever you don't like," Bubbles answered.

"But pixies are very picky on who they choose to trust," Henchberry said. "It's almost impossible."

"I think I know how," Bubbles said. "Just stay back. Let me talk to them first."

Bubbles hopped out of my pocket and walked down to the last cell. On her way, she passed by some terrifying creatures. One of them snarled at her, another growled. But Bubbles seemed unfazed and just continued on.

She got to the pixies' cell. They stopped moving and stared at her. And then pixies started making this strange noise. I couldn't mimic it even if I tried, but it sounded like a dolphin's squealing mixed with the calling of a peacock. But what surprised me even more was that Bubbles spoke it back! How did she do that?

They went back and forth, chirping in gibberish. Henchberry, Maria, and I had no clue what was going on, but judging from the fact Bubbles was still talking to them, we took it as a good sign.

About five minutes passed before Bubbles walked back to us. She looked a little nervous; her eyes faced the ground and her front paws dragged across the floor. Was everything okay?

"So, are they gonna help us?" Maria asked.

"Yeah, they will. But on one condition," Bubbles said. "They want to live in Strelit."

"Okay, well, that's not a problem," I said. "Let's go tell them that they can."

"Wait," Bubbles said. "You probably don't want to do that. They can't live in a kingdom because they cause too many bad things to happen."

I thought about that for a second. I mean, if they trusted everyone, then nothing bad would happen, right? Good things would actually happen instead.

"Well, do they want to live in Strelit?" I asked her.

"They love Strelit," Bubbles said. "They are actually really big fans of you and Maria. But we can't risk something terrible happening."

I pondered some more. There were only twelve pixies. If we just kept them around the people they liked, then there wouldn't be a problem, right? I explained this to the rest of the team.

"That's a good idea," Maria said. "And we don't have that much time left. A demon could come down any second."

"Okay," Bubbles said. "But I don't wanna be the one to blame if things go *KABOOM* at Strelit. You two hear me?"

We nodded as we all walked to the cell. The pixies were making that chirpy, squeaky noise when we got there.

The pixies looked at us. They started chirping excitedly. What were they saying about us?

Then they made eye contact with Henchberry. Their yellow eyes seemed to glare at him, as if they were wishing something awful would happen to him right then and there.

"Henchberry," Bubbles said. "You can't just walk up to them like a demon. Are you trying to get us killed already?"

Henchberry changed back to his normal form, and the pixies relaxed. They went back to their chirpy little selves again.

"Okay, can we get them out now?" I asked. Bubbles nodded.

We needed a key for the lock. I tried blasting it with water, but that didn't do anything.

"Move over," Henchberry said. He pushed me aside and grabbed the lock. He closed his eyes and started muttering stuff under his breath. I couldn't quite make out what he was saying, but it didn't sound like English. Was it … the scarred tongue? It couldn't be.

But the lock just disintegrated in his hand. He swung the gate open, and the pixies fluttered out.

"How did you?" I stuttered. My eyes were wide open, and my mouth was gaping. Blubba gubbas couldn't speak that language. How could he do it?

"I've learned how to speak it over the years, in case I ever needed to know it."

I didn't know that about Henchberry. It did help us, though. I didn't have much more time to ponder the scarred tongue because, as Henchberry was talking, a demon came down the stairs.

"I knew you were a traitor!" the demon shouted when he saw Henchberry as a blubba gubba. It was the same one that had been suspicious of him before!

The demon flew back up the stairs to alert the guards. We ran after him. I aimed my arm to blast him with ice, but before I did, he suddenly smacked into the wall.

He grunted, collapsed onto the stairs, and rolled down. *BONK BONK BONK BONK.* He was unconscious.

"That's pixie bad luck for ya," Bubbles said.

Wow. They *were* really useful.

"Now, let's get out before more demons come," she said.

"But what about the other creatures?" I asked.

I looked around at the cells. There were seven different types of creatures. They all looked like creatures we didn't want to mess with. But the demons had all locked them up. They didn't deserve to be down here.

"Some of them are deadly!" Bubbles shouted. "We can't do it."

"But we can't leave them here. The demons will probably kill all of them. We can't just let that happen. And plus, they can probably help us."

The locked-up creatures were angry-looking. But when I looked into their eyes, they all had a hint of sorrow in them.

I walked up to one of the cells. Inside, there was this huge gray and black wolf that was taller on all fours than I was standing. He looked down at me with narrow red eyes. His teeth were as sharp as daggers, and his tail encircled his body and thumped the ground hard.

"Um … hi," I said to him. Did he even speak English? "Um, how did you guys get captured?"

"We were taken from the forest," the wolf said in English. His voice was low and gravelly, but also slow, like he was mourning something. "The demons killed my mother and my sister. I don't have any family left. I just want to be free. We all do. And the demons hurt all of us and our loved ones. We want nothing more than to get revenge on them. We'll help you in any way possible."

I looked at Bubbles. "You're right," she said, with tears brimming in her eyes. "We can't just let them sit here. Henchberry, can you free them?"

Henchberry did his magic again and unlocked the cells. He unlocked the wolf's cage first. The wolf hesitated for a moment before he made his way out. He stretched his body, similar to how a dog would.

"It feels good to finally be out!" the wolf said as he raced around the room, his tail wagging. And then he floated in the air. He did flips and flew across the room ten feet up in the air.

"How is he doing that?" I said to myself, in awe.

"Ruko is telekinetic," Henchberry said to me. "He can move objects with his mind, including himself. The creatures are free, let's get out of here."

Around the basement, all the creatures were free and moving about, quietly though, while they tested their powers.

"Okay, everybody," I said. "We need to get moving. Henchberry is going to lead the way. Don't do anything until his command, okay? We are trying to find my sister, Rebecca. She's somewhere in this castle."

"I'm readyyyy," a creature said. It looked like a five-foot-long cobra with the upper half of its body upright. "I'm readyyyy to desstroy thossse demonsss."

"Okay, then let's go," I said.

Henchberry went up the stairs first, with Maria, Bubbles, and I following next, and then the rest of the creatures behind us. There was no point in Henchberry turning back into a demon, because walking around with a team of at least ten people and a horde of pixies wasn't exactly stealthy.

When we got back up the stairs, no one was there. Not a single demon in sight. I didn't know if this good luck was the pixies' doing or just something else, but I didn't want to test it. We needed to get moving.

We ran across the room and up the other set of stairs that led to the cells we had been in before. But, as we'd seen before, they were all empty. There were no demons either. Where were they all?

"We need to keep moving. She's not here," I said.

We all slowly crept up the next flight of winding stairs. I peeked my head to look at the next floor. It was full of empty jail cells, though different from the ones we were trapped in. How many cells did they need?

Alongside the cells, demons were crawling all over the place. Demond was there as well. And he was livid.

"Where are they?!" he yelled at another demon, who was quivering underneath his wrath.

"I-I don't know, sir," the demon trembled. "There was no trace of them."

"Well, they couldn't have disappeared!" Demond yelled. "You can't let them go past this door. Do you hear me?!"

On the other side of the wall was a wooden door. This door was different. For some reason, I felt as though Rebecca were right behind that door, waiting to be saved.

Demond turned his head toward the stairs. I froze as our eyes locked for a moment. A wicked smile spread across his face. "Didn't you learn your lesson last time?"

"I brought some reinforcements," I said. I came up from the stairs, and out emerged the army. When Ruko came out, the demons backed away in a hurry to the other side. About fifteen of the demons also blocked the door.

"Well, more fun for me," Demond said.

He blew fire out of his mouth. I dove away from the flames as they licked the back wall.

One of the serpent creatures started muttering something in a language I didn't understand. She turned blue and then, all of a sudden, the ground where the demons stood turned into a sheet of ice.

The demons started to slip and fall. Some went unconscious as they hit the ground, but most of them dodged the attack by flying away.

The demons charged at us with their spears pointed in front of them.

A demon came hurtling toward me. I dodged its spear as the demon rolled to the ground. He got back up, but before he did anything else, I managed to stab him in his neck with the sword Bubbles gave me. He howled in pain and collapsed to the ground.

Everyone else was fighting in a battle already, but instead of one-on-one, four or five demons were attacking one of us. This was not good.

My eyes darted around, trying to find something I could use to our advantage. And then an idea came to me. Half of the cells held pools of water.

If I could control that water, it could help us. I had never done that before and didn't know if it was even possible. But I didn't really have another choice.

I ran to the back cell, away from the fight. I closed my eyes and tried to calm myself down as much as I could.

I focused on the cells, and the water inside of them. I imagined the water rising and swelling. Growing and growing. I pictured the water becoming waves and surging through their cages. The water growing in quantity, spreading out and overturning the demons.

And then I heard someone yell, "Take cover!" I opened my eyes in a panic.

The water sure had grown. It was as high as the ceiling, which was about twenty feet tall. Five enormous waves were about to crash down to the ground.

"Get below!" I yelled to my team.

The creatures and I rushed down the stairs while the demons pushed through the door on the other side.

Just as we all made it down, we heard a thunderous crash. Water gushed down the steps, creating a waterfall between each one.

I went back up the stairs, sloshing through the water. The floor now looked like an ocean. The water bounced off the walls and created a current. The *SWOOSH-SWOOSH* of the little waves echoed throughout.

My eyes fixed upon the wooden door. I hadn't noticed at first, but there was a small window in the center. Demond's yellow eyes stared through it, looking directly at me.

Knowing that he had kidnapped my sister and held her hostage here for all this time fueled me with rage.

My fists balled up, and the current of the water grew.

"Charge!" I yelled to myself and the rest of us. I dove into the water and propelled myself forward.

I could hear my allies coming up behind me. I jetted myself across the floor. I could see I was creating another wave behind me.

The door got closer. It approached so fast that I didn't have time to stop. Instead, I crashed right through it.

The door splintered into a million pieces as the wave plowed into it. I rode the wave into the other room until it died down. No one was there. There were no doors or other ways the demons could've left, and the room was only about fifteen by fifteen feet.

The rest of the group came into the room.

"Where are they?!" Maria shouted. "Where did they go?"

"What's this?" Ruko said. He was looking at the ground. I fixed my gaze at the floor. The whole floor was mesh. It was made out of wire cable, and the gaps were woven so tiny that my pinky couldn't go through.

Multiple wires were tied to the mesh and were hanging from the ceiling and the walls. My mind started churning. What could this be?

And then I realized.

"It's a trap," I said. "Everyone get out!"

We all tried to run, but it was too late. A net came from the floor and swooped us up just before I could get out, and we were suspended in the air. I fell back and tumbled to the center of the net, squished with everyone else.

We were trapped.

I grabbed the dagger Bubbles had given me and tried to cut the wire, but it was no use. It was like trying to cut a rock with a butter knife. I tried using my powers, but those didn't work either. What were we going to do?

Before we could come up with a solution, a white smoke filled the room. We all started coughing and hacking. I felt as though I couldn't breathe, like my lungs were at full capacity already, but they weren't. My eyes danced with black dots, and my vision became blurry. Soon enough, I passed out.

* * *

I woke up again, to the sensation of warmth. It was like a blanket had covered me. Or like I was sitting next to a fire. But too close to the fire.

"Aaaah!" I yelped. I shot up but crashed into the mesh net. I was hovering above a huge pit of fire like some rotisserie pig. I backed away as much as I could.

I was outside now, on the roof of the demon castle. I was also by myself. Well, by myself in the net. The rest of the team were in separate nets, and they were all on the brink of death, like me.

Demons surrounded us. They carried their spears and wore armor from head to toe. Demond emerged from a set of stairs, with another creature standing beside him. The creature wore shiny armor and a helmet that seemed to be four times as thick as normal. The creature's head was held high, but hair covered most of their face. All I could see was a brown eye the color of coffee beans. But that's all I needed to see.

"I always loved family reunions," Demond said.

CHAPTER THIRTY-ONE

"**R**ebecca!" I yelled. I couldn't believe it was really her underneath the armor and helmet. After all these years, I had found her! I threw myself onto the net. "Rebecca! It's me!" Why wasn't she looking up?

"Ha-ha-ha!" Demond cackled. "You really think she remembers you?"

What did he mean? Of course she remembered. She couldn't just forget about me. But I was completely wrong.

"We have new captives," Rebecca said. Her voice had changed drastically. It used to be sweet and harmonious, but now it was scratchy and hoarse, similar to how the demons spoke. But every now and then, that distant melodious voice that I was used to came out, like she was a radio station that was just a little too far away. "How perfect," she said.

But the rest of my team must had heard a shrilling noise, because they winced when she said the last line. She knew the scarred tongue. That was how I was able to understand it. She was part demon, and I was related to her. It was just as Bruno said. Someone I knew must speak the scarred tongue. It was Rebecca.

"Rebecca, don't you remember me?" I pleaded. How could she not remember? "It's Leon, your brother!"

"I told you," Demond said. "She doesn't remember anything from her past."

"What did you do to my sister?!" I yelled at him.

Tears streamed down my face. My breath was shaky. I banged against the net with my fist, but it just started swinging.

I needed to get out of here, but how? I couldn't use my powers. There was nothing I could do. I racked my brain, trying to think of something else I could do, but I came up with nothing.

I screamed in anger. Demond smiled and laughed. I glared at him, my eyes as narrow as daggers. How could he do such a thing? How could he do that to Rebecca? He'd basically killed my sister and left only her body to be used for his twisted and corrupted ways. He was a selfish, lying—

All of a sudden, balls of water started forming in the palms of my hands. My eyes widened. How could that be? My powers didn't work in this net. And then it clicked.

This water wasn't my powers, it was my emotions. My anger was changing me, like it had when I turned into the water dragon at the ceremony. I could turn into the dragon and burst through the net. But what if I died? Bruno said I was *lucky* to come out alive last time. I had to try, though. It was the only option.

I shut my eyes and closed my fists. I conjured all the anger I possibly could. I thought of Demond over and over again, and how he'd ripped my sister away from my life. Not only that, but he'd made her forget who I was!

I opened my eyes. My vision was pulsing, and my senses grew more acute. I heard birds chirping in the distance, and I could see them too.

My hands and feet had turned into paws with claws as sharp as daggers. And I was growing. My line of sight was getting higher and higher. I touched the top of the net now. I could feel wings forming on my back and expanding. Pretty soon, I was fully formed. My claws slashed through the net and my wings did too.

I dove through the opening and zoomed out. I was free! I rose up into the sky and roared. Water spewed out of my mouth, and the demons went scrambling.

"Arggh!" Demond yelled. "Lower his friends into the fire!"

A groan came from the mechanism that held the rest of my team. All of the nets inched closer and closer to the flames. How was I going to save all of them in time?

The fire. I needed to put it out. But I was rapidly losing control of my dragon. I started cutting through the sky and spraying water out of my mouth. Come on, I needed to focus. My friends were in danger, and I was the only one who could save them.

I took a deep breath and regained control over myself. I flew down to the pit of flames and dove into it. My entire body was made of water, and so I extinguished all the flames I touched.

Once I put them all out, I slashed the nets, and my team was set free. They landed safely on the ground, but soon the demons started charging at them.

I swooped back down to the ground and stood in between my team and the enemies. The demons stopped in their tracks, and scurried back, but I charged at them and sent them reeling over the edge.

I looked at Maria. I was about three times as tall as her. She smiled at me. "Ready?" she asked.

I transformed back into my usual self. I hadn't noticed how tired I was. My body ached in all sorts of places. But I needed to push through.

"Ready," I answered.

The demons rushed at us. As soon as the adrenaline kicked in, all my pings and pangs were kicked to the curb. I wielded my dagger at a demon and stabbed its side. The demon fell down, and I blasted him with water, making him fall off the roof.

We were severely outnumbered, and more demons were charging up the stairs every second. But this battle felt different than the others. I didn't just hope we would win, I knew we would win. I thought my confidence was because this battle held more meaning. This was our last chance to get back Rebecca and finish off Demond and his crew once and for all.

The Palace had been taken over by demons. We were Strelit's only hope.

I threw icicles at demons, and swung my sword, all while dodging attacks and balls of fire.

But I kept glancing at Rebecca. What had happened to her? She was never very athletic, but now she was moving, sliding, and jumping all around.

She was also angry, which I had never seen before.

Out of nowhere, a demon swatted me with a club, and I fell to the ground. The demon swung his club again.

I managed to roll out of the way just in time. I got back up and pushed the demon away by blasting ice out of my hand.

Rebecca was throwing fire out of her hand. Who was she?

All of a sudden, the demon swung his club at me again. I miraculously dodged his attack and managed to freeze him on the ground.

I was getting distracted, but I couldn't help it. I didn't recognize Rebecca anymore.

She and Demond were running toward the stairs. They were going to get away!

I flew toward Demond. They were so close to the exit now. I wasn't going to get to them in time.

The stairwell was available only because the door was open. If I could close the door, then they wouldn't be able to get out. I just needed one lucky shot. Come on, pixies.

I steadied my hand out in front of me. I shot two balls of ice and watched them fly toward the door.

I held my breath as the ice soared through the sky. The first ball hit the ground in front of the door, but the second one hit the door and swung it shut just before Demond and Rebecca got there.

Demond turned around and glared at me. "Might as well kill you now," he said. "Even better to do it in front of your sister."

Demond lunged at me. I moved to the side as he skidded on the ground. I sprayed water out of my hand like a hose, trying to get him. But he kept dodging it.

All of a sudden, fire burned my legs. I yelped and shot up. They were in searing pain, but luckily the pain subsided a little. I turned around to see Rebecca lowering her arm.

She'd shot me. What was she doing?

"Rebecca, it's your brother," I said. "You don't need to fight me." But she blasted fire at me again. Was she trying to kill me? What if she did? Strelit would die and Demond would rule it, but also, I would never see Rebecca again.

Demond had found a sword. He charged at me with the gleaming tip pointed forward. I barely missed it, but then Rebecca burned my leg again. I hobbled in pain as I waited for my healing to kick in. I couldn't keep fighting both of them like this.

I was going to die.

It was as if someone had read my mind, because Maria suddenly teleported next to me. "Now it's fair," she said. "I've got Rebecca."

"Be careful," I said. Rebecca couldn't get hurt. But I trusted Maria. She knew what to do.

"I won't hurt her," Maria said. "I've got this."

We both went back into battle. I dodged Demond's sword, and then thrust with my dagger, but he ducked underneath it. We went back and forth with our weapons, neither of us landing a blow. But he came dangerously close at times. One of his blows nearly hit my neck, but I somehow saw it early enough to back away in time.

I managed to strike him first. My dagger knocked his sword out of his hand, and it soared through the air before clattering to the ground.

Demond didn't hesitate at all before he swung his claws at me. He scratched my face, just below my eye. I screamed in pain as I fell down. I held my hand up to the wound and flinched. My hand was all red. It was a bad cut.

CHAPTER THIRTY-ONE

Demond lunged for me again. I shielded my face, bracing for a collision.

I was going to die and fail everybody. I was going to fail Maria, Bruno, Bubbles, Rebecca, everyone. But the collision never came. What had happened? I looked up.

Demond was frozen in midair. How was that possible?

I saw Ruko next to me. He'd saved my life.

"Thank you," I said as I got up.

"No," he said. "You set me free. It's the least I can do."

Out of the corner of my eye, I saw three demons flying at Ruko and me, with swords outstretched.

I blasted them each with ice and they stumbled back, but they came charging again only moments later. I dodged all of their sword attacks and managed to hit one of them with mine. But the other two demons were still coming on strong.

My eyes were wide open, and my senses were as sharp as needles. I blocked attack after attack. I surprised myself with how well I was able to defend myself. I grunted as I hit the last two demons, and they collapsed on the ground.

I turned back toward Ruko, but he was nowhere to be found. Neither was Maria, Demond, or Rebecca. What had happened to them?

Next to the pit where we had been trapped were my allies, Demond, and Rebecca. Somehow, my team had managed to tie up all the remaining demons in the nets, including Demond and Rebecca.

"How did you guys do that?" I asked.

"You gave us our freedom," one of the creatures said. "That means more than anything to us. You gave us our life back. Of course we found the strength to help you."

I walked up to Demond. He struggled inside the net. "It's over," I said. "Give me back my sister."

"Too late," he said. "She's gone forever."

"No, she isn't!" I yelled. "Bring her back!" I started forming ice on my hands. "I'm warning you."

"Ha! You think I would bring her back?" Demond said. "And if you kill me, she dies too. So, are you going to kill me and end this once and for all, or is your sister going to stop you from doing so?"

Why should I trust him? He had tricked us before. But he was telling some sort of truth. If I did kill him, then the demons would die, and Strelit would win. I needed to kill him in order for this to be over.

I took a step closer to Demond. I raised my hands higher. But what would happen to Rebecca? Would she die also? I couldn't lose my sister. She was the only family I had left. But then I would keep all of Strelit in danger, just for my personal gain. What type of leader did that make me? I felt like I was being torn in half. Demond was trying to make me take a bet with my sister's life on the line.

"Don't listen to him," Bubbles said. "You need to kill him. Look."

Bubbles was indicating Rebecca's head. In the back of her head was what looked like a shard of glass, but it was black.

"That's a piece of the Orb of Impius. That's how she is getting her powers," Bubbles said. "That shard is basically a demon. And so if you kill Demond, then the shard just becomes a regular piece of glass. You have to do it, Leon. It's the only way."

"Why can't we just take the piece of glass out?" I asked Bubbles.

"It's too risky," she answered. "It could be hitting a nerve or something. Plus, that doesn't certify that there is no part of a demon left in her."

"What if you're wrong?" I asked her. "What if killing him kills her, like he said?"

"It won't," Bubbles said. "You have to trust me on this. No one knows the Orb and its powers better than me."

What if she was wrong? Bubbles was essentially telling me to put my sister's life in her hands. I trusted her, but was she completely sure, though? I didn't want to take a chance on Rebecca's life.

But there was no way to kill the demons *and* be confident that Rebecca would live. I had to trust Bubbles.

"Okay," I said.

I raised my hands, icicles forming on my palms. I mustered all the energy I could, but before I shot them, something happened.

I started walking uncontrollably toward Rebecca. How was this happening? I looked at Demond. He was muttering something under his breath. He was taking over my mind like the demon had in the desert. He was going to make me kill Rebecca.

I started thinking all these crazy thoughts. I was angry at Rebecca for not telling me that she had been hit with a shard when we were still in Boston. I was angry at her for not remembering me.

No, I had to fight Demond's manipulation. But it was too strong: I had no control over my body. What was I going to do?

I focused all my energy on thoughts of Rebecca. The ones where we were laughing together. The ones where we were playing at the park or eating ice cream. The memories of us goofing around or going to watch a movie together.

Those memories sparked something inside of me. I needed Rebecca back. I wasn't going to lose her.

My body slowly turned back toward Demond.

"What's going on?!" Demond yelled. "What are you doing?"

"It's over, Demond," I said. "Aaaah!"

The icicles came down and struck Demond. His head fell to the ground, limp. All the other demons wailed as they realized their time had ended. One by one, the demons collapsed to the ground.

But so did Rebecca.

We all rushed to her side. "Rebecca?" I said. I nudged her shoulder.

"Rebecca. Wake up."

I shook her again, but nothing.

CHAPTER THIRTY-TWO

Come on. Why wasn't she waking up? She couldn't be dead. She had to be alive. She was turning back to her human form and looked more recognizable.

But still, she didn't stir. It felt like it had been an hour since Rebecca went unconscious. "Rebecca!" I shouted, my voice shaking as tears rolled down my cheeks. "Rebecca! Get her out of the net! Get her out!"

We all lifted the net and moved her outside of it. Her skin felt cold to the touch. Her face was turning a light shade of blue.

"She's getting cold," I said. "She's cold. What do we do? What do we do?!" I was frantic. I looked around at our team. Maria was the only one with fire powers, but she was too drained. Rebecca was going to die. My sister was going to die in my arms.

I crumpled to my knees and lowered my head. This was all my fault. I had killed my sister. I sobbed.

A flood of memories of me and Rebecca came back to me. All of our times at the park, or when Rebecca would take me to get ice cream after school. Even just laughing together at dinner. That would never happen again.

My hands started getting warm, and then a realization struck me. I had fire powers, or something of the sort. Fire happened every time I thought of my family. It happened after I thought I saw her signature at the Lake of Luck and when I had the warm sensation when thinking about my family after battling Kimyo in the desert. I could save Rebecca.

I stuck out my hands and laid them on her. They shook uncontrollably, but I tried to steady them as best as I could. And then I closed my eyes and let all the memories of her flood my brain like a tidal wave. Every single detail, emotion, and feeling I had of her, I pictured as vividly as I could. My hands started to burn, but it didn't hurt me. The feeling crept up my arms and all around my body. And then *POP*.

I risked a peek to see the crackle of a fire. I had just made two fires in the palms of my hands. The rest of my team gasped in shock.

"W-wh—" Maria stuttered. "What's going on?"

I tuned her out and focused on the fire. I willed it to grow just a bit more, and it listened. I moved the flames over Rebecca's entire body, and slowly, her skin returned to its normal color.

And then she moved.

Rebecca groaned as I moved back. Her big brown eyes fluttered open as she sat up. "Whoa, this isn't Boston," she said.

My eyes became wide, and I gasped. "Rebecca!" I flung my arms around her. "You're alive! It worked, it worked!"

Emotions flooded my entire body. I was relieved, excited, grateful, and so many more emotions all at the same time. This reunion was a miracle. It was a dream come true.

"Hey, Leon," Rebecca said. "Where are we? And how did you grow so fast?" She started taking in her surroundings. "Aaaah! What are all of these things?!" Her brown eyes went wide with fear as she looked at the creatures behind me.

"These are my friends," I said. "And they are different creatures that aren't human. But don't worry, I will explain everything to you, even why I look older now."

Rebecca just looked at them with fear and horror. "Let's just get out of here, back to Mom and Dad." The rest of the team looked at me, confused.

Why had she brought up Mom and Dad? Did she forget that they'd died? She was also acting like she didn't know she had been kidnapped by the demons, and turned into one, and almost ended a whole kingdom. Was this even Rebecca?

And then it clicked for me. The Orb of Impius.

"Rebecca, what's the last thing you remember?"

"Eating ice cream with you," she said. "I had just finished working my shift at the parlor when you came in. I handed you a scoop of lemon and got one rocky road for me. And then I went to the back to grab my stuff, and then …" Rebecca was thinking. "I can't remember. The only thing I remember after that was sitting in Dad's car."

"That was eight years ago. You must've gotten hit by the shard at the ice cream shop," I said. "That's why you can't remember anything after that. And your arm was all red after that. Rebecca, how old are you?"

"Sixteen," she answered quickly.

"She thinks that she's in the past," I said to Bubbles. "She's supposed to be twenty-four. Does that make sense? Can the Orb of Impius do that?"

"If infused with too much energy," Bubbles said, "then it can overtake the person's old identity. That's what happened to her. She doesn't remember anything from that moment when she was hit until she recovered just now."

I was speechless. What did this mean? My sister was living eight years in the past.

She smiled at me and seemed to glow with happiness. Just having her here made everything seem okay. Though she didn't do it on purpose, she reassured me. She put all my worries behind me.

"It's okay," I said. "I have my sister back. And that's all that matters.

Now let's go."

I helped her up off the ground, and she took another look around.

"Ugh!" Rebecca squealed. "What are those things?" She pointed to the dead bodies on the ground.

"Demons," I said without giving it a thought.

"Demons?!" she shouted. "Leon, what do you mean, *demons*? Where are we?"

The rest of us laughed. I had gotten so used to being in Strelit, I didn't even think anything of the creatures that lived here.

"That's a long story," I said. "But don't worry about them. You have to trust me. Come on. I have to catch you up on the last eight years of my life."

We walked to the edge of the roof. But before any of us could get off, the whole building shook.

"It's going down!" Maria said. "The kingdom is disappearing!" There was a loud tremble, and we all fell back onto the roof.

"It's an earthquake!" Rebecca said. "Everyone stay calm. I know what to do. We all need to take three breaths first so we don't make irrational decisions!"

"This isn't an earthquake," I said to her. "Come on, you need to jump."

"No way," she said. "We're going to die."

"You have to trust me," I said. "I can fly. Hold my hand."

I thrust my hand out. She looked at me as if I were crazy. But that connection we had came back, and she grabbed my hand.

I blasted off with water, and we rocketed into the air. The ground crumbled beneath us as we took off, then landed safely on the ground.

"Wh-what? H-how?" Rebecca was bewildered. "What did you just do?! And where did that building go? There's nothing left."

The demon castle was gone. It was as if the building had never existed in the first place. All that was there was a plume of gray smoke rising into the sky.

We'd done it. We'd saved Strelit. A smile spread across my face. We were safe.

"Leon! Leon!" Rebecca was yelling. "What is happening? You can blast water out of your hand. That building just disappeared. Not to mention all of these creatures. I don't think we are in Boston anymore."

"No, we are definitely not in Boston," I said.

* * *

Rebecca, Maria, and I walked through the forest. We decided against Maria teleporting us because we didn't think Rebecca could handle it, and I wanted the chance to talk to my sister.

I introduced Maria and Rebecca, and we caught my sister up on where we were, why I had powers, why she couldn't remember the last eight years, and everything in between.

"Wait, so those creatures were your friends?" Rebecca asked when I told her about the team I had created. "And those creatures live here?"

"Yeah," I said. "It takes some time to get used to it, but you will."

We also told her that Mom and Dad had died in the car crash.

"Oh," she said when I mentioned their passing. "So they're not here anymore?" She started to cry. "I know they died a while ago, but to me, it feels like I was just with them yesterday." She wiped away her tears.

"It's rough, I know," I said. "I went through it. I'm here for you." I hugged and comforted her as she came to terms with the news.

Afterwards, I told her about the Orb of Impius and how it had shattered, which led to us getting our powers and me becoming the leader of Strelit.

"Wait, so you are the president?!" she said. "Do you have, like, an underground bunker?"

"I mean, kind of," I said, remembering the hidden place underneath the Palace.

"Wow!" Rebecca exclaimed. "So, is Maria the first lady?" Maria's face flushed red, and I assumed mine did the same.

"No, no, no," I said, embarrassed. "We're just friends. She's part of the Council of Strelit."

"Oh, okay," Rebecca said. "It's okay to admit it though, Leon." She winked at me and smiled.

"Nothing is going on between us," I said quickly.

"But it's crazy that you don't remember anything," Maria said, changing the subject.

"Well, it's just really patchy," Rebecca said. "It's kind of coming back slowly, like now I remember that there was another person in the back room with me."

"What did they look like?" I asked.

"I can't really remember," she said. "She had a huge nose and was really hairy. That's all I can remember."

"I mean, if it was a human, then I don't think they would've put the shard in you," I said. "But come on, let's hurry back to Strelit. This forest isn't exactly the safest place to be."

We ran through the forest, following my internal sense of where Strelit was. We hopped over creeks, climbed huge boulders, and scaled fallen trees. But then we heard footsteps. We all stopped in our tracks. What was it?

We heard someone say something, but we couldn't make it out. It sounded like a different language.

And then Mother Carla appeared. She was the same as always, but this time she had a crazed look on her face, like someone who was really angry and hadn't slept for days.

"Hello," Mother Carla said in her usual sweet tone. "What brings you to the forest at this hour?"

"We know what you did," Maria said. "So you can drop the act already."

"It's about time you figured it out," she said. "You two are a slow pair. Oh, and this must be Rebecca."

"Wait," Rebecca said. "Now I remember you. You were the person in the back with me at the ice cream shop!"

"Mother Carla was in the back with you!" I shouted. "She probably put the shard in you!"

"Why did you backstab us?" Maria demanded. "All of us. You betrayed us to go and work for the demons."

"Because they promised me the recognition I deserve," she answered. "For thousands and thousands of years, the citizens of Strelit and beyond looked down on me. They thought I was nothing but a crazed lunatic who made up prophecies."

"Maria, teleport us," I mumbled to her, hoping she heard me.

"I can't," she whispered back. "My powers aren't working."

I tried mine, but they weren't working either. The issue was the muttering we heard before. Mother Carla must have cast a spell or something.

"I will take over Strelit, and that will all change. Everyone will reply to my every command. It doesn't even matter that the demons are dead."

This last part shocked me. Why didn't she want the demons' help? I had to stall anyway to give us time to find a solution, so I asked.

"I thought you were working with the demons," I said. "Why do you want them dead?" I looked around everywhere, trying to find a way out.

"Because then I can be the leader. I don't want to work for someone anymore. I want to be the boss for a change. Plus, those demons made me do their dirty work for them! How do you think Rebecca got to Strelit? You think it was just a coincidence that the car crash happened and all of a sudden, she's missing?"

My eyes went wide. She'd caused the accident.

"You killed my parents!" I shouted. They're dead because of you!"

"Exactly!" Mother Carla said, her eyes becoming wild with anger. "I drove the truck straight into you and committed the murder."

How could she do such a thing?! She—she was a murderer. Now it all made sense, why the police didn't find the driver of the truck afterward.

"Yes, I killed your parents," Mother Carla said. "And I'm going to end the rest of the family right here."

She lunged for me first. I dove away just in time. But there was no way the three of us could fight back. We had no powers. We were going to die.

She swatted at Maria and knocked her to the side. Maria groaned as she lay there on the ground. Then Mother Carla turned toward Rebecca.

"You're next," she said.

"No!" I shouted. "It's me you want. Leave her. Kill me."

"If you insist," Mother Carla said. She shifted her attention from Rebecca and pounced on me. She grabbed me in her two front hooves and held me tightly.

"Leon, what are you doing?!" Rebecca shouted.

"I lost you once," I said. "I'm not losing you again."

"Don't kill him, please!" Maria pleaded. Both she and Rebecca had tears running down their faces. I was crying too. This was the last time I would see any of them.

Mother Carla's grip got tighter and tighter. It felt as though a million knives were stabbing me.

Knives.

I still had the knives that Bubbles had given me. And so did Maria.

"Maria," I managed to get out. "Your knives. Quick."

Maria looked confused at first, but then she understood what I was saying. She fished in her pockets frantically, searching for them. My vision started going black, and I didn't have any more oxygen left in my body. My body would be pulverized soon. She had to hurry.

She finally managed to grab one of the daggers. It shimmered as she held it in her hand.

"No," Mother Carla said. "Don't come near me with that thing!"

Maria charged at her. Mother Carla tried to run away, but she couldn't do that while holding me, so she ended up throwing me on the ground and running away.

Maria threw the dagger at Mother Carla as she ran. The dagger soared in a clean and straight line.

It hit its target.

Mother Carla froze and collapsed on the ground. We all ran to her. She was bleeding out of the wound. "You won't get away with this!" Mother Carla gasped as she took her last breaths.

"She's dead," I said. I let out a long sigh. She was really dead.

"She better be," Maria scoffed. "We should go back, they might still need our help."

I broke from my state of shock. The war might not be over yet. "You're right," I said. I picked up Bubbles and began running.

As we ran through the forest, I checked on Rebecca. "Are you okay?" I asked. "How are you doing with everything?"

"I don't know," she answered. "It still feels like there is this huge gap in my life. I don't think it'll ever go away."

"It's okay," I said. "I'm here. And we'll make the rest of our lives a million times better than anything that could've been in those years."

She smiled at me. That smile made my heart regain a piece that I hadn't even known was missing. I felt whole again.

As we kept trying to find our way out of the forest, we heard our names being called.

"Leon!" Bruno yelled. "Are you there?" His voice seemed to break in the middle of the sentence. "Leon!" He shouted louder.

"That's them!" I exclaimed to Maria. "We're here!" I shouted back to Bruno.

I heard a round of cheers and whoops rise from the right of us. I turned toward the sounds, and sprinted.

We were all racing, and finally we saw the light of a distant torch.

"I see them!" Victoria shouted. People gasped, cheered, and started crying—all sorts of emotions.

A crowd of people rushed to us, led by Bruno and Victoria. Bruno got to me and flipped me onto his back with his tail.

"You did it!" he shouted. "Strelit is safe!" He took me around the crowd while everyone praised me and shouted my name.

It was nice to see so many people thank me and appreciate me. I felt at home, and relieved from so much that had weighed me down. Everything was okay.

Victoria was hugging Maria and talking to her. Kienan was there as well, staring in awe at Maria and me.

Bruno put me down and looked at me. His tearful eyes were filled with joy, but I felt as though some of those tears were from sadness.

"Thank goodness, you're okay," he said to me. "I should've known about Mother Carla. I put your entire life at risk. I trusted her for too long. She was plotting this for an eternity. I was so blinded."

I was shocked. He really cared for me, beyond what was necessary for

CHAPTER THIRTY-TWO

Strelit's sake. "It's okay," I said. "No one knew about her."

"I suppose," he answered, but his voice still had a twinge of sadness. "But regardless, you saved us all."

"Well, I can't take the credit," I said. "Maria was actually the one who killed Mother Carla."

"Wow," Bruno said. "Very impressive, Maria." Though Bruno's reaction seemed calm, the rest of the crowd was over the top. They surrounded Maria, asking all kinds of questions, in awe of her. Maria beamed with all the attention, detailing everything that had happened.

It made me happy seeing Maria like this, seeing everyone like this. The war and everything else was over.

We had won.

CHAPTER THIRTY-THREE

Maria and I sat with Bruno in the office. The war was over, and everything was done. Well, everything was still a mess, but that was being fixed. Slowly but surely.

"I should have told you two about this sooner," Bruno said. "I just didn't know when the right time was."

"We just want to know everything," Maria said. "Why am I a huldra?"

Bruno cleared his throat. "Well, do you remember when I told you about the previous war with the demons and how a witch saved me?" We both nodded. "Well, when the previous war with the demons happened, it wasn't a witch that was with me, but a huldra. When the demons raided the castle, the huldra exploded, and caused the Palace to crumble and all of the orbs to shatter. Millions of people died, and this caused everyone to worry about huldras. And so, they were forced to go into extinction. But during the war, a shard of the Orb of Impius must have hit the huldra, and then hit your ancestor, Maria. As for you, Leon, a shard must've hit me first, and then your ancestor, which explains why you are the leader. The trait of leadership got passed down with each generation until now. This is how each of you received your ties to Strelit."

Maria and I both sat there in silence. I didn't know what to make of all of this. Bruno's tail thumped rhythmically as he awaited a response.

"Why did they all have to go extinct?" Maria asked. "Wasn't there any way to protect them?"

"I'm afraid not," he answered. "They were too dangerous and could've killed all of us if given the time. That's why we didn't want you to use your teleportation powers. We didn't want to awaken any abilities of a huldra. But it seems as though you have your powers very much under control. I am terribly sorry I didn't tell you this sooner. I didn't want you two to have to find out through Demond."

"That's why everyone was afraid and shocked about me," Maria said, her mouth hanging open. "I mean, it's a little weird to know my huldra ancestors are all dead, but at least I know now. Thank you."

Bruno smiled. "Of course. Now, you two have a celebration to prepare for."

* * *

I put on a tie and combed my hair. The celebration was soon, and I was getting ready.

I couldn't believe that I was where I was. There was no more war to worry about. No more team to prepare. No more demons to battle. It was done. We had won.

Of course, we still had to take care of many things. Like, figuring out where all the children who had lost their parents would go, and how we would build up the kingdoms that had taken a hit.

A knock came at my door. "Come in," I said.

Maria came in. She wore a black dress and had her hair down in loose curls. And her eyes glistened even more than they usually did.

"Hey," she said, "how are you feeling?"

"Amazing," I said. "To actually be done with the war. It's insane. How are you?"

"Okay," she said. "I mean, I'm happy the war's over, but I'm still a little shook about hearing about the huldras. But I came here to say thank you."

"For what?" I asked as I tied my shoes. I could hear creatures starting to gather and chat outside my window

"You changed my life," she said. "I met you as a snobby, bratty kid who was as rude as can be. I only cared about myself. But I feel like I've changed so much since then. I've become compassionate and caring. I've learned to help people, and to find joy in that. You helped me with that. And I never had anybody I could really call a friend until I met you."

"No," I said, "you helped me. You helped me find my purpose in life. I used to be a terrified little kid that was too scared to do anything. But now, I feel like I have the strength to do so much."

"So, I guess we helped each other," Maria said. "I guess it was a good idea to come here." I laughed. "Are you ready to go down?" she asked.

"Yeah," I said. "I have to just go get Bubbles really quick. I'll meet you down there?"

"Sure," she said. "Bye, Leon."

Once she had gone, I opened the door to look for Bubbles. I found her in the cafeteria.

"Bubbles, Bubbles," I said. "I need to talk to you about something."

"What, what's wrong?"

"Nothing is wrong. I want to make a decision. And I've thought about it for a long time now. Since before the war."

"Well, what is it?"

I knelt down and whispered something in her ear. She gasped in shock. Her eyes were wide, and her mouth gaped open.

"Are you sure about it?" Bubble said. "That's a big decision."

"Yes," I said. "I've thought about it for a long time, and I think it's the best decision I will ever make."

"Then go do it," Bubbles said. "I'll always be here for you."

* * *

I stood outside, in amazement. The party was huge. It seemed as though everyone had shown up. Crowds of dragons, blubba gubbas, and unicorns swarmed the lawn of the Palace, and chatted and laughed. Even Ruko and our other allies showed up!

To the left side was a giant food court with everything you could imagine. I could smell the delicious meals all the way from where I stood, closer to the right side. Music blasted from speakers behind me and seemed to echo throughout all of Strelit. The ground beneath the speakers shook with each beat of the song.

Bruno walked up to me. "I can't even believe all of the accomplishments you have had," he said. "You saved Strelit. I couldn't be prouder of you."

"Thank you, Bruno," I said. "I couldn't have done it without you. You mentored and helped me so much. I don't know where I would be if it weren't for you."

"It was my pleasure," Bruno said. "Now, are you ready for your speech?"

I hadn't been told about a speech. I had nothing prepared for it. Why did I never seem to know when I had to speak in public? But I was more at ease, knowing I would be okay. I wasn't as nervous as before.

"Yes," I said.

"Splendid," he answered. "Follow me."

I followed him down to a stage that had been set up. On my way, I was greeted by Carl, Sam, Heather, Emily, and many others. All of them congratulated and thanked me.

It was a whirlwind, with everyone praising me and giving me all kinds of compliments. A wide smile spread across my face. I had become a part of Strelit's family. I wasn't an outsider anymore.

I stepped up to the stage. Everyone looked at me with eager eyes.

"We won!" I shouted into the mic to start. Everyone clapped and hollered in excitement. "And this couldn't be possible without each and every one of you. Everyone played a role in keeping Strelit alive. There are some things that still need to be fixed. We will be creating better defenses around all of Strelit, with the demons gone, so these attacks will hopefully never happen again. And all the children who have lost their families will find homes. But I also have a big announcement to make. Maria, would you come up to the stage, please?"

Confused murmurs spread through the crowd as Maria stepped up. Her forehead wrinkled in confusion.

"What's going on?" Maria asked.

"Maria," I said into the mic, and to her. "Since we have been here, you have shown so much strength and bravery. And you have also shown an immense amount of love and loyalty to Strelit. You have cared for each and every one of the citizens here. You listened to all of our concerns and did your best to solve them. You have put your life at risk to save us. And you deserve this. Henchberry, could you bring out the Goblet of Green Fire?"

The crowd gasped.

Maria was shocked as well. "Leon, what?!" she exclaimed.

"Yes," I said. "I want to make you the leader of Strelit. I feel you would lead Strelit to amazing things and would be one of the greatest leaders Strelit has ever had. Would you take this honor, Maria?"

"Yes! Yes, of course!" she shouted. "I can't believe this is happening. Are you sure about this?"

"I am," I said. "I have Strelit's best interests at heart. And I want Strelit to grow and become the best it can be. You would do that better than I could ever imagine. You were meant to be a leader. I couldn't be happier to give you this. Are you ready?"

"Yes," she said.

I started with my lines. "I, Leon, resign my position as leader willingly and offer it to Maria."

"I, Maria," she said, "willingly accept the offer of leader."

And then, the fire turned green. It curled up to Maria and circled around her. And then the fire rested. It was done.

The crowd erupted in cheers. They started chanting, *MARIA-MARIA-MARIA*. She smiled and waved to the crowd.

I stepped off the stage, and let Maria bask in the glory of the citizens of Strelit. She saw me step off and ran after me.

Maria hugged me. "Thank you," she said.

"I couldn't be more grateful to have you as a friend," I said.

I couldn't believe it. All the hardships I had faced during my life had led up to this perfect moment. All those nights I cried about not having friends or someone to be with. They were worth it. I had the best friend anyone could ask for.

"Now go," I said. "They're all waiting for you!"

Maria smiled at me as she ran back up the stairs to the stage.

"That was a bold decision of yours," Bruno said from next to me. "What made you do it? Even after finding out she is part huldra."

"I took after my mentor," I said as we shared a smile. "You have taught me how to be a leader, and I feel like this is the best move. Maria is a natural leader, regardless of her ancestry."

"What is next for you?" Bruno asked.

"I'm not sure yet," I answered, but Maria read my mind.

On stage, she said, "Leon, I would like you to be the Head of Strelit Restoration. I want you to help build Strelit back to greatness!"

Everyone cheered and applauded. Maria beamed brightly at me and continued her speech. I looked at Rebecca, who was off to the side. She was smiling.

I thought about the person I was before I came here. I had been scared, anxious, and nervous. I would never take any risks and would hide in my room all day.

Now I was confident, strong, powerful, and so much more. I had become the person I had always wanted to be. I had won a war and gotten my sister back!

Now, Mother Carla's riddle about my life made sense. *Your life will not be a line, but an ocean. The feats will be big, but the crashes will be hard. But in the end, you will return home.*

My life did have highs and lows. I became a leader and won a war, but I also became self-centered, and lost appreciation for the people who had cared about me along the way. In the end, though, I found my home here in Strelit with Bubbles, Maria, Rebecca, Bruno, and everyone else.

I looked up at the sky. I thanked my parents. I felt like they had guided me through my whole journey here and would continue to.

Thanks, Mom and Dad. I couldn't have done this without you guys.

AUTHOR BIO

Sterling Davies, an aspiring author and a junior in high school, draws inspiration from the world around him and the wide variety of classic and modern books he comes across. Sterling uses writing as a means to use creativity and express his ideas and thoughts about different subjects. He hopes this novel is one of many to come. He lives with his mother and twin brother in California, and competes in both tennis and swimming, and enjoys playing the piano.